Sh
leane
up into his eyes and found a mix of emotions looking back. "Goodnight, Jackson."

As she drew her hand away, he captured it, pulled her into his arms, and kissed her.

His lips were warm, firm, and familiar as they settled over hers. They did not tease, they took possession. He kissed her like they'd never missed a beat. Like five years had never come between them.

Abby melted.

A moan from somewhere deep inside rumbled up from her chest and slipped into his mouth on a long exhale of breath. Then, like someone had flipped a switch, he was gone.

By Candis Terry

SWEETEST MISTAKE
ANYTHING BUT SWEET
SOMEBODY LIKE YOU
ANY GIVEN CHRISTMAS
SECOND CHANCE AT THE SUGAR SHACK

Short Stories
HOME SWEET HOME
(FROM FOR LOVE AND HONOR
AND CRAZY SWEET FINE)

Coming Soon
SOMETHING SWEETER

CANDIS TERRY

Sweetest MISTAKE

AVON

An Imprint of HarperCollinsPublishers

AVON BOOKS
An Imprint of HarperCollins*Publishers*
10 East 53rd Street
New York, New York 10022-5299

First Avon Books mass market printing: January 2014

Avon Trademark Reg. U.S. Pat. Off. and in Other Countries, Marca Registrada, Hecho en U.S.A.
HarperCollins® is a registered trademark of HarperCollins Publishers.

Printed in the U.S.A.

10 9 8 7 6 5 4 3 2 1

For John and Patty—
best and most fun brother-in-law and sister-in-law ever.
I love you both dearly. It's not a competition.

Acknowledgments

A very big thank you to M.L., a certain California fire captain who likes to fly under the radar and didn't want to be acknowledged (you know who you are). I had to thank you anyway for all the wonderful feedback and the time it took for you to answer all my crazy questions.

Special thanks to my good friend Tommy Collins—the hardest-working deejay on the Boise airwaves—for all the laughs and musical inspiration.

Heartfelt thanks go out to my readers who *always* come through for me to offer support and encouragement when I sometimes think I'm all alone. I appreciate you so very much. Special thanks to Valerie Lane for responding to my Facebook plea and coming up with a name for Miss Kitty.

Chapter 1

In the split second before hell exploded, Jackson Wilder picked up his weapon and pounded the bastard back. His hands were steady. His mind focused. Sweat rolled down his back from the heat and the adrenaline.

The memories.

He shoved away any weakness that taunted him from the edge and dared him to fail.

He would not.

Could not.

Ever again.

In his book, fighting a fire that threatened to destroy lives was no different than combating the enemy on the parched soils of Afghanistan.

Same battle.

Different villain.

The only variation? *This* war he had a better chance of winning.

He ignored the ache in his bones from the busy shift he'd just completed with the San Antonio Fire Department and gathered all the oomph he had left to fight this structure fire for the Sweet, Texas, volunteer station.

He'd do anything to protect his hometown. Hell, he'd even gone to war.

Still was if anyone paid attention.

Except he wasn't really the heart-on-your-sleeve kind of guy, so most folks couldn't see what went on inside his head or heart.

Those battles he fought alone.

On the battlefield, it didn't matter if the weapon was a hose or a military assault rifle—it felt good in his hands. Felt right. It gave him a reason. A purpose. An opportunity to help others and sink his thoughts into something other than his own colossal fuck-ups.

And he'd made plenty.

As fire licked up the side of the house, he moved forward—daring it to jump to the roof. Like a living, breathing entity, it paused, seemed to look at him, and accept the dare. When it made its move, he shook his head.

He who blinks first gets their ass annihilated.

One slight shift of the hose shot bullets of water that split the flame. Weakened its power. Forced it into submission.

Today, he could claim victory.

Tomorrow? Who the hell knew.

Minutes later, he finished helping with over-haul, then climbed back up into the engine. Head dropped back and eyes closed, he endured some good-natured ribbing on the way back to the station from the group of volunteers made up of ranchers, lawyers, and shop owners. The camaraderie he shared with them was different than the one with the guys from the big-city station. But no less important. He'd grown up with some. Learned from others. Respected the hell out of all of them.

Back at the station, he'd barely kicked off his boots and shrugged out of his turnouts before fatigue sank deep. Too tired to stop and shower, he tossed a wave to the crew, and, behind him, the steel door slammed shut.

Anxious for a quick combat nap before he picked up his baby girl for their Wednesday-night visit, he shoved his sunglasses on and headed toward the big silver truck parked in the back lot. Once inside the cab, he stretched, yawned, and stuck the keys in the ignition. The engine turned over with a low growl, and he eased out toward the road.

In his thirty-one years, traffic in beautiful downtown Sweet had never been more than a trickle or two of farm vehicles or mom taxis on their way to pick up the kids at school or shuffle those same kids off to soccer practice or a 4-H meeting. But lately, since a few businesses had been revamped by the TV show *My New Town*, tourism had picked up. The traffic flow as well. He didn't like it, but there wasn't much he could do.

The county sheriff's SUV cruised by, with its black deer guard gleaming in the late-afternoon sun. Jackson lifted his hand with the locals' two-fingered version of a wave. Instead of continuing down Main Street, the patrol car swerved into the fire station driveway and stopped. The window rolled down with a squeal.

"Been looking for you, Wilder."

"Aw, hell. What'd I do now?"

Deputy Brady Bennett—childhood friend and local chick magnet—chuckled. "I'm sure there's something. Lucky for you I don't need to haul out the handcuffs this time."

"Ever," Jackson reminded him.

"Only because you never got caught." Brady grinned, knowing he'd been in on some of those wild-ass and death-defying capers too. "And might I add that you aren't dead yet."

Jackson rolled his tense neck muscles. "Feel like it."

"Busy shift?"

"Four structures in the big city. Just mopped up one here too."

"Eckels's place." Brady pushed back his Stetson. "Heard that over the radio."

"Yeah. The missus set a hot pot of fryer oil next to the gas grill to let it cool off. The mister popped on the grill to cook some Brats for lunch."

"Poof."

"Yep." Jackson flexed his fingers on the steering wheel. "Caught it before it hit the roof."

"Lucky for them."

Jackson nodded. "So what's up?"

Brady squinted against the sun. "She's back."

"*She* who?" Jackson nearly shook his head at the pointless inquiry. He knew *who* by the immediate tingle up his spine. The instant rush through his heart.

"Ms. Abigail Morgan." Brady glanced down at the computer between the seats, then back up again. "Or I guess she's Mrs. Rich now."

In more ways than one. "When?"

"Rolled in yesterday around noon. She's over at her folks' place."

"They come back too?"

Brady shook his head. "Saw one of those personal storage containers and a foreign car in the driveway, so I stopped in to check on things. Renters moved out. Abby said she's there to fix up the house and put it on the market."

A tangle of emotion coiled in Jackson's soul. It took everything he had to stay cool. Keep his tone even. Neutral. "How'd she look?" Sheesh. That hardly sounded superficial.

"Smokin'."

Hell, he knew that too. Abby had always been beautiful. Ethereal. Like a woodland fairy. Even when she'd been missing her two front teeth or had the chicken pox all over her face.

"I meant did she look . . . okay?"

Brady gave an almost imperceptible shrug of his uniformed shoulders. "Seemed fine." Then he glanced down the road, narrowed his eyes as an F–350 zoomed past. "Well . . . got to go catch me a speeder. Just thought you'd want to know."

"Thanks."

While Brady put the patrol car in reverse, Jackson sat there staring out the windshield. His head buzzed. Heart tingled. He lifted his fingers off the steering wheel one by one, then replaced them in the same systematic manner. The breath that lifted his chest stuttered.

She was back.

With a calm defying the current scramble in his brain, he eased the truck out onto Main Street and turned toward home.

Every place he passed on the way reminded him of her. Brought back memories of good times. Town Square—where they'd sat on the lawn with friends and listened to concerts beneath a hot summer sky. The high school where they'd laughingly raced through the halls, late again for class. The Yellow Rose Cinema, where they'd often double-dated and fought over the last kernel of a shared tub of popcorn. The used bookstore, which had once been a pet shop where Abby had worked for several months before recognizing animal cruelty and quit. She then proceeded to break in and rescue several cats, dogs, and even a chameleon she'd named Rainbow Brite.

He laughed at the memory because he'd been an accessory to the cause. An accessory who'd thanked god that Sheriff Mackey excused their *indiscretion* when he'd been witness to Abby's grievance. The shop owner had been prosecuted, and Abby had personally found homes for all the animals.

Jackson's fingers curled over the steering wheel. Squeezed until the muscles in his forearms popped.

Abby had been his confidante.

His partner in crime.

She'd been his first kiss.

The first girl he'd made love to.

His best friend—until the day almost seven years ago, when she betrayed him. Completely cut him out of her life.

No explanation.

No apology.

No good-bye.

Stopped at the intersection of Main and Stone Creek Road, he waited for Gladys Lewis and Arlene Potter—two of Sweet's reigning gossip queens—to clear the crosswalk. A long, hard breath pushed from his lungs. He was exhausted and clearly not giving a whole lot of caution to his thoughts.

So what if Abby had hit the delete key next to his name in her book of life? No big deal that as his best friend she hadn't been there for him after he'd witnessed his big brother being killed in Afghanistan. No big deal that as his best friend she hadn't been there when his father had died from the heartbreak over the loss of his firstborn son.

No big deal.

He should be over it.

In his mind, he pictured her the last time he'd seen her.

Over it?

Yeah. Not so much.

When the crosswalk cleared, he put his hands on the wheel and flipped an illegal Uey.

She was back.

And he figured there wasn't a better time than now to fill in the missing pieces.

*T*he Morgans' modest, rock-faced, two-story house sat in the heart of Bluebonnet Lane, surrounded by other bungalows and family-style residences. Since Abby's childhood home had been rented out for several years it looked a little bedraggled. Other than that, there was nothing particularly unique about it.

Except for the huge storage container and the shiny silver Mercedes SL parked in the driveway.

With a pull of air into his lungs, he got out of the truck and moved up the concrete path that split the front yard. His heart worked overtime as he knocked on the door, slid his hands into his pockets, and stepped back to wait.

The last time he'd seen Abby, she'd stood with the rest of his family as he'd cupped her face in his hands and given her a quick good-bye kiss. At the time, he'd never imagined just how final the good-bye would be.

His mental wanderings snapped back as the front door creaked open and . . . *Holy shit.*

Everything about her had changed. Her customary cloud of ivory curls were stick straight and streaked with caramel. Her blue eyes were shaded with dramatic hues of pink, brown, and a slash of black eyeliner. A dark blue clingy top draped at her neckline, then clung like a second skin the rest of the way down. Hot pink skinny jeans hugged her long legs. And a sexy pair of open-toed skyscraper high heels flaunted her purple nail polish.

She'd been made up to look like she'd just posed

for a magazine cover. And like some of those cover girls, she looked like she hadn't eaten a slice of her favorite pepperoni-and-pineapple pizza in a long time.

Where did her luscious curves go?

As usual, his big mouth opened before the words connected to his brain. Luckily, they only hit on one of the wild-ass thoughts flying through his head.

"What the hell happened to your hair?"

For a long, breathless moment, Jackson stood on her doorstep. Five o'clock shadow dusting that squared jaw. Fists clenched.

Abby took that split second to drink him in.

As usual, his dark blond hair appeared carelessly hand-combed—reflecting a hint of the man she knew to be an act-first-think-later kind of guy. The outer corners of his eyes were slightly turned down and made him appear like he was in a perpetual state of concern. But the vivid blue made him look keenly intrigued, full of mischief, and wildly untamed.

The impressive breadth of his shoulders and chest were rigid beneath a deep blue SAFD shirt. The defined muscles of his biceps expanded from beneath the short sleeves, and dark blue pants hugged his slim hips and long, powerful legs. The man oozed sexuality as if at birth he'd been granted an extra ration of snap and sizzle.

Abby's heart gave a fierce thump against her ribs.

He'd changed.

He looked better. Older. Wiser.

And probably a little north of ticked off.

At his comment, she resisted the urge to lift a hand to make sure her hair was in place. During the extent of her marriage, she'd been expected to appear flawless at all times. To be the consummate hostess. Dedicated personal assistant. And loving wife. At least in the eyes of the world—or Houston society—whichever came first on any given day.

Her birth date might claim her age to be only thirty-one, but she felt ancient.

Tired.

Far from perfect.

Her heart leaped again as she looked up into the eyes of the man who'd *never* expected perfection. He'd seen her at her best *and* her worst, and he'd never looked at her any differently.

Until now.

Now, those dark blue eyes were narrowed.

Judgmental.

Curious.

She'd never met a man as outspoken as Jackson Wilder. He called it like he saw it. Spewed advice no one invited.

Guess some things hadn't changed at all.

"So . . ." His entire expression shifted. "It's been a while," he finally said, unable to hide the undertones of a low Southern growl.

She lifted the corners of her mouth into a practiced smile. "We're not going to argue in the first five seconds, are we?"

"Argue?" His gaze locked onto hers. "I don't know what you're talking about. Friends don't argue. And that's what we were the last time I checked . . . oh, say almost seven years ago. Except . . . wait . . ." He folded those massive arms, shifted the weight of that big strong body from one boot to the other. "Friends don't run off without a word, then never write or call, do they?"

"Oh goody. We *are* going to argue." She tried her best to sound blasé—though a blood-pressure check would have proven otherwise. She stepped back from the doorway. "Then I guess you might as well come in so the neighbors don't start erecting fallout shelters."

Without another word, he strode into the house filled with haphazardly placed furniture and stacks of boxes she'd had the movers bring back into the house from the storage container parked outside. Prep, stage, and sell, had been the request from her mom and dad. Oh, and while she was at it, would she mind going through everything and having a garage sale too? And then, of course, send them the money even though she'd been the one to pay for the movers *and* she'd be the one to cover any renovation costs to sell *their* house. Heaven forbid they take a break from playing Texas Holdem or yucking it up during martini happy hour with their fellow retirees.

Irritation crept up the back of her neck as she turned to look at the man in the middle of her living room—muscular arms folded across an amazing chest while he studied the current wall-to-wall catastrophe.

"Have a seat," she told him as she shut the door. "If you can find one."

"No thanks. I don't plan on staying long."

"Suit yourself." She wadded up the sheet covering the sofa and tossed it on top of a stack of boxes marked *Records*. "Hey, how about if you just stand there and glare at me while I make some tea. Or maybe you'd like a beer. The previous renters might have left one behind in their haste to vacate while skipping on the last month's rent."

"I'll pass."

"Great." She pushed a breath from her lungs. "You do that."

"You sound a little testy." The orneriness in his deep voice rippled up her spine.

"*Testy?* Whatever gave you that idea?" Her blood rushed through her veins, and, for the first time in a long time, she felt alive. She'd been on the run for so long, it was finally time to stop. Deal with the consequences. After all, she'd come back to Sweet to face her demons, hadn't she?

Might as well start with the devil himself.

"The way you're grinding your teeth," he said.

"My teeth were fine and dandy before *you* showed up at my door with your fists and jaw clenched and your Grrr face in full force. So why did you come here, Jackson? To argue? To throw a wad of guilt at me?"

He said nothing.

"Or . . ." Her hands slammed down onto her hips. "Were you looking for an apology?"

Denial darkened his eyes.

She'd always known him better than she'd ever

known herself. Which made her realize he hadn't come for a pathetic admission of guilt.

He'd come for answers.

The truth.

But she could never give him that. Not without losing a whole lot more of herself than she was willing to give.

Which just proved what a total weenie she really was.

So now it became about who played the game better. And since she'd just graduated from a hard lesson of Living a Lie 101, she had no doubt who would win.

"I'll take your silence as a yes. So here you go, big guy. *I'm sorry.*" Check. Mate. She folded her arms across her chest to mirror him. "Happy?"

"Ecstatic. Never been better." His eyes lowered. Then that penetrating gaze moved back up her body—stopping, inspecting, assessing. "How about you?"

"I'm great."

"Really? Cause you look . . ."

"Watch it."

"Different," he said, though she knew that wasn't his first word choice.

"Don't judge, Jackson."

"I know it's been a long time but . . . damn it Abby, you're different."

"Back atcha, bucko."

"A lot has happened since the last time we saw each other."

"Tell me about it," she mumbled, then went back into the kitchen and yanked open the refrigerator door. Cold air brushed her face as she peered inside. *Nada.* Not even a tray of ice existed in the freezer section.

What had she expected? For the past couple of years, her parents had been living the good life in the Florida condo her husband had given them. Scratch that. They'd been living the good life in the fully furnished Florida retirement condo her *ex*-husband had used as bribery. Or even more accurately, to remove them from any chance of their casting some kind of hillbilly blemish on his pristine status with the movers and shakers of Houston's high society.

Quite the opposite of their two relatively mild-mannered daughters, her parents had always lived on the wild and loud side of Partytown. They might never have been the loving and devoted parents that Jackson was privileged to have—but even Abby had been shocked to discover how quickly her mom and dad had been bought like Las Vegas hookers.

At the time, her young and handsome husband had just been handed the Houston Stallions NFL team by his ailing father, and he'd been out to prove himself both on the influential social scene and on the scoreboards. The man oozed charisma. Especially when he wanted something. She should know. He'd turned that charm on her, and she'd been blinded. Eventually, the rose-colored glasses had come off, and she'd quickly learned that money could not buy happiness. But by then it had been too late.

So really, who was she to criticize what her parents had obviously seen as a way to a better life? She'd done the same thing. She'd just been really misguided about the true definition of *a better life*.

Empty-handed, she shut the refrigerator door and turned to find Jackson right behind her—so close she could smell the remnants of smoke in his hair. See the smudges of soot near his hairline and the exhaustion in his eyes. Her instinct was to reach up and brush the hair back from his forehead and trail her fingertips down the lean lines of his face. Instead, she curled her fingers into her palms.

"Cupboard's bare?" he asked, with the hint of a smile that said he knew he was inside her personal bubble and was totally enjoying how much that made her squirm.

"Apparently." She ducked around him and found a spot with more room to breathe. He had her squirming all right. But she was sure he didn't realize in what manner. She didn't know what she'd expected it to be like the first time she saw him again, but this whole heart-thumping, nerves-tingling, dry-throat thing hadn't been it. "I don't know why I imagined there'd be anything resembling life around here other than dust bunnies or spiderwebs."

She leaned back against the counter—gaining at least another centimeter of personal space. "How'd you know I was back?"

"Ran into Brady. He said you'd come back to put the house up for sale."

"That's right."

His brows lifted. "And that's it?"

"Fishing was never your sport, Jackson. So why don't you come right out and say what you're thinking like you usually do?"

He gave her an honest smile, and her traitorous heart went all wibbly-wobbly.

"Thought maybe you'd finally come back to see *me*. But something tells me if I hadn't come by, you would have done what you needed to do, then skipped town without my knowing."

"Maybe." She shrugged. "I didn't really have a plan when I got here. Still don't. I just figured I'd do what my parents asked, then I'd be on my way."

"Back to Houston?"

A slow breath pushed from her lungs. "No."

His head tilted just slightly. "Why not?"

Everyone who read a newspaper, the Internet, or subscribed to *People* magazine knew *why not.* Was he just being cruel? She searched his face for a hint of spitefulness and came up short. "You know why."

"Tell me anyway."

A rush of air pushed the words from her throat. "Because there's nothing for me in Houston since my divorce."

In the long, awkward pause that followed, Abby heard the sound of a car door close. The bark of a dog. The chirp of a robin. The pounding of her heart.

"Yeah." There seemed to be more behind his single-word response. He glanced away. When he came back around, she still couldn't get a read on him.

"What happened?" he asked.

"I'm sure you don't want all the ugly details."

"There you go thinking you still know me." His lips flattened and disappeared within that gorgeous face. "How about you start with why you ran off, cut me out of your life, then married a man you barely knew."

She'd long ago accepted the circumstances that drove her from her hometown and into the big city. The reasons she'd taken the job in the Houston Stallions offices. The lunacy with which she'd married Mark Rich after only knowing him a few months. He'd been handsome, and attentive, and she'd thought it love at first sight. Kismet. An answer to her prayers.

Yeah. Maybe if she'd been praying to the voodoo gods.

"Why don't we just cut to the chase?" she said, determined to give him answers with only a few of the facts and none of the emotion. She couldn't and wouldn't lift the lid off that steaming pot of absurdity, or she might be in danger of losing any of the stable ground she'd regained in the past few months.

His broad shoulders lifted. "Sounds good to me."

"I left Sweet . . ." *And you.* "Because it was time. I was almost twenty-five years old and going nowhere in this town. I needed something different. Something new. Something that would make better use of my college degree. Something that would last a lifetime. I thought I'd found it."

She blinked. Looked away from the intensity in his eyes. "Clearly, I'd been delusional. Mark made that very apparent when he . . ."

"When he *what*?"

Crap. She'd fallen right back into the comfort of their old friendship and said too much. While she searched for the right words to recover from her mistake, his eyes narrowed.

"It's no big deal." She spouted the well-rehearsed propaganda she'd fed everyone else. "Really."

"Bullshit."

Jackson had always been someone she could trust. But she didn't know him anymore. And she didn't trust as easily as she once had. Oddly enough, when she finally opened her mouth, it had nothing to do with him at all. When she spoke, it was to face her devils, shake off the shame, and put the past behind.

However, the irony of the situation did not escape her.

She'd cut Jackson out of her life. No looking back.

Her ex had done the same with her.

"Mark ejected me from his life. Quick. Clean. No looking back." She forced her gaze to meet his and acknowledged the ugly truth. "Karma's a really vicious bitch."

In all the years she'd known him, Jackson had rarely been one *not* to have something to say.

But for the first time in her life, she'd rendered him speechless.

Chapter 2

Combat nap or any form of peace of mind long forgotten, Jackson pushed through the glass door of the Sweet Pet Clinic.

"Hey, Jackson." Andrea Davis, his brother's newest and most likely short-term vet assistant, greeted him with a flash of flirtatious smile.

Andrea was pretty and shapely, and by the time Jesse spun his magic, she'd have fallen in love and tumbled into his bed. Once she discovered Jesse had no interest in anything more permanent than his cable TV subscription, she'd be on her way like all the others. Eventually another Heather, Nicole, or Britney would take her place, and the cycle would start all over again. Jesse had *player* down to an art.

"If you're here to see Dr. Wilder," Andrea said, "he's in the back tending to Mrs. Purdy's Pekinese."

"Thanks." He shoved his sunglasses up onto his head and ignored the pounding echo of his boots as he strode across the yellowed linoleum floor that had existed since he was a kid and they'd brought their Australian shepherd Ralphie to be neutered by old Doc Michaels.

Poor Ralphie.

When Jackson reached the back room, he found his brother murmuring in a gentle voice to the petrified pooch as he snipped the stitches on her shaved belly. At the sound of footsteps, Jesse looked up.

"Hey, little bro, what's up?"

"*He* dumped *her.*" Jackson thrust his hands on his hips and expelled the breath he felt like he'd been holding since he drove away from Abby's house.

A frown pulled Jesse's brows together as he looked back down and carefully pulled a stitch with a pair of tweezers. "Who's *he*? And *who* did he dump? And you'd better not say Reno, or I will personally kick his stupid ass."

Their oldest brother had fallen in love—hard—and gone after his lady love—the host of the TV show who'd come in and renovated half their town, including Reno's hardware store. As far as anyone knew, all was sunshine and lollypops on that front. "Not Reno. I'm talking about Mark Rich."

"Uh-oh." Jesse's tweezers paused midair as he looked up again. "Are we talking about—"

"Abby. The son of a bitch dumped her like she was dirty underwear."

"And we know this how?"

"She's back."

"Shit."

"Yeah." Jackson pushed another breath from his lungs. "Came back yesterday."

"And you've already been to see her?"

The almost invisible nod he gave didn't make his little visit to her any less lame. He'd sworn he was done the day she'd cut ties and got married. He'd sworn he wasn't going to think about her. Wasn't going to miss her. Wasn't going to lose sleep over her.

What a load of crap.

He'd done all of the above and more. And didn't that just make him Mayor of Loserville.

"Why?" Jesse tossed the tweezers on the towel-covered metal tray and lifted the little, flat-nosed dog into his arms with a comforting stroke of his hand.

The question was legit though that didn't make Jackson want to answer it in any hurry. He shrugged. "Don't know."

"Bullshit." Jesse baby-talked to the snorting pooch, telling her what a good girl she'd been. Then he called for Andrea to take the dog back into the exam room, where her nervous owner waited.

"You've been waiting for her to come back ever since you found out she left," Jesse added.

"I just wanted an explanation."

"You get one?"

"No."

Jesse folded the metal tools up in the towel and tossed it into a pile on the counter. "You *try* to get one?"

"Of course. What kind of idiot do you think I am?"

"The kind who's been hanging around her as far back as when he thought giving her a frog he'd captured in the creek was a good idea. The kind who devoted himself to her but never took the time to explore what that meant until it was too late. The kind who—"

"Jesus, Jess, you don't have to hammer into my head what a fuck-up I am. I came here to talk. Not get a lecture."

His brother balanced his closed fists on the front pockets of his jeans. "I never said you were a fuck-up. But I'd have thought you'd learned your lesson by now."

"Which is?"

Broad shoulders lifted beneath the white jacket with SWEET PET CLINIC monogrammed above the pocket. "When it comes to fighting fires or the enemy on foreign soil, your actions are about two steps ahead of your thoughts. When it comes to women, they're about two steps behind."

Good point.

Taking in mind the woman he'd married.

His now ex-wife.

He loved Fiona. He'd always love her. But *in* love was different. She'd been crazy to marry him—even if she'd been pregnant with his baby.

At the time, they'd both agreed it was the right thing to do. If he could have handpicked a woman who'd be a perfect mother to his little girl, he'd have chosen Fi. She was an amazing woman. But she deserved a man who would marry her out of love, not obligation.

From the moment his baby had taken her first breath, she'd become the light and purpose of his life. But he'd wronged her too by never allowing himself to even try to fall in love with her mother. He'd been too busy living in the past. Too busy thinking of a woman who'd made her feelings perfectly clear the day he'd been tiptoeing through the rugged terrain of Afghanistan dodging IEDs and she'd pushed pedal-to-the-metal out of his life.

"So what are you going to do?" Jesse asked.

In the last hour, he'd imagined every possible reason for Abby's divorce. He thought maybe she'd finally come to her senses. But to learn it had been Rich who'd ended the marriage?

Game changer.

"Nothing." Jackson shrugged. "Let her do her thing here and go on with my life status quo."

"Seriously?" Jesse's eyebrows jacked up his forehead. "How about you give that a little more thought. Maybe then you could actually make a plan that might make sense and put it into action. You and Abby were inseparable most of your lives. Spent a whole lot of time in that old tree house figuring things out."

And she proved how much he'd meant to her the day she cut ties and took off. The devastation he'd felt when his brother had been killed almost destroyed him. If she'd been his best friend, she would have been there for him the same as he had for her when she turned sixteen, and her parents decided she could fend for herself and her little sister.

The agony of Jared's death washed over him like it had happened just yesterday. He'd loved his big brother. Idolized him. From the moment he'd been able to recognize faces, Jared's bright eyes and ever-present smile had been one of his favorite sights. He'd been a hell of a baseball pitcher. A superstar poker player. And the one person Jackson had always sought out for good advice.

Abby had been the perfect complement to his own personal Yoda. She'd always been there to share and listen. Even as a young girl, she'd handed out some solid solutions to the many scrapes he'd gotten himself into over the years.

When she and his brother both vanished from his life, he'd lost a piece of himself that he didn't think he'd ever get back. When his father died, the losses became too great. And like the rest of his grieving family, he'd been devastated and retreated from everything that had once brought him joy. At that awful time in his life, all he'd wanted—needed—was his best friend to talk him off the ledge.

Only she hadn't been there.

"Shit happens," he said.

"Yeah, well, something tells me this might not be over between the two of you."

"Oh, it's over all right. Hell. I don't even know her anymore." He scratched his head, and a lingering hint of smoke filtered past his nose. "She doesn't even look the same."

"Oh?"

"Hair's all straight like that Jennifer Aniston's, and a different color too. And she's too thin.

Like she hasn't eaten more than carrot sticks for months."

Jesse laughed.

"What's so damn funny?"

"You were her best friend when she had pimples, braces, and was flat-chested. You expect me to believe straight hair and a few pounds thinner is going to make a difference?"

"It's more than that, and you know it. Too much water under the bridge. Besides, she's just . . . different."

"Then why don't you try to get to know her again?"

"What?"

"Get to know her. Like you would any other woman you might be interested in."

"I'm not interested."

"Find out what makes her tick," Jesse continued as though he hadn't spoken. "What she likes. What she doesn't like. Find out if you're even compatible anymore. You're either going to find out you are or aren't. What have you got to lose?"

Not much, he thought. He'd pretty much already lost it all. "What makes *you* so smart?"

"Check the diplomas on my wall." Jesse grinned. "I've always been smart. And you should be clever enough to pay attention to my words of wisdom."

"So says the man with the revolving vet assistants because he shags them all."

"Not *all*."

Jackson laughed. "Right."

"Seriously, Jack, you've got to ask yourself

'What's the story?' Why would a man as shrewd as Mark Rich *seemingly* dump a woman as gorgeous and nice as Abby?"

Jackson glanced out the window to the canine exercise yard beyond. "That's a damned good question."

At the Touch and Go Market, Abby pushed the shopping cart with the wiggly wheel down the juice and water aisle. She kept her head down. Tried to make herself invisible as much as possible. She'd even changed into an older pair of jeans, a plain white tee, and a Cowboys ball cap, hoping everyone would focus on the two-for-one wiener sale and not the newcomer scoping the aisles.

Unfortunately, at the checkout stand, the current issue of the *National Enquirer* was plastered with seen-before photos of celebrity cellulite so there was an excellent chance that all the behind-the-hand whispers were focused on her. In Texas, gossip came as big as the hairdos. And everyone in the Lone Star State knew that the higher the hair, the closer to God.

Humiliation humbled a person even if that person already considered themselves modest. It wasn't just the divorce that shamed her. It was that she hadn't trusted her instincts. Hadn't listened deeply enough to her heart. The day Jackson left for Afghanistan, she'd run like a rabbit. She regretted ever taking that job in the Houston Stallions' administrative offices. She regretted allowing herself to get tangled up with someone who'd obviously sensed her weakness or desperation and played her for a fool. Someone who'd kept his emotions—if he had any—locked up tight. She'd left Sweet to find love. To make a familial connection. To start a family of her own.

She'd walked away from the experience shaken, lost, childless, and lonelier than she'd ever been before she left Sweet.

While the sound system played a Muzak version of Foreigner's "I Want to Know What Love Is," she scanned the shelves for her favorite brand of flavored water before she remembered the T&G didn't offer a wide variety. She should have known that having worked in the local grocery-store office for the two years prior to moving to Houston.

Mark had forbidden her to shop anywhere but Whole Foods. He'd completely banned her from Walmart—which was a sin to anyone who'd been raised to watch their pennies. Money had never been an issue for him. Not even when he'd been a kid. He'd never had to get out and figure how the other ninety percent of the nation lived. Never had to perfect the Fryolater at McDonald's. Never had to bag feminine products at the CVS. His opulent tastes ran from Persian rugs to Salvador Dali originals. Kobe beef to Italian white truffles. He'd even been particular about his brand of toilet paper, for God's sake.

Toilet paper.

No matter how much she tried to excuse that, there was just something freakish about the war between single sheet and two-ply.

She'd always had simple tastes—a real beer-and-hot-dog kind of girl. The first time he'd handed her a cracker piled high with caviar, she'd about died. She'd barely managed to get the slimy stuff down her throat. She didn't even want to think about the whole-raw-oyster incident.

Over time, she'd learned to swallow the *delicacies* without dashing to the bathroom in full gag mode. But no matter how many times she'd been told it was an acquired taste she'd learn to love, she'd never moved beyond the *yuck* phase.

Should have been her first clue she didn't fit.

Had she been paying attention.

She grabbed several bottles of lemonade-flavored water, then pushed her wobbly cart farther down the aisle. In front of a P.M.S. survival kit display of Cocoa Krispies, Cool Ranch Doritos, and Cheez Whiz, she crashed head-on into another cart. Apology danced on her tongue as her gaze jerked upward.

"Abby?" The woman tilted her big blond Texas-sized hairdo, dipped her head to peer below the brim of Abby's ball cap, and smiled. "Sugarplum, what are y'all doing back here in Sweet?"

Great.

If Jackson Wilder had been number one on her "Be sure to avoid" list, his mother Jana was number two.

Not that Abby hadn't always adored the woman. She had. Still did. She'd always wished she could have been lucky enough to have been born into the Wilder family and had a mother like Jana. At one time, she'd wanted to be a part of that family more than she'd wanted anything. But those hopes and dreams had turned into a self-imposed nightmare.

Being Jackson Wilder's best friend had been one thing.

Falling in love with him had been no-no numero uno.

A chill from the nearby dairy cooler settled in her spine while her brain scrambled in a zillion directions for a response. One that wouldn't be too curt. One that wouldn't be too leading. One that would be just right. Like maybe a hint of the truth without all the *"I'm searching for who I am"* part.

"My parents have decided to sell their home," she said, "and they asked me to come put it up for sale. My sister Annie just found out she's going to have a baby, and—"

"Oh, that's wonderful news." Jana edged her cart a little closer. "Last I heard she and her husband had moved to Washington."

"They're not married, but yes, they live in Seattle." And as far as Abby could tell, her little sister should run far away from her loser musician boyfriend.

"I hear Seattle is beautiful. I've never been but a friend of mine recently moved here from there." Jackson's mother gave her a disarming smile. One that said her thoughts were not connected to her lips, and whatever she was saying was a pure diversion from what she really had going on in her mind. "I'm sorry for interrupting. You were saying?"

"Just that someone needed to clean up my parents' house and put it on the market."

"So you'll be staying here in Sweet?"

"Temporarily. Then I'll go . . ." Where exactly? She didn't have a home to go back to. Before Mark had issued her walking papers, he'd gone out and purchased a high-rise condo for her—his former star quarterback Dean Silverthorne's condo to be exact. When the Pro Bowler injured his shoulder, he decided to hang up his wristband, get married, and start a family. Perfect timing for Mark to get a good deal on a posh piece of property.

As part of their divorce settlement, he'd put the condo in her name only—a going-away present so to speak. Abby called it what it was. A bribe. She'd since sold it to the CEO of a Houston-based Internet company at a tasty profit from what Mark had paid for it.

"Wherever the wind takes me," she said in an unbelievably chipper voice for someone whose heart was about to hammer out of her chest.

"Well, doesn't that sound interesting." Jana's smile quivered at the corners as she glanced down into Abby's cart. "Looks like you're stocking up on water, carrots, and . . . celery. All you need now is a nice chunk of roast. How about you drop by on your way home, and I'll pull one from the freezer for you. You know you can't get meat here at the store equal to what we raise on the ranch."

Abby had been restrained from eating comfort food for so long, she'd forgotten what real down-home cooking tasted like. Her stomach grumbled. "I wouldn't want to bother you."

"Nonsense." Jana waved her hand. "Actually . . . now that I think of it, there's a better selection of cuts over at Reno's place. He has a big chest freezer out in the barn. How about you drop by there on your way home and grab a few packs?"

"Does he still live out on Rebel Creek Road?"

"He does. Built a space above the barn a couple years back. Just take the stairs up and go on in. Make yourself at home and take as much beef as you want. Lord knows we've got plenty. And you know I've always thought of you as family."

The comment struck a sour note in the center of Abby's chest. Jana had never been one to lay on the guilt. Abby didn't believe she meant to do so now. But being thought of as a member of the family and being a member of the family were two different things. And as much as she'd run out on Jackson, she'd done the same with the rest of his family. So, at the moment, it was easier to think about rib roast, brisket, or a thick juicy tenderloin than how many people she might have hurt with her selfishness.

"That sounds wonderful. If you're sure you don't mind."

"Don't mind at all."

"I'll make sure to stop in and thank Reno. Are he and Jared still roommates?" Abby asked, regarding the two oldest Wilder sons.

"Oh. No, sugarplum." The light in Jana's bright blue eyes dimmed. "Jared was killed fighting in Afghanistan."

"What?" The air was sucked from Abby's lungs.

"And Joe . . . well, he died the following year."

Abby's heart missed several beats. Her stomach rolled. Her ears buzzed. And her entire body trembled. She backed up and almost nailed the stack of cereal boxes on the end cap display.

Why hadn't anyone told her?

And exactly who would that have been? she chided herself. She'd cut *all* ties with anyone in Sweet.

"I'm so . . ." Abby bit her lip. Tried to catch her breath. "I . . . I don't know what to say. *I'm sorry* just sounds pathetically lame."

"It's not." Jana reached out, took her hand, and gave it a reassuring pat. "And I appreciate it. I know how much you always loved Joe. And Jared was just like a brother to you."

Abby nodded, feeling foolish that the woman who'd lost so much was giving *her* comfort. It should be the other way around. "If I'd known, I would have been there. I swear I would have."

"I don't doubt it for a moment." With another reassuring pat, Jana took control of her grocery cart. Wrapped her fingers around the steel handle. "You make sure you stop by for that beef. Then you come by and see me first chance you get. We can have ourselves a little chat. I'll make us some cobbler."

"I'd . . . really like that."

While Abby tried to recover from the devastating news, Jana wheeled away and turned down the canned-vegetable aisle. It took Abby several deep breaths to quiet her pounding heart and clear the moisture from her eyes.

Joe Wilder had been a handsome, bigger-than-life individual who spent most of his time teaching his five sons how to ranch and be good men. The rest of the time he focused on his devoted wife or helping out the community. Everyone knew Joe Wilder, and Joe Wilder knew everyone. And when Abby had needed fatherly advice, she often sought him out instead of the man under whose roof she lived.

Jared had been blessed with his daddy's good looks, kind eyes, and thoughtful smile. He'd been the troop leader of the band of rowdy brothers. He'd been the calm in the storm. The voice of reason.

She couldn't believe both he and Joe were gone.

Or that Jackson hadn't mentioned it.

On a shaky exhale, she pushed her cart with the wonky wheel toward the wine aisle. She might only find a bottle of Boone's Farm on the shelf, but damn if she couldn't use a drink.

An hour, six bags of groceries, and a reasonable diversion of gossip at the checkout counter later, Abby aimed her Mercedes toward Wilder Ranch. After squeezing tomatoes and poking at cantaloupes for freshness, she'd debated whether to take Jana up on her offer. The knowledge that two people whom she'd considered an important part of her younger life had died weighed heavy in her heart. She battled with the truth—that *she*'d walked away from them. They'd never pushed her away. Well, that wasn't exactly true. Jackson had extended that long arm, but the decision to walk away from everyone had been all her own.

With the horrible news still barely registering, she turned her Mercedes down Rebel Creek Road and cruised beneath the tunnel of live oaks that led to Reno's place. A long look over this portion of the family ranch brought back so many happy memories of the times she'd spent with the wild Wilder boys and the hours they'd all spent playing make-believe about what they wanted to be when they grew up.

Jared, the oldest and customary peacemaker, had always wanted to be a sheriff or a Secret Service guy. Reno and Jesse had wanted to be cowboys. Jackson had always wanted to be a fireman. And Jake, the baby, had wanted to be Batman. Yet Abby hadn't been surprised when after 9-11, they'd all joined the Marines.

Patriotic blood ran through their veins. But as Jackson had told her the day he went off to boot camp, he hadn't joined solely based on an honor-bound duty. He'd felt a need to do something for all the people lost that day because they were someone's mother, father, sister, brother, or child. And because someone out there needed to care enough to make a difference.

The Wilder boys and many more young men from Sweet had enlisted. They were all heroes. Some gave all. All gave some. And that just made her heart ache all the more. Because besides chairing a few Junior League committees, what had *she* done with her life in the past few years?

Certainly nothing so honorable.

Alongside the big wooden barn at Reno's place she parked the car and stepped out into the hot afternoon sun. Though she was only going into an empty barn to grab some packages of beef, as a habit she smoothed her hands down her shirt and checked her hair in the window's reflection. Appearances had been everything to her ex.

Everything and the *only* thing.

As she climbed the stairs to the loft, she realized the absurdity of her high heels. Everyone in Sweet wore boots, tennis shoes, or flip-flops if they were down at the lake. So who was she trying to impress with her Tory Burch sandals? The busy spider in the corner? The pigeon cooing in the rafters? The mouse diving into the bale of hay?

She reached down and yanked them off. In an affront to the *rules* she'd once lived under, she tossed them over the handrail. They hit the ground with a thunk and a puff of dirt.

The pine boards beneath her feet were rough and cool. She flexed her toes, smiled, and climbed the remaining steps to the HOWDY doormat. At the top, she reached for the handle and the door swung open . . . into a roomy apartment.

Not a storage room.

Not a vacant loft.

Granite countertops highlighted the open kitchen and island bar. Exposed ceiling beams gave the place a country atmosphere without benefit of horseshoe lamps or a black velvet John Wayne painting.

In the center of the hardwood floor, amid tasteful leather furniture and décor, sat Jackson . . . with pink barrettes in his short hair, gobs of bright blue eye shadow on his eyes, and peppermint pink blush on his cheeks. Never mind the cherry red shine on his lips, which were open in surprise.

"Daddy pweety." The little girl at his side had golden curls and . . . Jackson's deep blue eyes. The big grin on her little cherub face said she was obviously proud of her handiwork.

Abby laughed before reality crashed the party. *Jackson had a child.*

A breath-stealing ache burrowed deep into her heart.

"What are you doing here?" he asked in a deep masculine voice that was in direct conflict to the clownish makeup on his face. He did not jump up and try to wipe off the mess; he merely sat there while the cherub went about rearranging the sparkly Disney princess barrettes in his hair.

"I . . . uh . . ." All thought flew from Abby's head as she watched those tiny fingers groom. "What?"

"*What* are you doing *here*?" he repeated in a tone that leaned more toward a demand.

"The . . . um . . . freezer." Abby's heart tumbled as the cherub's chubby hands cupped Jackson's face, and she kissed his cheek. "Your mother. A roast."

Jackson looked at her as if she'd bet all her marbles in a game and lost. Then, as if he could read the questions scrambled up inside something that might resemble her brain, he said, "This is my daughter, Isabella. We call her Izzy." He lifted one baby hand to his lips and kissed the backs of her tiny fingers. "Say hello to Abby, sweetheart."

Adorable blue eyes lifted and a smile parted Kewpie-doll lips. "Hi."

Like she'd been hit with a blowtorch, Abby's heart melted into a pile of goo. "Hi."

Izzy held out her little hand. Opened and closed it in a *come here* gesture. "Come pway."

"Oh." Surprised by the request, Abby was dumbstruck. "I don't think . . . I'm not . . ."

"Abby can't stay and play, baby girl." Jackson looked into his daughter's face. "She has better things to do."

When he looked up, Abby couldn't tell if she saw challenge in his eyes or accusation. The moment Izzy's mouth pulled into a sad little pout, Abby forgot all about the groceries in the backseat of her car, melting in the hot sun.

"Are you kidding?" She closed the door behind her and walked into the room. "I've always got time to play."

When Abby sat down on the floor across from him and crossed her legs, Jackson noticed she was barefoot. *That* was more like the Abby he knew. Not the Barbie doll who'd opened her parents' door just a few hours ago.

At the moment, she looked a little frazzled. Her stick-straight hair had developed a little bend to it as though those amazing curls had grown weary of being forced into submission. Her makeup looked a little the worse for the wear. And her red eyes revealed a hint of recently shed tears that anyone who didn't know her well might have missed.

He didn't.

So what—or who—had made her cry?

Not that it was any of his business.

Izzy got up and toddled over to the toy box and the little makeup kit he'd made the mistake of buying her. At the time, he hadn't noticed the recommended age on the plastic box had said 5+ years. Which meant his baby girl had little to no control over exactly how much blue stuff she shoveled onto his eyes. Yeah, he probably looked like a total ass sitting there with glops of goo all over his face and his hair sticking up all over his head with colored plastic poking out at all angles. He didn't care.

Since Izzy had come into his life, he'd learned that little girls played completely different than little boys. He'd learned to lift the tone of his voice when they played dolls, and to sing quietly while My Little Pony was trying to nap. He'd learned to sit patiently when Izzy wanted to use him as a guinea pig for Play-Doh cupcakes, or, as she had today, her beauty makeover victim. In the world of a three-year-old, playtime often equaled disaster.

But the rewards of being a daddy to a three-year-old girl?

Priceless.

He'd learned that cuddling took on an entirely different meaning when it came to naps and a little girl who fought sleep until he'd gently stroke her forehead, and she'd finally drift off. And when she'd wrap her little arms around his neck and lay her head on his shoulder? Yeah. Heaven.

When he and Fiona had divorced, he'd lost the

right to tuck his own child into bed every night. To give her tickles and hugs, then watch her float away to dreamland. And that had killed him. Pounded home the reminder of the mistakes he'd made. The regret he'd live with forever. Though he and Fiona shared custody he didn't get to spend nearly as much time with his daughter as he wanted.

Thus she ruled his world.

"I like the sparkles on your pink barrettes," Abby said to him with a complete straight face.

"You should see me decked out in the purple Dora ones. They have bows."

Abby's knockout smile finally appeared.

"Yeah," he said. "Izzy has totally put me in touch with my feminine side. But if you tell anyone, I'll have to kill you."

That got him a laugh, and he couldn't help but smile.

"She has quite the creative flair."

"Uh-huh." He noticed that Abby had changed her clothes from her earlier flashy pants and top to what he figured the rich and famous deemed *casual.* And he had to admit, jeans and a fitted tee had never looked so good.

Izzy plopped down between the two of them and stuck a Popstar Barbie in his hand.

"Shoes, Daddy." In her plump little hand Izzy held out a hot pink pair of miniature stilettos. Obviously, the makeup kit had been long forgotten in the quest for plastic pumps.

"You keep these out of your mouth. Okay, baby?"

Though Izzy nodded, he watched her like a drill sergeant whenever she played with such small items. Part of being a firefighter meant he was also an EMT, and he'd been on enough 9-1-1 choking-child calls to know to never take things for granted.

While he pried the small pieces onto the unrealistically arched doll feet, he watched Abby's expression. Her eyes darted from Izzy to him and back to Izzy again. Questions. Curiosity. And something else he couldn't read darkened the tropical blue. She looked back up at him again.

"How old is she?"

"She turned three a couple months ago."

A slight nod tipped her chin as she calculated time and circumstance. Then she glanced around his oh-so-male-dominated apartment. "Where's her mother?" she asked in a voice so soft he barely heard.

"Does it matter?" He wasn't about to discuss his child, his ex-wife, his failed marriage, or anything else. Especially not in front of Izzy.

He handed Izzy the doll, then got up and lifted her into his arms. Since it was a ways till dinnertime, he figured he'd give her something to tide her over. And since he needed to get away from Abby and her probing curiosity, he headed toward the kitchen. "Are you hungry, baby girl?"

"Yeth," she answered with a nod and a bounce of her soft shiny curls. "Coney dawg pweath."

Izzy favored corn dogs, mac and cheese, and ice cream. Anything else was up for debate. "You want ketchup?"

Izzy nodded.

From the living-room floor, Abby watched him while he wished she'd just get up and leave. But she didn't. She just sat there. Watching him.

He didn't know what she wanted. He wished he didn't care. But the hell if he didn't.

He set Izzy down on the floor. "Can you go wash your hands please?"

"Yeth." He watched her toddle off to the bathroom, where she had a pink plastic stepstool already in place.

Izzy liked her independence. Of course that didn't mean she wouldn't get sidetracked or try to fill the sink with water and pretend it was an ocean for the three floating ducks in the bathtub toy container. And it didn't mean he'd give her any more than about a minute before he'd need to run Izzy patrol.

As she disappeared into the hallway, he smiled. He didn't know what he'd done with all his time before she'd been born, but he must have been bored out of his mind. She kept him busy. On his toes. And he loved every second.

"She's adorable."

Jackson's gaze swung back into the living room, where Abby was picking up the forgotten toys and dropping them into the princess toy box. "Thanks."

She gently set a Lalaloopsy doll inside and closed the lid. "I didn't know you had a little girl."

"Guess news from Sweet doesn't travel as fast and far as from Houston." He pulled the box of corn dogs from the freezer and removed two.

"You're still mad," she said. She leaned her tan arms on the granite counter and watched him stick the corn dogs in the microwave above the stove.

He barked a laugh. "I blew past mad when I realized you'd cut me out of your life like I was some kind of poison." He shoved the cardboard box back inside the freezer. "At the time, I was tromping through the mountains in Afghanistan trying to stay alive and wondering why you'd do such a thing."

The timer on the microwave dinged, and he took out the corn dogs to let them cool. "But that was a long time ago, and I'm over it." He tossed the pot holder down on the counter. "I need to check on Izzy."

As he walked away, he felt her eyes burn into his back.

Mad?

No.

Heartbroken?

Absofuckinglutely.

Inside the bathroom he found Izzy on her little pink stool washing her hands with about half a bottle of bubbles foaming in the sink.

"I wash, Daddy." She grinned up at him.

"Let me see those cute little hands."

She held them up for his inspection, and he kissed her little fingers.

"Perfect. Let's get you dried off. Your corn dogs are ready." He knelt beside her and wiped her hands with the soft towel. When they were dry, she lifted them to cup his face.

"Pwetty Daddy."

He stood and glanced in the mirror.

Shit.

Hard to look like a total badass when you looked like a drag queen.

"Thank you, baby. Now let's go eat."

As she sprang out the bathroom door, he snatched her up and carried her upside down to the kitchen. Her giggles and squeals made him smile. Warmed his heart. When he got back to where Abby stood at the breakfast bar, he wondered why she didn't have any kids. She loved children. Or he'd thought she did. Maybe she'd changed more than just her hair and her clothes.

Her blue eyes darted between him and his daughter as he sat Izzy up on the counter and grabbed the ketchup from the refrigerator.

Izzy held up her corn dog and offered it to Abby. "Bite?"

Surreptitiously, he watched Abby's reaction.

"Oh." She smiled. "No thank you. I know you must be very hungry."

Izzy shook her head and thrust the corn dog closer to Abby's face. "Bite."

Abby hesitated.

A second later, she smiled, and said, "Thank you." Then she leaned forward and something weird moved in Jackson's chest as her mouth opened and her white teeth flashed just before she took a bite. While Izzy giggled, Abby covered her mouth and laughed.

"That's really good." She looked at him. "Are you eating the second one?"

He shook his head.

"Mind if you give it to Izzy and I take this one?" She shrugged. "Guess I missed lunch."

Silently, he handed the new dog to Izzy and marveled at his little girl's acceptance of the stranger in their midst. As much as he hated to admit it, Abby was just as much a stranger to him as well.

"Mmm," Izzy said.

"Mmmhmm," Abby responded.

While he watched Abby's white teeth dig in again and tear off a chunk of the breaded coating, he stood there wondering what the hell had just happened.

Bonding over a microwaved snack? That was a new one.

At a total loss, he folded his arms and leaned back against the counter. He wasn't sure he liked that his daughter was so accepting of Abby. She'd changed. Where once he'd known everything about her, he now knew squat.

Hell, her husband could have divorced her because she'd become some kind of total whack job. Maybe she belonged on that show *Snapped*. Not that he would ever watch such a ridiculous program, but they'd done an episode on a Texas millionaire's wife who conspired to kill her husband. Everyone at the station had talked about it ad nauseam. Tim "Meat" Volkoff, the driver of Engine One had said the episode gave him nightmares. And while they'd all laughed, Jackson had wondered what it would take for a woman to lose her mind like that.

Holy crap.

He needed to get a hold on his ridiculous thoughts. The Abby he'd known—the one he'd spent nearly a lifetime with talking about everything from history pop quizzes to which core classes to take in college. From politics to religion. From whether Jack should have died in *Titanic* to whether the guy in *My Best Friend's Wedding* should have ended up with Julia Roberts or Cameron Diaz. Abby had never even been the type to kill a spider. She'd had a gentle soul and a loving spirit. And she'd been the best friend a guy could ever ask for. Outside of his brothers, who often and every chance they had, gave him nothing but grief.

"I have to take Izzy home soon," he blurted out. Both females looked at him as if he'd just announced the sky was made of dog poop.

"Oh. Okay. I'm sorry for taking up your time." Abby took the last bite of her corn dog, wrapped the stick in the napkin, and tossed it in the trash. She ruffled Izzy's curls as she passed by. "Thanks for sharing your snack, cutie pie. And it was very nice meeting you."

His daughter smiled, and something tugged at his heart.

As Abby headed toward the door, he watched in fascination as the rhinestones on the back pockets of her jeans winked at him with each step. When she got to the door, she stopped and turned. He lifted Izzy from the counter to the floor, where she gave Abby an open and closed "bye-bye" hand. Then he walked to where Abby stood by the door. Waiting. Watching.

He opened the door, and she stepped out onto the landing.

She looked up at him and answered his unspoken questions. Well, some of them anyway.

"I didn't come over here to bother you, Jackson. I ran into your mother at the Touch and Go. She noticed the carrots and celery in my cart and offered me a roast to go with them. She told me Reno had a freezer up here and just to come help myself. I had no idea that this was an apartment or that you lived here."

He folded his arms. Rocked back on his heels. His mother was always up to something. Why had he thought she wouldn't glom onto Abby the minute she'd discovered her back in town? She'd always loved his ex–best friend.

"You were tricked," he said.

"Obviously." She glanced away.

When her eyes came back to his, a jolt of electricity hit his spine.

"But I'm not sorry I came," she said. "I'm glad I met your daughter. She's adorable. She looks just like you." Then she gave him a smile that trembled at the corners. "Your mom told me about Jared. And your dad." Her eyes misted. "I'm so sorry. I had . . . no idea."

She hadn't known?

All this time he'd thought she just hadn't cared.

A chunk of his bitterness chipped away.

"I know this is late," she said, "and you may not care what I think, but I am deeply sorry for your loss. Your father was a wonderful man. And if I could have ever custom-ordered a brother for myself, Jared would have been perfect. They both meant a lot to me."

As much as he'd like to think otherwise—even if the mist in her eyes wasn't telltale enough—he knew her words were sincere. She'd tagged along after Jared and admired him just like the rest of them. And his dad had always treated her like the daughter he'd never had.

"I hope you'll accept my sympathy," she said.

"Of course." It took everything he had to keep his voice level. To keep his hands at his sides instead of reaching out to take her in his arms. "And thank you."

Like she had when she'd studied for a final or pondered over which calf to take to the fair, she snagged her bottom lip between her teeth. Then a long sigh pushed from her lungs.

"We got off to a bad start earlier," she said. "I don't want to fight. I know there's a lot of water under the bridge. But if it's possible, I'd like to make things right between us."

Was it possible?

He didn't know.

"I guess time will tell."

Abby gripped the handrail as she went down the stairs from Jackson's apartment. When she reached the ground, she picked up the shoes she'd tossed over the rail earlier. It was then she noticed the chest freezer against the far wall, tucked into a corner away from the empty horse stalls. At least Jana Wilder hadn't completely bamboozled her.

She opened the lid and took out a packaged roast and some ground beef. She didn't care that the icy packages stung her arms as she carried them to the car. She didn't care that the bottoms of her bare feet were picking up dirt, dust, and God only knew what else the horses had left behind. She didn't care that half the groceries in her car were most likely warm and melted.

She tossed the beef into a bag, got inside, and sat behind the wheel. Heat rolled across the back of her neck as she stared out across the open meadow and rolling hills where she and the Wilder boys had once played, rode horses, and lived like there was no tomorrow.

Though she'd had troubles back then, with her mom and dad's constant lapses in parenting and the task of taking over raising Annie, she'd had some of the best times of her life. And throughout whatever troubles she'd faced, she'd had Jackson right there beside her. What they couldn't figure out together his parents had jumped in to help. The Wilders had always been more of a family to her than her own.

Jackson.

She hadn't been there for him when he'd needed her most.

Before that, she'd always been there.

From the time he'd broken both arms falling off his horse, and she'd hand-carried his homework to him each day, to the time they'd studied for the SATs until dawn broke. He'd been her best friend . . . until the day she'd walked away thinking she could find something better.

What a joke.

There was no better.

And he now had a child.

A child he'd had with someone else while she'd tried to make herself believe the man she'd married could ever truly love her. Or that a child could save her pathetic ghost of a marriage.

She'd been wrong.

Seeing him again brought back everything wonderful she remembered. She'd meant it when she'd told him she wanted to make things right between them. Even if that only meant a general ease when they'd see each other instead of the gut-gripping intensity she felt now.

The expression in his eyes hadn't given away what was in his mind or his heart.

Time will tell.

He hadn't said yes.

But he hadn't said no.

Which left a whole lot of room for hope.

Chapter 3

$\mathcal{J}$ackson knocked out his shift at the San Antonio station with thirty minutes remaining. He'd never been a clock-watcher before, but with Reno still MIA, the family was taking turns to keep Wilder and Sons Hardware & Feed going until he returned. Jackson's shift at the store was due to start in two hours—providing the fire bell didn't ring before then.

Last time he'd talked to his big brother on the phone, Reno and Charli had packed up her apartment in L.A. and were driving back home via Sin City. Jackson hoped that didn't mean they were stopping off at a twenty-four-hour wedding chapel. Not that Reno shouldn't or wouldn't put a ring on Charli's finger, but because if their mother was denied throwing a big shindig of a wedding, the shit would fly.

While the rest of the A Shift lay sprawled out in the blue firehouse dayroom recliners watching

Chopped and talking smack about which of them would do better on the show, Jackson perched on a stool and dealt a playing card to Mike "Hooch" Halsey. He waited for the man with the nickname unbefitting to his nondrinking lifestyle to stay or scratch for a hit on a card that would either relieve him of dish duty or whether he'd be assigned to the kitchen until the pile of pots and pans were scrubbed clean. When Hooch smiled, Jackson knew Captain John Steele was about to roll up his sleeves.

One of the best things about their captain was that he didn't put himself on a different level than the firefighters. They all worked together whether it was washing the station windows or folding hose. They were a team. A unit. Just like Jackson and his brothers. Just like his fellow Marines.

"Flash 'em," Hooch said with the grin he'd been known to give while raking in a pot of poker cash.

The cap laid out his cards. Ace of spades. King of hearts.

"Ha!" Jackson hooted a laugh. "He kicked your ass."

"Hell." Hooch tossed down his king and queen and stood. "I just took pity on him, that's all."

Cap stood too and the men were eye to eye.

"Don't forget to wear your cute little apron," Cap said with a smirk and a poke at Mike's wide chest.

"Don't you think it's a little pathetic that you're only willing to bet on some cups and plates and not throw down some hard cash, old man?" In good humor, Hooch poked at their captain, who was hardly ancient enough to be called an *old man*.

"I just wouldn't want to see you crying like a little girl when I took your lunch money."

Jackson laughed and stuck the playing cards back in the box.

"Crash?"

At the sound of the nickname he'd received as a rookie with his *act first, think later* approach, Jackson looked up.

"My office," Cap said, then headed in that direction.

"Shit." Hooch clamped his hand over Jackson's shoulder. "What'd you do now?"

"Don't know." He shrugged. "Been keeping it clean."

"Apparently not enough. Want me to go get the donut for you to use on the ride home after the ass whoopin'?"

"Ha-ha." Aside from his brothers, he considered Mike one of his closest friends. They'd leaned on each other when they'd both gone through divorces. Lost their man cards by whining a time or two. And they never failed to razz the other whenever the opportunity arose.

He glanced up at the big clock on the cinderblock wall, hoping whatever problem Cap intended to take out of his backside would be quick and painless. He still had a thirty-mile drive home and a shift slinging bags of horse feed left in his day.

"Shut the door," Cap said as he dropped down to the creaky chair vacated the previous year by his predecessor.

Shit. In the firehouse "Shut the door" usually meant a suspension or at the very least a warning. Jackson didn't have a clue what would constitute a behind-closed-doors discussion, but he guessed he was about to find out.

"Sit down," Cap said when he remained standing. Suddenly feeling like a middle-schooler who'd gotten busted throwing firecrackers down the bathroom toilets, Jackson crossed the room and dropped down into one of two worn chairs in front of the desk.

The captain watched him with a cool expression that worked well with the light gray color of his observant eyes. At only thirty-nine years old, the captain looked as young and rugged as the rest of the men at their station. Lil Bit and Mighty Mouse, the two female firefighters on staff, had been known to declare the cap as "hot." Especially after they'd had a few after-shift beers. Jackson didn't know about that, but he did know that the man had earned and deserved respect from every soul in their company.

"So how's life treating you outside *the box*?" The captain leaned back, and the chair gave a groaning squeak.

Jackson smiled at the term given to the station many years and many firefighters before. "Can't complain."

"Still helping out at your brother's store while he's gone?"

"Yep. Rumor has it he'll be back next week."

"And you're still helping out your mom on the ranch?"

"Me and Jesse. Until Reno returns. Then he'll step back into place."

"You've got quite a full plate."

Jesus. Where the hell was this heading?

Had he done something wrong? Had there been complaints against him? In the past year and a half, he'd been busting his ass to stay out of trouble. No bar brawls. No one-night stands. He hadn't gotten so much as a parking ticket.

Jackson shrugged. "I can handle it."

"I know you can." Cap leaned forward and braced his thick forearms on the desktop. "Which is why I'm about to throw more on you."

Great. "Okay."

"Once upon a time I'll admit I thought you were headed downhill on roller skates. I know life served you up a bad hand there for a while, but I've been impressed how you've handled yourself when others might have taken the easy way out."

"Thank you, sir. That means a lot coming from you."

"So tell me . . ." The intensity in his superior's eyes made him shift in his seat. "How do you feel about being a firefighter?"

"Aside from my family, sir, it means everything to me."

"I'm glad to hear that. So what are your plans?"

"Plans?" Other than trying to be a good dad and putting one foot in front of the other, he hadn't thought much past next week. But with Abby's popping back into town, he'd sure given a hell of a lot of thought to his past. "Unless you're trying to tell me I'm skating on thin ice, I plan to be a firefighter until I'm too old to lift a hose."

"No complaints about your job performance. I'm asking about your plans because I want you to move up."

"I'm happy at this station, sir."

"Not move stations. Move up the ranks."

"Me?" Jackson flinched. "All I know is how to fight fires. It's what I love to do."

"Understood. But you've got leadership qualities, and I think you'd be even more satisfied with your career if you put them to use."

Jackson laughed. "I think you've got the wrong man. I've always been a follower."

"The hell you have. Just because you're one of the youngest in that band of brothers of yours doesn't mean you weren't meant to lead." He pushed a battered, dog-eared folder across the desk. "This is the study material I put together when I started thinking about moving up the proverbial ladder. Take it. Look it over. And start putting together a plan. I'd like for you to apply to be an engineer. Get the whole spectrum of duties under your belt. It will make you a better captain when it's your turn."

"Captain!" Jackson sat up straighter. "Me?"

Cap gave him a smile. "Yeah. You." He nodded toward the folder. "Take a look. I hope it will whet your appetite. Help you make a decision."

"I . . ." Jackson looked at the folder, then back up at the man he held in the same high regard he'd given to his military superiors. "I don't know what to say."

"I'm not going to bullshit you, Crash. It won't be easy. Studying takes time away from your family and all those little things you might do, like watch TV. But it's worth it. And the fire service is always in need of smart, strong, dedicated individuals like yourself. You just have to fight your weaknesses to make it happen."

The captain stood, pushed the chair away with the backs of his knees, and offered his hand. Conversation over. Jackson rose and accepted the gesture. Then he picked up the folder and tucked it beneath his arm. "Thank you, sir."

"I believe in you. Don't let me down."

"I won't." Knowing his superior believed in him meant a lot. Trouble was, Jackson didn't always believe in himself. He was great in a pinch. Worked like a champ off his instincts. But when he had to think about something first, then react, he tended to stop cold in his tracks.

"Hopefully the woman in your life will understand she may have to share you with the books for a while," Cap said with a good-natured clap on the shoulder.

"No problem," Jackson countered. "No woman."

Not even the prospect of one.

*S*everal days after she'd taken the plunge to come back to Sweet and face-plant into her past, Abby stood in the center of her parents' living room, taking notes on what needed to be done in order to put the house up for sale.

After she'd gotten the furniture put back in place, she'd taken a couple days to reacquaint herself with the area by taking a long drive through the Hill Country. Each mile had reminded her of how much and why she'd missed the quaint little towns and the friendly smiles of people who didn't know or judge her.

In Houston, she'd never gotten used to the glares from other women at the mandatory social gatherings that made her feel as though she had toilet paper hanging from the back of her dress. Or the ogling she'd receive from the men, who'd assess her breasts, waist, hip size, and intelligence all in one quick scan.

On the arm of the man who'd briefly chosen her to be his wife, she'd been judged often and harshly.

From Highways 87 to 290 to 46, she'd stopped at antiques stores and tourist sites and walked out with bags of trinkets and geegaws. She had no place to keep any of it. She didn't exactly have a permanent home or even a plan on where she wanted to settle down yet.

One thing she'd learned about herself in recent days? She was great at making lists.

Everything else she pretty much sucked at.

She glanced at the dingy living-room walls and couldn't recall the last time they'd seen a brush and new coat of paint. And even though she'd never been allowed to decorate in any of the homes her ex had owned, she'd developed a sense of what worked and what didn't. With her mind focused on keeping things neutral for a quick and easy sale, she jotted down some color ideas. Then, pen poised above paper, she moved into the kitchen.

Paint. Curtains. New stove. New faucet. Her gaze dropped to the yellowed linoleum. Uck. New flooring. She might not know how to install or apply anything on her list, but she was determined to give it a go. She'd take it slow and learn.

She had nothing but time on her hands.

A quick study of the rest of the house told her each room needed new paint, and the bathrooms would need new sinks, faucets, and flooring as well. She'd replace the worn carpet with a hardwood type of laminate and call it good. By the time she was done with her parents' house, hopefully she'd have an idea of where she wanted to go and what she wanted to do when she grew up.

Though she held a degree in business, her occupational skills ran the gamut from clerical to flower arranging. Of course, this was ranchland. She could always fall back on the talents she'd developed as a member of the 4-H and FFA, but she wasn't sure there were any current job openings for a calf chaser or poop picker-upper.

Which led her to the conclusion that until she discovered where she was going, she needed to guard the remains of her divorce settlement. Unless she happened to find that one thing she just couldn't resist buying.

Then all bets were off.

A rush of exhilaration tickled her stomach as she grabbed her purse and, list in hand, headed toward one of those big-box stores in San Antonio.

Maybe she'd even treat herself to lunch at Whata-burger. She hadn't been to one in years. Hadn't been *allowed*. Her mouth watered just thinking of a thick, juicy jalapeño cheeseburger with a side of onion rings.

Typically, the noon traffic in downtown Sweet was the same as morning rush hour or the afternoon rush. Compared to Houston, it was virtually nonexistent. As she leisurely drove down Main Street, she recognized the changes that had recently taken place. Town Square—where birthday parties, weddings, and the Sweet Apple Butter Festival took place had been given a complete overhaul. Instead of a plain patch of grass, some overgrown trees, and a few beat-up picnic tables, there now stood a Victorian gazebo, walking path, water features, and a colorful playground.

Farther down the road sat the building that housed Goody Gum Drops, the candy store she and every other kid in town saved up their pennies to invade on Saturday afternoons. The one-time candy-striped building had been repainted crisp white and given a modest turn-of-the-century appeal. Several other stores had been given a face-lift as well.

Namely Wilder and Sons Hardware & Feed.

Abby's foot hovered over the brake as she passed by at a crawl.

Why was she taking her business to San Antonio when she could keep her dollars right here in town and help out a family friend at the same time?

She flipped a Uey at the corner of First and Main and parked in front of the cedar-sided Western-style building. A revamped sign hung above a shiny corrugated metal overhang, and a display area now perked up the front window. Daisy-filled red feed buckets hung on the posts out front, and the boardwalk was brand spanking new.

After a quick smoothing of her hands down her clothes to make sure she was put together, she pushed open the glass door. A bell tinkled her arrival while Kenney Chesney sang about "Reality" on the radio. Several other people were milling about the store—an elderly man with a plastic handbasket filled with small boxes and packages of unidentifiable hardware goods and a woman with big hair and painted-on jeans at the paint-samples display booth. Abby vaguely remembered the woman.

Lila Ridenbaugh had been a wild child back when they'd been in high school. Though Abby had tried never to get sucked into the local gossip about who was doing who in the backseat of someone's car, Lila's name did happen to come up quite often.

While Abby waited for Reno to appear, she checked out the inside of the store, which felt as new and fresh as the outside. Yet somehow it still managed to preserve the spirit of Joe Wilder, the man who'd given the place life.

She pulled off her Dior Piccadilly sunglasses, shoved them up onto her head, and glanced up at the sepia-toned photos framed by aged barn wood. The pictures were of Joe and his five boys at various stages in their lives.

One was of Jackson, with a grin that displayed

his missing two front teeth as he stood on a stool at the cash register with Reno and their father looking into the till. It was cute and animated, and Abby well remembered that toothless smile. Jackson's teeth had grown in straight and white and gave him that knockout beam she was sure brought women to their knees.

Not that she wanted to think about that.

"Sorry that took so long," a male voice said, and Abby shifted her gaze to the man coming through the doorway of the stockroom carrying a red box with BALL COCK printed in bright yellow letters down the side. Jackson, not Reno, headed over to the gentleman with the handbasket. While they conversed about toilets, she couldn't stop her appreciative gaze from traveling down that tall, lean, muscular body.

A gray V-neck T-shirt hugged his wide shoulders and broad chest, then hung loose over his tight abdomen. A pair of worn Levi's lovingly cupped his generous package, embraced long legs, and broke across the tops of well-worn cowboy boots. Jackson had the type of physique that made a woman's girl parts tingle. She'd have to be dead not to include herself in that party. Especially since her girl parts had been told "*No*" way too many times in recent years.

As a deterrent, she joined Lila—who clearly didn't recognize her—at the paint-sample display. Abby's fingers immediately plucked out a sunny shade of yellow from the display. She loved color. Especially after being subjected to an all-white everything in Mark's homes.

"I wouldn't pick that color if I were you," Lila said with a frown pulling her dark and a bit shaggy brows together.

"Oh?"

"Uh-uh. I painted my kids' room with that and the color about blinds me every time I walk in there. Plus crayons and felt markers are impossible to get off. I don't even want to talk about all the grubby handprints those brats make."

Abby had no intention of letting Lila know that unfortunately she had no concerns over those types of stains. Or the fact that she was horrified to hear a mother call her children brats. "So you're here to choose a new color for them?"

"Oh hell no." Lila's broad shoulders and double D's came up. "They're all with their dads, and . . ."

Dads? As in plural?

"I had a little time to kill and came in for the scenery."

While the inside of the store was neat and welcoming, Abby glanced around and didn't see anything that would draw people in unless they had a need for screws or dog food or . . .

"Yeah. I'm talking about the Wilder hunk," Lila clarified.

"Oh."

"Didn't know which one would be working today, but it doesn't matter. They're all gorgeous. And since I haven't had a man in my life for a couple months . . ." Lila leaned in and Abby almost choked on her overpowering floral perfume. No doubt bought at a Dollar Store two-for-one special. "I'm way overdue and looking for somebody new to fill the empty spots."

She nudged Abby with a sharp elbow. "*If* you know what I mean."

Abby was pretty sure Lila wasn't talking about anything related to the vicinity of her heart except for those massive breasts straining beneath a way-too-tight tank top.

Booted footsteps and a deep voice rescued her from responding to Lila's remark.

"What are you doing here?"

"I came to buy supplies." Abby looked up at Lila's walking bull's-eye and waved her shopping list. "I thought my money would be better spent here in town than heading into San Antonio. What are *you* doing here?"

"Covering for Reno till he gets back in town." The corners of that sensuously masculine mouth lifted. "Your business is much appreciated."

"Hey. I was here first." Lila's displeasure came out in a perceptible foot-stamping pout.

"I'll be with you in a minute, Lila. Let me help Abby real quick." He tossed her a smile. "Then you can have all my attention."

Lila's spiderweb lashes fluttered. "Now you're talkin'."

He came closer to Abby, bringing with him the scent of a fresh shower and subtle lemony aftershave that made him smell as delicious as he looked. Casually, he took her arm and led her away from the paint-chip display. And Lila's bodacious self.

"Now," he said. "What can I help *you* with?"

"You sure you don't want to help Lila out first? I'm thinking it might not take much."

He chuckled. "Sugar, what Lila's looking for, we don't sell."

Abby's heart gave a little tumble. He hadn't called her *Sugar* in years. She did her very best not to let the endearment warm the pit of her stomach or, heaven forbid, travel any farther south.

"Good to know." She handed him her paper. "But I do think you might be able to cover everything on there."

"This is quite the list." His eyes scanned the contents, then came back to her face. "You plan to do all this by yourself?"

"I could hire someone to do it all but . . ." She left the real reason hanging in the air. *She had nothing better to do with her life right now.*

"Landscape lights. New sinks and faucets. New flooring. New . . . paint?" One brow jacked up his forehead, and he grinned. "*That* has disaster written all over it."

"Seriously? I figured that was the easiest one."

"Guess you've forgotten about the time we painted your bedroom blue. Which first started out pink. Then pink with white stripes that looked like a racetrack. And ended up with more paint on us than the walls."

The memory and the laughs they'd shared that crazy weekend her parents had decided to fly to Vegas came rushing back. Once again, he'd come to her rescue when her parents had bailed on her and her sister. In those days, he'd always had her back. And she his.

"That's because *you* decided we didn't need to tape things off," she said.

"Proof positive you should never follow my lead."

"And you should have told me *that* before the time you talked me into ice-block sledding down the hillside."

"Yeah. We were quite a pair after that. You with a sprained ankle and me with a sprained wrist."

She grinned at the easy smile on his lips. "Good times."

"Yeah." His eyes met hers. "We did have a few."

When his smile slipped away, she knew he was thinking about more recent times. And because she didn't want to get back into that ugly discussion, she said, "I guess if I screw up the paint job this time, I'll only have myself to blame. So maybe I should stick with neutral colors."

He dropped his gaze back down to her list. "You sure you don't want to hire someone to do all this? We've got a corkboard over by the cash register with a slew of business cards on it."

She ignored the edge to his tone that might hint that he was curious about her hefty divorce settlement. Or maybe he was only suggesting that since her parents *should be* footing the bill, she shouldn't have to do all the work. Heaven forbid he was suggesting she couldn't handle the work herself.

"That might be easier. But my parents can't afford it, and neither can I." How much money she did or didn't have was nobody's business. But even that wasn't the issue. Until she figured out what to do with the rest of her life, she had to be careful. Eventually, she wanted to buy another house—a home actually. Not just four cold, sterile walls like the ones she'd shared with Mark Rich.

The man owned two residences, and neither exuded any warmth. Several times she'd tried to bring things in to make them cozier or to personalize the spaces. But each time, the following day the new object would disappear without a word. When she'd finally gotten up the courage to ask why he'd disposed of them, he'd told her they were tacky and didn't suit his lifestyle.

She didn't suit his lifestyle either. He'd made that clear. Just like the lovely cashmere throw she'd found for the foot of the bed or the hand-embroidered pillows she'd picked up for the den, he'd disposed of her as well.

"I wasn't trying to pry about your finances," Jackson said, bringing her thoughts back to the here and now.

"I didn't think you were." She slid the paper from his fingers and looked at it again. "This *is* a pretty convoluted list. Maybe I should break it up into projects."

"You on a time crunch?"

"Not really." *Not at all.*

"Good."

Good? She searched his eyes and found he was a difficult man to read anymore. Maybe too much time had passed for them to ever reestablish the connection they'd once shared. But then what did he mean by *good*? Could he, deep down, be happy she was back? Dare she allow her heart to go down that path?

"Because some of these tasks are going to take a while to figure out and complete."

"Oh." Crash and burn.

"So maybe . . ." He reached out and gently lifted her hand with his big palm. She could swear something snapped.

Slowly, he took her list back without looking at it. "We get started by finding out what color of paint you want. And then . . . who knows. We'll just go from there."

Even after he'd retrieved the list, he still held on to her hand. The gradual smile he gave her suggested he might mean more than just faucets and laminate flooring.

"I'd like that." Pleasure floated through her chest. "Very much."

After closing time, Jackson carried several five-gallon buckets of Baked Scone paint to his truck, then came back for the boxes of drop cloths, brushes, masking tape, and cleanup rags. It had taken a couple hours for Abby to gather her supplies and decide on a neutral, updated color. In the end, her selections were classic and no doubt would make the house attractive to potential buyers.

On the other hand, every second she'd spent in the store heightened his senses, drew out surprising responses, and literally had him so distracted he barely recognized the moment she finally pulled her credit card out, paid, and left.

He'd had to sit down and compose himself with

a cup of coffee before he could complete the task of closing up shop.

For the first time since she'd walked in, he'd been able to breathe without capturing the warmth of her scent. He'd been able to concentrate without all the little oohs and aahs she made as she pondered over various shades of beige.

She'd been his first in many pleasures of life. They'd shared a first kiss merely by being curious kids. At the time, she'd had braces, and the experiment between best friends had been ridiculous and so funny they'd both laughed their asses off. After that, they'd saved further experimentation for their significant—or at least temporary—others.

Unfortunately, Abby had a tendency to choose guys who walked all over her. When her so-called boyfriend had broken up with her the day before their junior prom she'd been so sad it had crushed his heart. Though he hadn't planned to stick himself in a monkey suit and join all the other yahoos at their school for the ridiculous *How Sweet It Is* themed dance in the high-school gym, he'd done it for her. Afterward, they'd taken the bottle of sloe gin she'd snuck from her parents' liquor cabinet out to their tree house. When they got a little tipsy, things got a little amorous. Clothes came off, and they became each other's firsts. Even as a guy, he knew the experience had been something amazing and memorable.

That had been the first time something inside him had felt different with her. Something that at the time he'd tried not to look at too deeply.

The following day, after he'd battled a gnarly hangover and finished his chores around the ranch, he'd called her to talk it over. See how she felt about everything, so they could figure out where to go from there. At first there had been an awkward silence, then she'd made no mention of the night before. So he hadn't either. Later in the conversation, she mentioned that the douche bag who'd dumped her before prom had called and wanted to get back together.

End of story.

They never discussed doing *it*. Never discussed how they felt about *it* or each other. She'd been his first, and yet she'd walked away from him without any mention that maybe, just maybe, that might have been a pretty important event in their lives.

Eventually, he pushed away the new feelings he'd discovered for her in order to dodge the relentless teasing from his brothers, and he moved forward.

Then college came, and they headed in different directions. With miles of separation, their friendship somehow endured, but it had never been the same as all those hours they'd spent together holed up in the tree house talking. After college, they'd both moved back to Sweet. They'd been focused on careers and jobs and everything in between. They might never have regained the rhythm of their friendship as it had been in those early years, but they hadn't forgotten each other either, and somehow they'd managed to stay close.

When 9-11 happened, he and his brothers enlisted and headed off to boot camp. After the

most mentally and physically challenging twelve
weeks of his life, he and his brothers had graduated in San Diego. During those long, exhausting
weeks, he and Abby had stayed as close as possible. When he'd come home before he deployed
to Afghanistan, they'd gone out to the tree house
to catch up on each other's lives. Somehow they'd
ended up in each other's arms. And they'd made
love.

He rubbed the ache in the center of his chest.

It hadn't been until a few weeks later, when
he'd been lying on a cot staring up at the canvas
tent above his head, that he'd realized his feelings
for her might have changed. But by then, it had
been too damned late.

So here he was, trying to figure out how to
move forward.

Today, the problem escalated when she realized
her Mercedes might have been built for comfort
and speed but not hauling hardware supplies.
Without success, she'd tried to figure out how to
get all her purchases inside the two-seater, and
he'd found himself offering to drop everything
off on his way home. He'd tried to assure himself that delivering purchases for her wasn't any
different than if she'd been Arlene Potter, presi-
dent of the Sweet Apple Butter Festival. Or Ray
Calhoun, local good guy. Or even Chester Banks,
Sweet's oldest living playboy.

He tried, but knew it was a damned lie.

He'd realized that the moment he'd reached for
her shopping list and touched her hand instead.

He'd tried to ignore that she smelled as sweet

and fresh as a field of bluebonnets. Or that her skin was so soft. Or that he could still remember how all that soft, scented skin felt beneath his young, greedy hands.

He slammed the tailgate shut on his truck, jumped in the cab, and hit the gas. Minutes later, as twilight burst across the sky in tequila-sunrise hues, he parked in front of the Morgan home, grabbed the buckets of paint, and headed up the walkway.

The front door stood open, and the hard-country edge of Jason Aldean's "Take a Little Ride" spilled outside. With no door to knock on, Jackson walked into the living room, where he spotted Abby in the kitchen. She'd changed from the pair of silver-studded designer jeans she'd had on earlier to a ragged-at-the-knees pair of Levi's that fell loose over her slender hips and looked sexy as hell. Like all he had to do was slip his hands down the waistband and slide them off her long legs.

The expensive silk blouse she'd worn had been traded in for a cropped T-shirt that showed off a tanned wedge of firm belly and smooth skin. Her feet were bare, and her hair had been pulled up in a messy knot on top of her head.

His hands tightened around the handle grips on the buckets, while everything south of his belt came to life.

"Hey," he called. She turned midsip of something pink and icy and gave him a warm smile.

His heart did a drop and roll.

Stupid heart.

What the hell did it know?

"Come on in," she said.

He looked behind him at the open door. "Kinda am already." He held up the buckets. "Where do you want these?"

"Just set them down right there. I'm not sure which room to start with yet."

"There's no way you're going to be able to carry these heavy buckets upstairs."

"Hmmm." She came into the living room. "Maybe I should just have you carry one upstairs then. Do you mind?" She looked up, and those big blue eyes mesmerized him.

"Just tell me where you want it," he said.

"If you don't mind, could you put it in Annie's room?"

"No problem."

He fell in behind her on the way up the stairs, paying no attention to the steps beneath his feet and instead focusing on the rise and fall of the back pockets of her jeans. "Annie coming home to help you out?"

"No. She just found out she's pregnant. Apparently, she has morning sickness pretty bad."

"I remember when—" Damn. There's no way he'd bring Fiona into this conversation.

Abby stopped on the step ahead of him, turned, and he found himself at face level with her high, firm breasts. "When what?" she asked.

"Nothing."

"You don't have to watch everything you say around me, you know." Her delicate brows pulled together. "You might want to keep everything private, and I'll respect that. But in case you've forgotten, this is Sweet. And gossip runs faster than water from a faucet around here."

"Any gossip concerning me has been spent a long time ago," he said.

She gave a little laugh, then continued up the stairs. "I wouldn't bet on that if I were you."

He followed her down the hall, knowing the layout of the house as well as he knew his own. He'd been there enough to feel like he belonged. To get to her sister's room, they passed Abby's. The light was on. An open suitcase sat on the vanity chair he'd once helped her reupholster. They'd antiqued the French-provincial frame, then put a pink-and-white floral print over the existing seat cover before Abby had added crystal beads.

At that point in time, Abby had been in a super girly bohemian mode. She'd worn gauzy floral dresses that hit just above her knees, and she'd finished off the look with cowboy boots and lots of dangly bracelets and earrings. She'd been pretty damned hot and never suffered for the lack of attention from the guys at school or around town. She'd just always been the good girl who seemed to pick the wrong guy.

"Just set the bucket anywhere," she said. "I can drag it wherever I need to later."

He set the paint near the door and laughed as he noticed the hot pink carnival prize monkey propped up in the center of her bed. It still held the long-stemmed daisy in its hand and still had the same silly grin as the night he'd won it for her at the fair.

"What's so funny?" she asked.

He pointed. "The monkey. I can't believe you still have that."

She walked into the room, picked up the toy, and hugged it to her chest.

Good day to be a toy monkey, he thought.

"This is Cha-Cha." She smiled first at the monkey, then at him. "Short for Chiquita—as in banana."

He raised his eyebrows.

"You don't remember I named her that?"

He shook his head.

"Then I guess you don't remember what *you* wanted to call her."

Again he shook his head.

"You wanted to call her Spank."

"Ah." He grinned. "I was an ingenious devil in those days."

"*Those* days?"

"I know that the Wilder Boys have a reputation, but you can't believe everything you hear."

"True." She settled the monkey back on the girly bedspread, then turned to him, arms folded across that really nice chest. "But some of us have seen you in action. And everyone knows that actions speaks louder than words."

Annnnnd, time for a diversion.

"With all the furniture back in place, it's hard to tell the house has been rented for a couple of years," he said. "For the past couple of months, my mom's been on a redecorating tear."

"Don't tell me she's getting rid of the John Wayne stuff."

"Hell, the Duke was the first thing to go. Mom got a little too cozy with Charli and—"

"Charli?"

"Charlotte Brooks, the host of *My New Town*. The folks at the senior center sent a letter into the show. You probably noticed the changes when you drove down Main Street."

"I did. It looks great."

"It was an adventure, all right. At least for Reno. Charli's kind of a whirlwind of energy, and she swept Reno right off his stubborn foundation."

"But I thought he and Diana were . . ."

"Yeah." His chest tightened. "You missed that one, too. A few months after Dad died, Reno and Diana were set to get married. The week before the wedding, she and her sister were killed in a head-on on Highway 46."

"Oh my God." Her hand went to her mouth, and her eyes widened.

"Reno pretty much crawled inside himself after that. Charli found a way to bring him back to life."

"She must be a very special woman."

He nodded, knowing he'd thank that girl for the rest of his life for rescuing his big brother. "She's a helluva decorator too. Mom took her up into the barn loft, and—"

"Ah. Your mom's antique treasure trove."

"Yep. Wasn't long before mom was ripping out furniture, painting walls, and tossing *the Duke* out on his ear. She's got a crazy sense of style, but, somehow, it all manages to work."

"Well, whatever makes her happy, right?" The smile that lifted her luscious mouth zapped him with 220 volts.

At the moment, his mother's *new friend* Martin Lane seemed to have accepted that job. He and his brothers still weren't sure how they felt about that. "Guess I'd better let you get back to making dinner or whatever you were doing in the kitchen when I got here."

"I had a protein shake earlier," she said, leading the way back down the stairs. "Figured I'd start tonight deciding which pieces of furniture would be the best to stage the house for the sale. The rest will go into storage."

"A protein shake?" When they reached the bottom of the stairs, he studied her and couldn't seem to tear his eyes away from that wedge of skin bared between the bottom of her shirt and the top of her jeans. Before he'd left for Afghanistan she'd been all soft, rounded curves. Now she looked toned to the point of having her own fitness show. "Who the hell can survive on that?"

Her gaze cruised down his body. "It's a sad truth that not all of us can afford to snarf down large quantities of food without paying the price at the altar of the elliptical gods."

"Did you just call me fat?"

She laughed. "Quite the opposite."

"You got shoes?"

"Shoes?"

"Yeah. Those things you wear on your feet."

Her head tilted, and she looked at him like he'd taken too many hits to the head. "Of course."

"Get them."

"Why? I'm not going anywhere."

"Yeah." He reached into his pocket and pulled out his truck keys. "You are."

She folded her arms across her chest. "You're not the boss of me, Jackson Wilder."

He took a step closer, looked down into her eyes, and responded to the familiar obstinacy he found there. "You didn't used to mind when I took charge."

"Things have changed."

"No shit." He headed toward the door. "But I'm still taking you to get something to eat."

"Why? You don't even like me."

He stopped and turned. "When did I say that?"

"Sometimes, words aren't necessary."

He shook his head. "Have you ever known me not to say what I'm thinking?"

"No."

"Then why the hell would I start now?" He reached down and picked up the pair of high heels she'd obviously kicked off earlier. "If you don't want to wear these or go barefoot, you'd best grab another pair."

"Why are you doing this?"

"Because a protein shake isn't a meal. And with all the manual labor you're about to put in on this house, you need to build up your energy."

"I hate to disappoint you, but protein shakes are filled with vitamins and—"

"Yeah. I know. Protein." He leaned close and pressed the high heels against her chest. "Shoes. Now. Then get in my truck."

Her eyes narrowed. "What are you going to do if I refuse?"

Hell, he had a million solutions to that problem. "*Are* you refusing?"

Five seconds of jutted chin silence gave him his answer.

God, the woman drove him crazy.

Completely destroyed him.

Melted him like he was a goddamned bar of cocoa butter in the tropical sun.

He tossed her shoes on the floor, then picked her up in his arms.

"What are you doing?" Her voice squeaked an octave higher.

"Taking action." He closed the front door behind them. "Because that's the kind of guy I am."

"I need my purse. My keys!"

"No worries." He stuffed her into his front seat and hooked the seat belt over her lap. "I'll just climb in your bedroom window like I always did."

On the way into town, Abby kept her mouth shut against the temper tantrum boiling inside. Which outweighed the million questions she wanted to ask. Which dwarfed the crazy exhilaration leaping through her chest because even though she'd foolishly treated him like someone who didn't matter, he still cared about her.

Oh, she wouldn't go so far as to expect him to believe the reason for him to physically pick her up and put her in his truck to take her to eat even though she'd already eaten was because he cared. She was certain he thought he was just being a Good Samaritan, like when he'd drop a dollar into the Salvation Army red kettle at Christmas. Or when he'd rush into a burning building to save a family. She knew he'd probably put her on his list as just another person he needed to rescue.

She hoped it was more.

As his big silver truck pulled into the parking lot of Bud's Nothing Finer Diner, Abby glanced into the back and noticed the pink car seat, which held a fluffy bunny all strapped in for the ride. She didn't know any man who'd keep such a feminine statement in his car. Even if it was a necessary one. Her ex sure wouldn't have.

But, of course, Jackson wasn't just *any* man.

While he set the big truck in PARK and got out, she sat there trying to figure out how this was going to work since she wasn't wearing shoes. Which was really only an excuse to explain the absolute panic clawing at her stomach. She hadn't had the best experience at the Touch and Go. The last thing she wanted to face right now was a restaurant full of the people she'd left behind thinking she deserved something better. The people who'd watched her "supposedly" make something of herself only to watch her collapse like an avalanche of utter stupidity.

They'd laugh at her.

Or give her those pitying looks they reserved for people who were either too stupid to live or people who had limited time on earth.

Maybe Jackson would just get an order to go. No sooner had the thought emptied from her head than he opened her door and held out his hand.

"I can't go in there," she insisted.

"Why not?"

Fear.

Humiliation.

Shame.

Among a million other issues.

"No shoes." She pointed to the sign on the door that read "NO SHOES. NO SHIRT. BIG PROBLEM. Y'ALL KEEP OUT."

"You've got on half a shirt," he said. "Half out of two isn't bad. I'm sure they'll make an exception."

"But—"

He reached in, unlatched the seat belt, and lifted her out of the truck the same caveman way he got her in.

"This is ridiculous."

"You want to walk?"

She looked down at the rough-pebbled parking lot. Ouch. "No."

"Then open the damn door," he said with a nod to the steel handle. "My hands are full."

With a long sigh, she reached down and pulled. He blocked the glass door from closing with his big body and carried her into the diner, where all heads in the busy place turned in their direction.

Great.

There went any hope they could sneak in unnoticed and grab a seat by the door.

He set her down in the only available booth in the old-time eatery lavished with "Don't Mess

With Texas" décor. The *only* booth that happened to be in the center of the diner, where everyone could see them.

And condemn.

In less time than it took for the waitress to look up and get their water poured, Ethel Mayberry, former high-school P.E. teacher turned legendary loan officer at the Sweet Credit Union stood at their table.

Abby wished she could make herself disappear. Not because Mrs. Mayberry wasn't a nice person but because Abby knew she had on inappropriate clothes, no shoes, messy hair, and most likely the makeup she'd carefully applied that morning had melted off in the afternoon heat. She was ill suited for receiving company in her own home, let alone being out in public.

She tugged down the short T-shirt, then crossed her ankles and tucked her bare feet as far beneath the booth as possible.

"It's so nice to see you, dear." Mrs. Mayberry's crinkly lips lifted into a smile as she gave Abby a pat on the hand. "When did you get back in town?"

"A few days ago. My parents decided to put the house up for sale. I agreed to get the place ready to put on the market."

"Well, that's just so nice of you to take the time from your busy schedule to help out. My sister Adelaide lives in Houston, and says you've been in charge of some really nice projects down there."

Whatever Abby had suffered through with her marriage, she was proud of the community-service projects she'd been involved with for the

Junior League. "Thank you. But I . . . no longer live in Houston." *Wait for it . . .*

"Well, their loss is our gain." Mrs. Mayberry smiled.

Abby exhaled. Relieved there'd been no mention of her divorce.

"I hope you'll come by the bank for a little visit. Maybe open up a new account? Fridays are best. Barbara Jean Beckenbauer, bless her heart, brings in schnitzel that's to die for." Mrs. Mayberry gave a wink. "So nice to see you two back together."

"Oh." Abby rushed to explain . . . what? That she'd been hijacked? That she and Jackson were barely on speaking terms? That most likely he'd throw a parade if she decided to drive out of town? "We're not—"

"I was sorry to hear about the divorce, dear," Mrs. Mayberry interrupted. "But you were never really meant for that pile of pretentious excrement anyway. Best you found out his true colors before you had children."

Abby's heart slunk into her curdling protein shake. "Yes. I suppose it was."

With a cheery "Please stop by" and a "See y'all soon," Mrs. Mayberry made her way back to her table of gray-haired companions while Abby tried to recapture her breath.

She looked up at Jackson, who was intently watching her. "Can we please go?"

He glanced around the diner at the faces that all seemed to be staring at *them*. "You're not afraid of these people, are you?"

"Afraid?" She glanced up and met a bounty of quizzical expressions. "Not the right word."

"So what *is* the right word?"

Another scan of the room. "Intimidated?"

"You asking me? Or telling me?"

She leaned into the table, and whispered. "*Please* get me out of here."

"Face the dragon, Abby. You've got no reason to hide."

She rubbed one cold bare foot over the top of the other, wishing the action could calm the breath-stealing wallop in her chest. "Shows how much you know," she mumbled.

A pretty blond waitress appeared at their table with glasses of ice water and a smile. "Hey, Jackson." As she set a glass down in front of Abby, she said, "I'll bet you don't remember me."

Abby looked up and admitted it took her a few seconds. "Paige Walker?"

"Paige *Marshall*." She wiggled her left hand and flashed a wedding ring. "Aiden and I got married last month."

"Congratulations." Abby sipped her water to soothe the Sahara developing in her throat. "I didn't know you two were still together." *Because really, how would she?*

"Well, we weren't. Aiden gave me up when he joined the Army."

Sounded familiar.

She glanced across the table at Jackson.

Just insert *Marines* in the place of *Army*.

"But I never gave up on him," Paige said.

Oblivious to the irony, Jackson chuckled. "Damned lucky for him."

"I know. Right?" Paige grinned. "It's nice to see you again, Abby. Maybe we can get together while you're here."

Abby felt a little of the pressure in her chest ease. Paige Walker had always been ultranice. "I'd like that."

"So what can I get you?" Paige asked, lifting a little order book from the pocket of her apron. "As long as it's not the meat loaf. Chester snatched up the last of it."

"I'm sorry. We really haven't had time to look at the menu," Abby said, reaching for the laminated piece tucked behind the condiment bottles. "Can you give us a couple of minutes?" Not that she had an appetite.

Paige flashed a smile. "Sure."

"Two Diablo burgers—extra chipotles," Jackson said. "Sweet potato fries. A chocolate banana milk shake for me. And a Butterfinger shake for her."

"Perfect." Paige jotted down the order and smiled. "I'll get that right up."

After she walked away, Abby leaned in, and whispered, "Are you crazy? I can't eat that."

"Why not?"

"Do you know how many calories are in all that?"

"About a bajillion," he said. "Who's counting?"

"Me!"

Jackson folded his hands together on the table and leaned in. Abby couldn't stop the little trip her heart took at the half smile that lifted his sensuous mouth.

"Why?"

"Because when you stop counting, you put on weight. And when you put on weight, your expensive clothes don't fit. And when your expensive clothes don't fit, you have nothing to wear to the party. And when you have nothing to wear to the party, you never hear the end of it," she explained with a silent "Duh" attached to the end before she realized she'd just given away way too much information.

"Lucky for me I've got nowhere to go but home after this." He leaned back, casually spread his arm along the back of the seat. "Why are you so worried about eating a normal meal?"

"*That* was *not* a normal meal you just ordered. That was a gastronomical nightmare waiting to happen."

He unrolled his silverware from the paper napkin and set the napkin on his lap. "A Diablo burger used to be your favorite late-night indulgence."

"Those were in the days when my metabolism worked overtime."

"Shit happens." He shrugged those broad shoulders. "People change. Why does it matter?"

"People talk, Jackson. And sometimes they say nasty things out loud as well as behind your back. Everyone in this diner is watching me. Wondering why I came back. Why my marriage disintegrated. Why I'm here with *you*." She pushed out a frustrated breath. Not that she thought she was all that important or anything special, but Sweet was a small town, where gossip was bigger than NASCAR. "As sure as I live and breathe, everyone

in this place is snacking on a deep-fried something and judging *me*."

He glanced around the place.

Surely he could see all the people studying
them more closely than the eye chart down at Eye
Carumba Vision Care.

"Chester's not judging you," he said. "But I'm
pretty sure he's wondering how to get you out of
those jeans."

She took a sip of water and choked. "Chester's a
million years old."

"But he's still trying to figure out how to get
you out of those jeans." Jackson smiled. "Just because the pistons don't work doesn't mean there's
no fire in the engine."

She laughed and gave a little shudder. "Now
there's an image I don't need burned into my brain."

The blue in his eyes darkened, and his strong
masculine features softened. He reached across
the table and laid his hand over hers. His thumb
swept across her skin. "*I'm* not judging you."

And there it was.

That overwhelming sensation in her chest that
made her want to cry for all the mistakes she'd
made and for the love of a man who would never
belong to her.

He'd made that very clear the night before he'd
left for the war. The night when he'd made love to
her with such passion it had brought tears to her
eyes. The night he'd helped her back on with her
clothes, then pushed her away, and said "Thanks"
as though she'd merely given him some quick
good-bye nookie.

The night she'd realized that while she might love him with all her heart, in his eyes she'd never be more than a friend.

A really convenient, ready to rip off her clothes for him, friend.

Yay her.

Abby leaned back in the front seat of Jackson's truck and laid a hand over her full stomach. As usual, he'd talked her off the wall, brought her down to a level where she could take a deep breath and think a little clearer. By that time, Paige had brought their Diablo burgers, fries, and shakes, and Abby hadn't been able to refuse the mouthwatering aroma. You could keep your designer perfume; nothing beat grilled, fried, and spicy.

Somehow, amid all that grease, she'd found a way to ignore the eyeballs focused on her enough to enjoy herself. Midway through the pile of sweet potato fries, she and Jackson were laughing about old times and even some stories he told about the guys down at his fire station. By the time they left Bud's Diner she felt like she knew the guys named Hooch, Meat, Hot Rod, and other various oddities that no human should ever be called.

When Jackson's big truck rolled to a stop in front of her parents' place, Abby glanced out at the house. "It's going to be fun watching you climb the tree and crawl through the window."

"I didn't lock the door."

"Oh. Darn."

"Learned my lesson the last time I fell out of that damn tree and took out my ankle."

"Yeah, and you milked the life out of the sympathy you got from those crutches too. Seems like you were always busting something."

He chuckled. "It's a curse I live with."

"Or that 'Ready, set, pull the trigger' way you have about you."

For the past hour they'd sat across from each other at the diner and exchanged small talk. Now, tucked into the cab of his truck, she realized the tension between them had seemed to melt away. At least on her part.

"Thank you," she said.

He looked up. "For what?"

"For looking after me. For making some of my reentry into Sweet less painful."

"You don't get a Get-Out-of-Jail-Free pass, Abby. I'm still pissed. You weren't there when—" He sucked in a lungful of air and yanked back his words before they spilled from his mouth. The last thing he'd want to do in front of her was sound like some pansy-ass crybaby.

"I know. And I'm deeply sorry for that." She sighed. Shook her head. "But that's what I've always loved about you. You can be pissed off yet still manage to do something very nice."

She cupped his cheek with her hand then leaned over and gave him a brief kiss. She looked up into his eyes and found a mix of emotions looking back. "Good night, Jackson."

As she drew her hand away, he captured it, pulled her into his embrace, and kissed her.

His lips were warm and firm as they settled over hers. They did not tease, they took possession.

Abby melted.

A moan from somewhere deep inside rumbled up from her chest and slipped into his mouth on a long exhale of breath. Then, like someone had flipped a switch, he was gone. His big hands wrapped around her arms and he set her away— back to her side of the truck.

"Holy hell." He looked at her like *she'd* gone crazy. "What was that?"

Okay, not exactly the words a girl wanted to hear.

Ever.

The muscles in her neck tensed, and her heart slammed against her ribs. "You kissed me."

"No I didn't."

She swept her fingers across her moist mouth. Her lips still tingled from his sensuous assault.

"Yeah. You did. You totally kissed me."

He made a sound of disbelief. "You leaned."

"I what?" She attempted to harness the frustration building like a bonfire in her gut.

"You. Leaned," he said.

"You grabbed me."

"I did?" His brows shot up like the idea was completely outlandish.

"Yeah. So now what are you going to do? Something completely offensive like apologize?"

"Apologize?" He pierced her with a long hard look. "Hell no. Apparently I've wanted to do that for a long time."

She let her guard down with a magnificent plunge. The breath she'd held pushed from her lungs on a long whoosh of air. The beginnings of a smile danced in her heart.

"Doesn't mean I'm happy about it, though," he said.

The air exploded from her party balloon.

"You need me to walk you to your door?" he asked like he hadn't just rocked her world.

"No thanks." Pushed away again. Looked like things were status quo in the land of Jacksonville. Confused, aroused, and ticked off, she pushed open the truck door, slammed it shut, and stomped up the walkway. Her bare feet made a slap-slap sound against the warm pavement.

Behind her, the truck engine idled, and she heard the whir of the electric window slide down.

"Hey," he called. "Don't go away mad."

"I know. I know." Her hands jerked her upward. "Don't go away mad. Just go away."

She escaped into the house and shut the front door. Yanked it open and yelled, "Thanks for dinner," then she slammed the door again.

Emotionally exhausted, she leaned back against the hard wood and waited until Jackson's truck roared off into the night. It could have been minutes or hours that she stood there in shock, disappointment, and utter humiliation.

But she would not cry.

No way would she cry over Jackson Wilder.

Never again.

Chapter 4

For two days, Jackson had put out fires, hit the books, and watched *Despicable Me* with Izzy for the millionth time. He'd washed the horses, bucked the hay, and chased wayward cattle back to the herd. He'd done anything he could to stay away from Abby and escape the big damn lie he'd told her.

What the hell had he been thinking when he'd pulled her into his arms and kissed her?

He'd done his damnedest to get over her. To stay pissed off at her for cutting him out of her life.

But then she'd touched him.

Kissed his cheek.

And he lost his mind.

When his brain cells had started to reassemble in his head, he'd panicked and allowed the first scrambled thought to leap from his mouth.

He'd blamed *her*.

Ha!

As a matter of pure survival, he'd kept his tires off Bluebonnet Lane and his mind off big blue eyes and soft lips. His attempts to stay busy, however, did not include avoiding the amorous attention of his mother's pet goat, Miss Giddy, when he rode into the barn.

With daylight waning, he took the headstall off Ranger—the most stubborn horse on the planet—while Miss Giddy bleated her discontent and butted his leg with her horns. He glanced down into the beady eyes glaring up at him.

"Seriously, goat?"

Miss Giddy—currently decked out with a red satin bow around her brown neck—bleated, "Meh-eh-eh."

Which he took to mean "Seriously."

When she pawed at the ground he gave in, reached down, and gave her a brisk rub between her horns. "What is it with you females always wanting attention?"

"We wouldn't have to ask for it if you men were more observant."

Loosening the cinch on the big bay gelding, Jackson dropped his chin and laughed. "Sorry, Mom. Didn't know you were standing there."

"Actually, I was on my way up to the loft." She lifted to her toes and gave him a quick peck on the cheek. Her big blond hair had been fluffed and sprayed into place. She looked like she was ready to go out on the town. "Just got a call from Charli. She and Reno are about a half hour out. I made some quick calls to gather folks up to welcome them home proper. Everybody should be here soon."

As she talked, she stroked the top of the goat's head. "I found something in the loft the other day I wanted to give them as a homecoming present."

"Not a wedding present?"

"Not as far as I know. 'Course your brother's been nothing but surprises lately, so it's hard to tell." She reached forward and tied up the saddle strings into a scaffold knot. "You don't look like you've slept much lately."

"Nothing gets past you, does it?"

"Sugarplum, I've been the mother of five boys for most of my life. Each one of you was wilier than the next. I had to be one step ahead, or you'd all take control of the universe." She gave Ranger a pat on the rump. "So what's on your mind?"

For two days, he'd kept himself busy. But for two nights, all he'd been able to think about was having Abby in his arms. Then he had to open his big mouth and lie his ass off so she wouldn't see how much it affected him. He'd be damned if he'd give his mother any ammunition against him. He shrugged. "Just been studying all the material Captain Steele gave me."

"I'm proud of you, son. I've always believed you could do anything you put your heart into."

"I haven't done anything yet. Haven't made any solid decisions." He lifted the saddle and pad from Ranger's back and set them on the stand near the stall. "Just considering the possibilities right now."

"You do that." She patted his back. "You take your sweet time. Just like you did with Abby. We'll see how that works out."

He turned and jammed his hands on his hips. "What the hell brought *her* into this conversation?"

"*You* did."

"I never even mentioned her name."

"Didn't have to." His mother gave him that grin that said she wasn't just two steps ahead of him, she was a whole damn mile. "But you'd better get used to the sound of it because here she comes right now."

"What?" His head whipped around at the sound of tires on gravel. Sure enough, Abby's slick silver Mercedes cruised past the open barn doors. He looked back at his mom, who stood with arms folded and a smirk on her lips.

"If I left it up to you boys, y'all wouldn't find the loves of your lives till I was dead and gone. And I want some more grandchildren before I take a dirt nap."

"Are you crazy? That's never going to happen with—" A car door closed, and he bit off an expletive.

"Abby!" his mother called. "In here, sugarplum."

"*You* . . ." He pointed. "Are nothing but trouble."

To his disappointment, his mother grinned.

"I've been called worse." She pointed back. "*You* mind the manners I raised you with."

The sound of unsteady footsteps over gravel came closer. Jackson blinked. When he opened his eyes again, Abby stood there, dressed in a soft white sweater, black skinny jeans, and red high heels. The outfit did nothing to deter the sudden hot flush that climbed his body and made him ache in specific areas.

Judging by the scowl on her face, he'd have to say she hadn't expected to see him either and that since the other night, she was *not* residing in Happy Camperville.

"I didn't see your truck," she said.

"Rode Ranger over."

"Oh." She pressed her glossy lips together.

Translated, he figured "Oh" to mean she wouldn't have gotten out of the car had she known he was there. Surprise. That street ran two ways.

"It's so good to see you again," his mother interjected at the silence dripping with animosity. Then she pulled Abby in for a hug.

He wasn't a bit surprised when Abby glared at him over his mother's shoulder.

"We've got so much catching up to do," his mother said. "But first I want you to come up into the loft and help decide if you think the clock I've chosen is a good gift to give Reno and Charli."

"What's the occasion?" Abby asked.

"They're coming home," his mother said with a big smile. "Haven't seen them for a couple of months, and we're about to celebrate with a little family gathering. They should be here in about half an hour."

"Oh." A spiderweb of anxiety appeared on Abby's forehead. "Then I should probably leave."

"Nonsense." His mother took Abby by the

hand and drew her toward the loft stairs and the treasure trove of antiques and collectibles she'd amassed over the years. "You're family too."

Jackson knew by the look in Abby's eyes that she didn't feel that way. But what his mother said was true. Abby had practically grown up in his house. He knew his family had always thought of her as one of them.

He wasn't sure how they all felt about her now, but it looked like he'd find out. Because the death grip his mother had on her hand was a sure sign she wasn't about to let Abby go anywhere anytime soon.

Climbing the stairs Abby looked back down at him. He knew her well enough to know that if she thought she could get away with it, she'd stick out her tongue. Or flip him off.

Her eyes narrowed.

Yep, she'd definitely flip him off.

When she and his mother disappeared at the top of the stairs, he heard Abby's enthusiastic exclamations over the ever-growing collection of junk his mother had discovered at estate sales, yard sales, and abandoned properties. He heard his mother explain how she and Charli planned to open a collectible and design shop once Charli and Reno got settled. And then all he heard were murmurs that made him wonder what was being said.

He opened the stall door, and Ranger wandered inside, giving Jackson's shirt a nip as he passed by. "Damned horse."

He received a horse laugh and snort in response

as he dumped a flake of hay into the feeder and closed the door. Miss Giddy reappeared when she heard the thunk of food. She gave him a "Meh-eh-eh" bleat until he dropped some hay into a bucket for her too.

While he brushed off his hands, he heard Jesse's truck pull up outside and park. Jackson went out to greet his brother, hoping he wouldn't have girl-of-the-moment with him, so they could have a little man-to-man talk before everyone else arrived. When he rounded the corner of the barn, he sighed in relief to find Jesse alone.

"When are you gonna get that hair cut?" he asked. "You're starting to look like Brad Pitt in that *Legends* movie."

Jesse grinned. "Brad has been pretty lucky with the ladies. So I'm good with that."

"Getting lucky? That all it's about with you?"

Jesse glanced over at Abby's Mercedes. "You got something you need to discuss, little brother?"

His brother knew him too well. "I might."

"Then how about we take a walk before we go inside?"

Exactly what he hoped Jesse would say.

Ordinarily he'd go to Jared first, him being the most levelheaded. In Jared's permanent absence, he'd taken his troubles to Reno, him now being the oldest. But Jackson didn't think it would be fair for his brother to come home to a bucketload of *his* problems. Jesse, on the other hand, might not always give out good advice, but he had an objective ear.

And at that moment, that was good enough.

$\mathcal{B}$y the time Abby came out of the barn with Jana Wilder and the antique clock chosen for her son's return, there were trucks and cars parked all over the place. Indeed, it looked like a party was in full swing.

Abby knew she needed to find a quick escape. She wasn't ready to face the entire Wilder family.

"I really should go," she said. "You don't need a party crasher."

Jana took her arm and gave her a comforting smile. "Nobody's gonna bite, sugarplum," Jana said. "Don't you worry about a thing."

She wasn't so sure about that.

Abby took deep breaths to calm the dread and stepped up onto the veranda that surrounded the big ranch-style home. Before they even got to the door, enthusiastic chatter from inside drifted through the screen. Reluctantly, she followed Jana into the house. Behind them, the screen door banged. All heads snapped in their direction.

Yikes.

Their entrance was met with the echo of crickets.

A quick scan of the crowded room revealed that not only had the impromptu celebration included a spread of take-out pizza and tin containers piled with salad mix, it had also gathered everyone in one place to easily pass judgment. Then again, to most of the people in this room, Abby wasn't much more than another body taking up precious floor space. So who was she to think she'd warrant such curiosity?

To her relief, Jackson appeared conveniently absent. He'd probably bailed the moment she'd gone into the barn. She couldn't blame him. She'd like to pull a vanishing act too.

Jana broke the brittle silence by sweeping into the room with a grand gesture of welcome to Reno and the gorgeous brunette on his arm.

Abby took the moment to inconspicuously inch toward the door. Surely in the commotion of welcoming Reno back to the fold, no one would notice she'd bolted. They'd probably be glad. Relieved.

When Jana moved on to greet others in the room, Reno stepped forward in all his dark-haired handsomeness and put a halt to her escape. "I knew you'd come back someday."

She noticed he didn't say he was happy to see her. "Well, I certainly didn't."

A brief smile tipped his mouth. "I can see that by the sheer panic on your face."

"Me? Panicked?"

"As your old friend, take it from me, Abby. Everything happens for a reason."

"Everything?"

He nodded. "Just make sure you pay closer attention than I did. Because it took me a while to realize that some of the best things in life are surprises."

The gorgeous brunette appeared at his side. "I hope you're talking about me," she said with a smile. Then she extended her hand. "Hi. I'm Charli. Reno's surprise."

Abby returned the gesture of the woman she'd seen once or twice on the cable design show.

"As soon as we unpack and get settled," Charli said, "I'd love to meet up for lunch."

"I'd like that," Abby returned. "But I'm not really sure how long I'll be here. I only came back to fix up my parents' house and put it on the market."

"Really?" Reno lifted a dark brow. "That's the *only* reason?"

"Of course."

"You keep thinking like that, sparkplug," he said, using the name he and the other Wilder boys—minus Jackson—had always called her. "And I guarantee you'll be in for a surprise."

Charli gave her a wink as, arm in arm, she and Reno walked away to chat with a silver-haired gentleman Abby didn't recognize.

As polite as Reno and Charli had been, Abby couldn't help feeling like the ugly stepsister at the prince's ball. She gave another longing glance to the front door and the freedom beyond.

"Hey, sparkplug." Jesse came forward, wearing his typical woman-eating grin. "Good to see you."

Really? Jesse had always been a professional bullshitter, so Abby wouldn't know if he was sincere or lying to the bone. "You too." How was it that all the Wilder men had only gotten more breathtaking over the years? "How are things at the clinic?"

"Keeping me on my toes. Old Doc Michaels finally retired. I bought the place from him about a year after my time with the Marines ended."

"I was really sorry to hear—"

"I know." He lifted a hand. "Dad and Jared

both adored you. They'd be happy to see you back home, where you belong."

"Oh. I don't—"

"Sure you do." He gave her a kiss on the forehead. "And now it's time for you to figure out the rest." He gave her arm a squeeze, then wandered off to join the others in the pizza line.

Random.

And weird.

Jesse had never been the philosophical guru type. But now both he and Reno had made ambiguous comments that had her scratching her head.

Before she could take that thought any deeper, the silver-haired man came up and shook her hand. He introduced himself as Martin Lane— "Jana's friend." The smile on his face when he made the claim had Abby wondering exactly what kind of "friend" he might be. And then she caught Jana's affectionate smile from across the room.

Ah. Well, good for Jana.

Chatting amongst themselves were a few neighbors plus Gladys Lewis, with her cottony blue hair, lipstick-smeared mouth, and traditional floral dress and, of course, old bowlegged Chester Banks, who'd given up on eyebrow waggles and was now tossing Abby a few winks. Lost in the shuffle, Abby figured it to be as good a time as any to get the hell out of Dodge.

Before she could get her feet in motion, Jackson came into the room with adorable little Izzy in his arms and a stunning, statuesque blonde at his side.

Abby's heart shattered.

Her eyes darted from Jackson to the child to . . .
yes . . . the mother.

Dressed in boot-cut jeans and a simple cotton
tee, the woman took casual cool to another level.
She wore little makeup, and her long hair fell in
loose waves around her shoulders. Her curves
were made by God—not a plastic surgeon—and
she looked completely at ease in her environment.

Beside her, Jackson, in his black T-shirt, jeans,
and finger-combed hair, accented her beauty with
his masculine good looks. Between them, Izzy, in
her frilly summer frock with her golden curls tied
up in a high ponytail, looked like the perfect combination of her parents.

Together, the three of them resembled the perfect little family.

Young. Vibrant. Gorgeous. Breathtaking.

At that moment, Jackson glanced across the
room and caught her eye. His brows pulled together. His lips flattened into an unyielding slash.

His silent message hit home.

She did not belong there.

No shit, Sherlock.

Before disaster roared into Armageddon, and
she did something really crazy like cry, she esti-
mated how far it was to the door. She didn't care
how ridiculous she'd look if she made a run for it.
She'd already been Sweet's hot topic of the week.
There was only so much she could stand. Seeing
Jackson with the mother of his child took her over
her limit.

She took a step backward and plowed into a
wall by the name of Reno.

At that moment, Jana clapped her hands together. "Can I have all y'all's attention?"

While everyone quieted, Reno leaned down and spoke into Abby's ear. "Looks like you're just going to have to stay a while longer. Can't hardly bolt in the middle of Mom's little speech."

As she turned to tell Reno she intended to do just that, she caught Jackson's eye again. Brows pulled tight over those blue eyes, his shoulders remained stiff—even when Izzy leaned her little golden head against his.

When Jana cleared her throat, Abby pulled her attention back to the woman who'd seemingly conned her for the second time. As Jana spoke, Abby controlled her disappointment and counted the seconds until she could escape.

"I have so much to be grateful for today I feel like it should be Thanksgiving," Jana said. "I'm so happy to welcome Reno and Charli back home. And if y'all haven't noticed, my *future daughter-in-law* is wearing an enormous diamond on her left hand."

Everyone applauded. Charli obliged by flashing the ring for all to see while smiling up at the man she obviously adored.

"I made Reno and Charli promise they wouldn't step foot in one of those twenty-four-hour wedding chapels in Vegas," Jana continued. "If they want tacky, we'll give it to them right here in Sweet." She grinned her happiness, and everyone laughed.

Chester Banks winked at Abby again, and she directed her gaze across the room.

Big mistake.

Jackson was looking right back. If there had ever been a moment in time where she felt more out of place, she couldn't name it. Even the moment she'd made the most heartfelt request of her husband, and he'd laughed in her face. Even the following day, when she'd come home from her committee meeting with the Junior League to discover the locks on her home had been changed and the bombshell waiting for her on the front step.

The note taped to the top of the white box had been brief.

And demoralizing.

Abby,

I realize now that the objectives in what we wished to achieve in this marriage are vastly diverse. Therefore, I seek to revoke the arrangement.

Inside this box are settlement papers and the keys to a condominium I have purchased in your name. If you choose to contest this petition for divorce, be aware that you will lose.

Please evacuate the premises at once. If you refuse, I have instructed the hired help to contact the authorities.

M.R.

Abby shuddered at the memory. At the absolute devastation and humiliation she'd felt when she'd reached down, picked up the box, and walked back to her car.

What had she done that had been so awful?

All she'd wanted was a baby.

A child to hold in her arms.

To love.

To have that love returned—a love she'd never receive from the man who'd put a ring on her finger and pretended to the world to be a loving and devoted husband. To him she'd never been more than an employee—someone to host his parties, wear on his arm, and attend the charity events that made him look like a man with a heart.

He hadn't been.

She'd been nothing more than a paid companion.

Mark Rich had discovered her working in the offices of his newly acquired team. He'd found her pleasant and pliable—someone who could be molded into what he needed to impress—or at least fit in—with the other married members of his peer group. She'd been educated, trained, and polished to be Mrs. Mark Rich. But she had never been loved or valued.

Across the room, Jackson snuggled the little girl in his arms, and when the stunning woman at his side leaned against him, looked up, and smiled, he smiled warmly back.

All Abby had ever wanted was exactly what stood right across the room—a man to look at her like *that* and a child to hold in her arms. Scratch that. Not just any man.

Her throat went as dry as the South Texas plains as she took a step backward. The wall behind her wouldn't budge. As though he could read her mind, Reno laid a hand on her shoulder. Gave her a squeeze.

"Extra points for bravery," he said.

Extra points?

She didn't give a damn about points.

She wanted the hell out of there.

"As if Reno and Charli's engagement isn't wonderful enough," Jana said, "I heard from Jake, and he'll be home for a visit in a few months. And even our Abby's back home."

Everyone's eyes cut to Abby. Including the woman at Jackson's side.

Abby imagined the woman might have heard her name mentioned through the Wilder family's talk of old times, and she couldn't imagine Jackson would have been kind if he'd mentioned her. So when Abby expected to see animosity from the woman or maybe even a hint of jealousy because of the close relationship they'd once had, she was surprised to find only a mild curiosity.

"Annnnd," Jana continued, "a little birdie told me that Jackson's superior at the fire department has requested that he start working his way up in the ranks. So it looks like U.S. Marine Sergeant Jackson Wilder will soon be San Antonio Fire Captain Wilder."

The woman beside him smiled up at him and rubbed his arm affectionately. His affectionate response made Abby's stomach roll like she'd eaten bad sushi. Obviously, he and the mother of his child had a very special bond. And why wouldn't they? She realized as guilt rammed headfirst into reason when all she could think of was the way he had kissed *her* the other night in his truck.

"So y'all eat up," Jana said. "We've got a lot to celebrate tonight."

Conversation and congratulations took off at high speed while everyone gathered around the table grabbing plates and slices of pizza.

Abby turned toward the human wall. "I'm very happy for you and Charli." She pasted on the same smile she'd used countless times in challenging societal situations. "But I really do have to leave."

She didn't care about extra points, or Brownie points, or any other kind of points—including knives—that would force her to *be brave* and stay to watch the man she'd always loved be in love with someone else.

Sure, she'd known a woman existed, but imagination and reality were not compadres. So before Reno could block her way again, she sidestepped him and slipped out the door.

She couldn't imagine anyone in the Wilder family had intended to be cruel. Then again, maybe she'd asked for this slap of reality by being naïve enough to believe they could forgive the way she'd cut Jackson from her life when he'd been in harm's way. She didn't know. She couldn't even think straight except that maybe the demons she'd come back to face had just taken a big-ass bite out of her ever-growing behind.

With a wobbly leap off the veranda, she expelled the air she'd held trapped in her lungs. Relief to be out of the home and away from the family she'd once loved to be a part of rushed over her as she dug in her purse for her keys and hurried to her car. She hit the button on the key fob and reached for the handle.

"Abby."

Shit.

"Wait."

She squeezed her eyes shut. Mentally spouted off every four-letter expletive that burst through her brain, and opened the car door.

Keep going. Keep moving. Get in the car and drive, drive, drive.

"Sorry. Have to go." Before she could get in the seat and start the engine, Jackson was right there, putting himself between her and her path to freedom. Her stomach pretzeled. What the hell was it with these Wilder men and their diversionary tactics?

"Hold on a second." His big hands captured her by the shoulders and turned her to face him. His voice rumbled deep in his chest the way it always had when he was edgy.

"No. Really." She shook her head. "I've got to go."

"Just give me five seconds. Okay?" His finger tucked beneath her chin and gently lifted so she had nowhere to look but in his eyes.

Big mistake.

One look into that piercing gaze, and her legs morphed into Jell-O. In response, she inhaled a stuttered breath that probably gave away all her emotions with little effort on her part.

For what seemed like an eternity he stood there—forehead crinkled, outside corners of his eyes pulled down. He searched her face as if trying to pull the thoughts from her head. In those anxious moments, her heart did a superlative job of attempting to Evil Knievel its way from her chest.

"That wasn't easy in there," he admitted, stroking his thumb gently across her chin. Tingles ensued.

Stupid tingles.

"No joke."

"For either of us," he added. "Be assured, I'll have a word with my misguided mother."

She nodded. Acknowledged and appreciated that at least the emotional impact of the awkward moment hadn't been one-sided.

"I didn't recognize her," she said. The *"her"* she referenced was met with a nod of immediate understanding.

"Fiona." His big hands slipped down her shoulders and butterflies hit her stomach at warp speed.

Stupid butterflies.

"I met her—actually we rescued her—at a traffic accident on I-10," he said. "She was trapped in the car. It took us an hour to get her out."

"That's scary."

Soldier. Fireman. Rescuer. Hero. Before he'd even been trained, he'd always been a first responder. A man who took care of things without thinking of himself. An act first, ask questions later kind of guy.

Of course, Fiona had fallen in love with him.

"Luckily she escaped with only a few bruises," he said, lowering his hands to cup her elbows. The heat from his palms seeped into her flesh and wound its way around her heart.

Stupid heart.

"I ran into her again a few weeks later and . . ." He shrugged. "The rest is history."

"How long have you been together?" And *why* was she asking? She didn't want to know all the details.

"We're not together anymore." He looked away. Dropped his hands to his sides. Exhaled. "Our divorce was final about a year ago."

Married.

While the idea of him married to someone else threatened to crush her, she sensed his feelings of loss. Failure. Heartbreak. Her selfish emotions became null and void.

She reached out—dared to touch him—and found warmth beneath her fingers. "I'm very sorry to hear that. Divorce with a child must be devastating."

"Divorce. Period." His eyes met hers. "*You* know that."

"Yes." She nodded. "I do." But not because she'd been so in love with Mark she couldn't bear to think of a life without him. Judging by the anguish etched on his face, Jackson didn't share that same feeling with Fiona.

So what had gone wrong?

His shoulders lifted on an inhale. In the moonlight, his eyes glittered. "I'm still pissed at you."

"Yeah. I get that."

"I still don't understand why you cut me out of your life."

"You probably never will." She didn't mean to sound flip, but that small part of her that hoped somehow they could put everything behind them and be friends again died in a fiery crash. The kiss in his truck had been a fluke. Some kind of twisted payback on his part? Who knew. Not something for her to try to figure out. At least not without a lot of pain, anguish, self-blame, and heartache.

Stupid heartache.

She'd beaten herself up enough about her grievous errors in judgment. She had to move forward with her life. She had to accept that while it had always been the one thing she'd always desired, needed, and craved, she was *never* going to be a part of the Wilder family. She was never going to have the love of the man she'd spent half a lifetime dreaming about. She might have made mistakes in her past, but didn't she deserve to find happiness? Didn't she deserve to be loved?

Ironically, she realized that today was no different than the day she'd tossed her bag in the back of her car and headed to Houston. She still had no one. And nothing. And that had to change.

Starting right now.

"Abby—"

His five seconds were up.

"I have to go." Before he or anyone else in that house could stop her, she dropped down into the car seat, yanked the door closed, and cranked the engine.

In her rearview mirror, she saw him stand there in the glow of her red taillights, watching her drive away.

In her heart, she said another silent good-bye.

Chapter 5

The sun blazed overhead, scorching the crew in their fireproof gear as Jackson and two other guys finished flat-loading the hose back onto the engine. Earlier, they'd been activated to a working structure fire on Pioneer Road. Engines 1 and 11 arrived to find the back section of the house fully involved. Three hours later, while the captain met with the homeowners and explained the overhaul operations, Jackson went to help Hooch search for hot spots.

"I think we got this bastard beat." Hooch pulled back the baseboard with a pike pole as Jackson came in through the kitchen door.

"We were lucky with this one. The wind's coming up pretty strong now."

"And no patients to package up either."

"Always a good thing." Jackson looked up at the soffit. "You check this?"

"Yeah. Hot Rod came through a few minutes

ago and did his usual white-glove treatment. I'm just running the boards one more time to make sure. You give any more thought to Cap's request of taking on some new challenges at the station?"

"Been thinking on it."

"Well, think a little harder," Mike said. "You're not getting any younger."

Pulling a baker's rack away from the wall and checking for heat, Jackson laughed. "Jackass."

"I am that. But all bullshit aside, you'd make a hell of a leader. Can't figure why you haven't moved up already."

"Maybe because I don't see myself in a leadership role."

"Seriously?" Mike looked up. "Guess you're the only one around here who doesn't."

To know he had the confidence of his peers touched him deeply. "Then maybe I'll give it some further consideration."

Mike gave him a grin. "Damned straight you will."

"You give any more thought to the auction?" Jackson pushed aside a utility cart so he could run his hand along the wall.

"Got nothing planned that night so . . ." Mike shrugged. "Sure, count me in."

"Thanks. The Emergency Center really needs the funds to expand."

"This isn't one of those auctions where the guys have to strip down in front of the audience and flex, is it? Because I don't do that Muscle Beach shit."

"And you think that's something *I'd* do?"

"I think you've either got an evil plan forming in that pretty-boy head, or all those deep-thought frowns you've been giving have something to do with a female."

When Jackson didn't respond, Mike lowered the pike pole to his side and nailed him with a look.

"What?"

"Holy shit. It's *her*, isn't it?"

"Don't know what you're talking about."

"Bullshit." Mike pointed the pole at him. "She's back. Right?"

Jackson considered lying through his teeth, but since he and Mike had spent more than a few hours commiserating over their failed relationships, losses, and regrets, he didn't bother. "Yeah."

"So, you get over your mad with her, or what?"

"*Over* might not be the proper term. We've talked."

"And what? You agree to be friends or some crazy shit like that?"

"We didn't agree on anything. But if she plans to stay in town, it's a possibility."

Mike leaned his head back and let go a laugh. "There's no such thing as being *friends* with a chick."

"Apparently you missed *When Harry Met Sally* or *He's Not That Into You* or—"

"All right. That's it." Mike laughed again. "Hand over your fucking man card for even knowing those movies."

"Date movies, brother."

"Whatever." Mike's eyes darted away for a

moment, then came back dark with memories. "Sometimes, it's best to just let 'em go. You know?"

Jackson understood the heartache behind his friend's bitter words of wisdom. Mike had loved his wife from the bottom of his soul. But during his long work shifts, she'd found someone else to keep her company. The day she left Mike was the day a little bit of the easygoing man he'd been had died. So far, he'd not recovered.

"What happens if you're not sure?" God, Jackson hated to play the pity card, but from the moment Abby had walked away, his life had been shit. His brother—his role model—had been killed right in front of him. His dynamic father had died shortly after—seemingly from a broken heart. He'd met an amazing woman and married her. But by then he'd been so disconnected from everything, he'd lost her.

The only thing that brought him to life was Izzy's smile. And the memory of the close relationship he'd once had with his best friend.

Jesse might be right. Maybe he should get to know her again. Get past what had happened between them. She sure seemed like someone who could use a friend. And, frankly, so could he.

Seeing her in the middle of chaos at his mother's house the other night had hammered home the reality that while he might not like what she'd done, he'd known her almost his entire life. He'd spent countless hours with her, talking, laughing, planning, and dreaming. There were times he thought he knew her better than he'd known himself. He'd always valued her opinion, shared in her common beliefs, protected her when she'd needed to be, and trusted her when the roles had been reversed.

"After what happened, you're not sure if you should let her go?" Mike asked.

Jackson shrugged.

Mike shook his head. "Then, man, you are totally screwed."

As the sun dropped low in the sky, Abby blew out a breath at the ridiculous amount of work to be done in her parents' house. Certainly, painting walls had never been big on her list of super-duper fun things to do. The last time she'd picked up a brush had been way back when she and Jackson had painted her bedroom.

At the time, her parents had been on another of their numerous out-of-state party excursions, and she and Annie had been left at home alone. Again. Jackson had been dying to get away from the chaos at his house and practically begged for the peace and quiet at her place. So she'd put him to work.

While Annie had crashed on the living-room sofa watching the battle of the wits between Mulder and Scully on the *X-Files,* she and Jackson had painted long into the night. It wouldn't have taken so long had they not screwed it up the first time and had to repaint. During those hours, he'd talked about his brothers. And though Abby had thought she knew them well, she'd been surprised at some of the crazy and ridiculous stunts they'd pulled—and survived. At the time, she'd decided that boys were a plateful of fun with a side order of gross.

At the moment though, fun—and especially Jackson—were out of the picture. And even though the buckets of paint were staring at her each time she walked through the hall, she planned to put off that particular chore for as long as she planned to put off trying to figure out her life—as long as possible.

Today's mind-preoccupation challenge?

Organization.

Toss. Donate. Pack.

Those were all the decisions she needed to make today.

Easy cheesy.

No more thoughts about Jackson or the fiasco at his mother's house. No more thoughts about when her feelings for him had changed or why. No more thoughts about him at all.

Today, she was all about getting crap in order and moving on.

As she stood in the middle of the living room, holding up her mother's old COFFEE, CHOCOLATE, MEN . . . SOME THINGS ARE JUST BETTER RICH T-shirt, Abby thought of just how misguided her mother really was and tossed the shirt into the *donate* pile. Gave it a second thought and reassigned it to the *toss* pile.

In her mind, rich was *not* better.

No need to pass on a false declaration.

The stack of old clothes and odds and ends stored by her parents when they'd moved to Florida made no sense. Why anyone would keep half the stuff she kept finding shoved into cardboard boxes would confuse a member of Mensa. Abby had a pretty good idea that by the time she was done, there wouldn't be much to fill that gigantic storage container parked in the driveway.

Still, she couldn't condemn too harshly as she had a storage container of her own back in Houston. And the moment she'd figure out where she'd land for the rest of her life—or at least the foreseeable future, she'd have it hauled out and put in her own driveway.

The only thing she could be assured of was there would be no bizarre-slogan T-shirts to sort through. The only T-shirt she owned was the long-sleeved SWEET HIGH SCHOOL SCORPIONS one Jackson had loaned her the day a bunch of kids had gone to the creek to swim in the man-made pool the Wilder brothers had constructed from rock. By nightfall, she'd gotten cold, and Jackson had handed over his shirt while he sat by the campfire—bare-chested—with his arm around busty Bridget Hunter.

Wonder whatever happened to her?

And why was she thinking of Jackson again?

With another woman.

Good grief.

All this organizing, decision making, and reminiscing had made her thirsty. Abby went into the kitchen and reached into the refrigerator. She pushed aside the flavored water and grabbed the liter-sized bottle of Dr Pepper—Jackson's favorite soft drink. She didn't know why she'd bought it. It wasn't *her* favorite soft drink. And yet somehow it had ended up in her grocery cart.

And why did he keep popping up in her mind?

Deep in denial, she twisted off the cap, poured some into a glass, and took a long drink. The sugary liquid splashed into her empty stomach, and she realized she'd been too busy to eat all day. Maybe she should whip up something before she delved into the rest of her parents' load-o-crap.

A knock on the front door diverted her attention. Too much to hope a pizza-delivery guy had read her mind, she supposed.

She opened the door. Surprise forced her to take a step backward. Jackson stood on her front porch, looking casual in a pair of cargo shorts and an unbuttoned plaid shirt over a black T-shirt snug enough to display the definition of his wide chest and rippled abs. Below his tanned muscular legs, his athletic shoes looked more on the side of well used than new. He looked amazing and was the last person she'd expected or wanted to see.

"What are you doing here?" she asked.

He held up two white paper bags. "Peace offering."

"For what?"

He cocked his head. "You didn't get a chance to eat pizza at my mom's the other night."

"You don't owe me anything." She curled her hand around the door and began to close it.

He stuck a gigantic foot in the way. "Not even Sweet Pickens."

"Barbecue?" The spicy-sweet aroma drifted beneath her nose, and her empty stomach took that inopportune moment to growl. Loudly.

He nodded.

"I don't know why you keep feeling the need to feed me," she said, even as the tempting aroma wafted farther into the house.

"Two words—*protein shake.*" He gave a visible shudder that made her laugh even though she didn't want to react.

"They're not that bad."

"This is *not* powdery protein. And it's delicious." He held the bags up again and gave them a little shake. "Just sayin'."

"Fine." Her growling stomach made her cave and step back. "Come on in."

"Wow," he said, scanning the piles of clothing and crap in the living room on his way into the kitchen.

"Yeah. I thought I should clear stuff out before I started painting, but I feel like I'm just making avalanches of junk."

"Maybe you need to reconsider getting some help."

She glanced around at the overwhelming amount of work to be done. "I should be okay if I don't get too many projects going all at once."

He stopped when he reached the kitchen table—yet another surface piled high with stuff— and shoved aside a tower of Nancy Drew books she intended to keep to make way for the take-out bags.

"You know," he said, "I wouldn't mind helping. All you have to do is say the word."

She couldn't stop her hands from sliding to her hips and popping off a smidge of attitude. "Why would you want to help when you're still pissed off at me?"

He turned toward her. Even while the blue in his eyes darkened, a smile lifted those masculine lips. "So women are the only ones who get to be complicated?"

"We're better at it."

"Amen to that." He laughed without actually giving her an answer, then set the bags down on the counter and reached inside. "I didn't know what you'd want so I got a variety. We've got chicken, pulled pork, and brisket. Fries and coleslaw and . . ." He pulled out a white Styrofoam container and handed it to her.

She flipped up the lid. "Fried pickles! Oh my God, I haven't had those in forever." That he remembered how much she loved the Southern delicacy stirred something crazy inside her heart. Before she even knew what she was doing, she curled her fingers into the front of his T-shirt and kissed the corner of his mouth. "Thank you."

He stood stone still.

Oops. She stepped back, prepared to issue an apology.

His heated gaze lowered to her mouth, lingered, then eased back up to her eyes. Without his even touching her, a punch of something hot and electric zapped her from the roots of her hair down to all the interesting places along the way to her toes.

"Are you okay?" she asked.

"I don't think so."

"I'm really sorry about that—"

"Yeah." He dropped the container of coleslaw to the table, and his arms went around her. He pulled her in and kissed her.

There was no tongue involved, but the kiss was far from sweet. It was possessive, hot, and needy, and it packed a wallop.

Though it had only happened a couple of times in her life, everything inside her remembered how it felt to be in his arms. In that moment, she knew she was in deep. Because there was no place on earth she'd rather be. She lifted her arms around his neck, pressed her body close, and clung to him to keep her knees from buckling.

His big hands slid down her spine, cupped her bottom, and pulled her against him. The long, hard erection beneath those cargo pants proved he was definitely intrigued with what was going on above their shoulders.

A car horn honked reality onto their heads.

He backed away, eyes locked onto hers in disbelief.

Uh-oh. "Do *not* blame me for that!" she said while at the same time her lips were begging for more.

"Nope." He shook his head. "That was all me."

"Look. If you're sexually frustrated I'm sure there are a million—"

"I am *not* sexually frustrated."

Although his expression disagreed, she had to hope he wasn't just man-whoring himself around town. She hoped that while he might not understand why he kept kissing her, she wasn't just another one of the many he did kiss who meant nothing. She hoped she was special.

"Then what was that all about?" she asked, wondering just how far down the River of Denial he'd floated.

He shoved a hand through his hair. "I have no damn clue."

Well, if he didn't know, how the heck was she supposed to know?

As a momentary diversion, she grabbed the Styrofoam container of fried pickles and sank her teeth into one. *He* might not be frustrated, but *she* certainly was. Sexually or otherwise. "That's the second time you've done that and had no damn clue."

"I know."

When he sank down into a chair and looked up at her with complete and utter bewilderment, she noticed he again didn't apologize.

And like a fool, she wondered what *that* meant.

You are a moron.

Jackson wanted to bash the message into his head. Because obviously his brain wasn't going to be of any help in the matter. And God knew his *friend* that lived behind the zipper of his jeans was clueless.

For Christ's sake, she'd given him an innocent little kiss.

An expression of gratitude. A simple demonstration of excitement over being given one of her favored snacks, which she hadn't had in a long time. The same kind of kiss she might have given her mom or dad or even her great aunt Tessie who had a huge mole on her cheek that sprouted all kinds of weird shit.

But when Abby had come close, her sexy floral scent had wrapped around him with promises of soft skin, and warm, wet, slick places.

And sighs.

And moans.

And greedy hands all over his body.

When that warm mouth touched his, he'd lost it. Completely. Fucking. Lost it.

Again.

What must she think?

Judging by the frown pulling those delicately arched brows together, she thought he was a complete nut job. Hell, *he* thought he was a complete nut job.

He hadn't come over here to try to jump her body-although it was a damned fine body. He'd come over to try to figure out if there was a way to salvage their friendship. A way to get rid of the grudge that still lingered in his soul. A way to just figure out some things about the two of them.

For most of his life, she'd always been a safe place for him to land. But all these other feelings that kept cropping up on him? *Holy shit.* Now he was more confused than when he'd walked in. Luckily, she didn't push for an explanation.

"So . . ." He stuck a wrapped sandwich in her hand. "Chicken?"

She blinked, like the abrupt change of focus spun her head. "Sure."

"Want to eat out back?"

"It's kind of a mess out there." She blinked again, and her eyes refocused. "Then again maybe you could give me some pointers on how to improve the backyard without sinking a couple grand."

Ah. He smiled. That was more like it. A mundane conversation that wouldn't make him wonder what color panties she wore beneath those pink running shorts. Something he had no business wondering. He snatched up the remaining sandwiches off the table and left the coleslaw and pickles for her to grab. "Jake's the one with all the landscaping knowledge, but I'll be glad to give it a go."

She picked up the containers, and he let her lead the way.

Big mistake.

Those running shorts were short, and her long legs were toned and tan and . . . His gaze lifted just slightly, and he immediately became happy his hands were full of barbecue. Otherwise, he'd be smacking himself on the forehead for watching her firm ass instead of watching where he was going.

Jesus. What was wrong with him?

Like so many Texas yards these days, Abby's was comprised mostly of rock and concrete— easy maintenance and drought resistant. When they reached the patio set, he opened the canvas umbrella before they sat down.

"I imagine you'll be happy to see Jake when he comes home," she said.

"Really glad. It's been a while since he's made it back to the U.S. Pretty sure he's a lifer."

"A *lifer*?"

"Career military."

"And you and Reno and . . . Jesse weren't?"

He noticed her hesitation and quick step around any mention of Jared. "Nope. We did what we felt we needed to do. And when Jared was killed, everything changed. Plus it gets too political. Charli's dad is a general, and she said she barely got to see him while she was growing up."

"That wouldn't be good for Izzy."

He shook his head, took a bite of brisket sandwich, and let the tangy barbecue sauce roll over his tongue before he answered. "The long shifts at the fire station are hard enough. I'll be glad for Jake to see Izzy again. She's growing up so fast."

"She's a beautiful little girl."

"Thanks. All the credit goes to Fiona."

"What happened between the two of you, if you don't mind my asking?"

He shrugged. "We were never in love. I mean, we love each other. But there's a difference."

She nodded, and something in the darkening of her eyes said she understood.

"We had a nice, easy thing going. Nothing serious. Then she got pregnant."

"And you were raised to do the right thing."

"I wanted it to work. We both did. It just . . . didn't." He still lost sleep over the failure of their relationship.

"We never really fought or argued. There was just something . . . missing. Eventually, we realized we were just meant to be friends."

Abby picked up a napkin and wiped the barbecue sauce from her fingers. "Maybe like us?"

No. Nothing like them. He couldn't define *them*. He couldn't stop thinking about her—not even when he'd been so pissed off he couldn't see straight. But here they were chatting like old times. Like all the hours they'd spent tucked up in the tree house he and his brothers had built, solving the world's problems—or at least their own.

Maybe he felt he needed her friendship again because of all the loss he'd faced. He shrugged. "Maybe."

She glanced away. Pretended to watch the hawk circling overhead. But he knew her well enough to know something deeper was going on inside her mind.

"That all you're going to eat?"

She glanced down at her half-eaten sandwich and pushed the paper toward him. "You can have it if you want it."

They'd shared food more than once, but that wasn't what he meant. "I'm asking because you've barely touched it."

Her slim shoulders lifted. "Guess I wasn't as hungry as I thought."

"Want to talk about it?"

Her gaze came up, and in the bright sunshine, her eyes faded to an icy blue. "Not much to talk about."

"Isn't there?"

"Not really."

"I told you what happened between Fiona and me. Your turn." He wiped his mouth with the napkin, tossed it on the table, and asked the question he wasn't sure he really wanted to know. "So what happened between you and Rich? All bullshit aside."

After several seconds of awkward silence, she planted her hands on the arms of the chair and got up. He sat there while she went to stand beneath the old live oak. Her hands went to the hips of her pink running shorts, and the shoulders beneath her fitted white T-shirt visibly slumped. She tilted her head and looked up into the leaves.

"I saw a robin building a nest out here yesterday," she said. "I kept thinking it was too late in the year for laying eggs and hatching babies."

Random? He wondered. Or trying to make a point?

"Guess when the instinct hits home, you have to follow your heart's desire," she said. "Even if you're a bird."

He got up and joined her beneath the shade of the tree. He cupped his hands over her shoulders and turned her until he could look down into her eyes. He ducked his head. Looked closer and . . . yep. She'd been trying to make a point. "What happened?"

She snagged her bottom lip between her teeth while she weighed the consequences of admitting her failure. Just the same as he had when he'd had to look at himself in the mirror after Izzy was born and admit he could never be the kind of husband

Fiona needed. Or wanted. Or when he'd failed to keep his brother from dying. Or Abby from expelling him from her life. With Abby, he'd had every opportunity to keep her close. In those days, his fears and probably immaturity had deceived him into thinking she'd always be there.

He'd taken that for granted.

Above their heads, the hawk screamed as if to say "Get on with it." Apparently, Abby took the message to heart.

"My marriage was a complete mockery from day one."

"How so?"

"You want all the ugly details?" She looked up at him, a feeble smile trembling at the corners of her lips. "Or just the CliffsNotes?"

All of it. "Whatever you're willing to share."

Still, she hesitated.

"Or maybe you'd feel more comfortable talking to my mom. She's always had a soft shoulder."

"Nooo." She shook her head. "Your mom is on my list right now for being sneaky and conniving."

"Yeah. She is that. But you know she means well."

"So did the captain of the *Titanic,* and look where that got him." She wrapped her arms around her waist, closing herself off. "Mark Rich married me because he thought I was easy."

She looked up and laughed at the obvious surprise on his face. "Not *that* kind of easy. He thought I was naïve and submissive—someone he could train and control. He'd just been handed the team from his father, and he needed to prove himself to his new peers. So he had to give up his wild bachelorhood and find someone to settle down with. He needed someone respectable to wear on his arm. To oversee his charity connections. To throw spectacular parties that made him look like a god in front of his business associates."

"I'm sorry, Abby. I really am." He smoothed his hands down her arms. "I'm sure when you love someone like that—"

"Love had *nothing* to do with that marriage." She choked out a strangled laugh. "He *never* loved me. Not even for one second. For him, our *union* had been nothing but a business deal."

Maybe he and Fiona hadn't been in love, but at least there had always been genuine affection. Sounded like that had been missing for Abby.

"I didn't mind handling the parties or the charity events," she said. "I actually really liked that part. What I did mind was feeling like a stranger to the person who bullshitted me into thinking he cared about me. I did mind that I was assigned to a bedroom on a different floor from the one he slept in. I did mind that he only came into my room when he obviously couldn't find anyone else to sleep with him. Obviously, I was too *mild* for his tastes in women which—from what I overheard— often stepped outside the boundaries."

Mild? That's not what he remembered about her.

The more she spoke, the tighter her jaw clenched, and the more the anger rolled off her in waves. Abby had always been passionate. About everything she did. And he couldn't believe someone like Mark Rich could be so blind as not to see it.

"And I did mind that when I got so lonely, and I finally got up the nerve to ask him if we could have a child so I'd have something—someone—to love, he laughed at me."

"What?" His head whipped around so hard his neck cracked.

"The next day, he locked me out. I found a box on the doorstep with a note saying he'd filed for divorce."

"Whoa. Wait a minute." Jackson's heart backed up into his throat. "Rich divorced you because you wanted a *baby*?"

"Yes. But I'm sure that was just the final straw. After all, he constantly had to remind me to watch my weight. Or how I needed Botox even though I was only in my twenties. Or . . ."

The rest of what she said rolled over him in spurts of words he barely heard.

Her husband had divorced her because she'd wanted a baby?

Hell, *he'd* have given her a hundred babies if she'd been his wife.

He'd never have told her she was fat.

He'd loved her curves.

He'd never look at her beautiful face and think she needed Botox. Not even if she was eighty.

He'd always loved her just the way she was. Or at least the way she'd been before some arrogant, selfish asshole who'd never loved her had gotten hold of her.

He pulled her into his arms and held her while she trembled.

He'd always loved her.

Reality clanged in his head as loud as the fire bell at the station on a three-alarm call.

He'd always loved her.

Ironically, now they were barely friends.

Suffocating heat. Choking dust. Blinding flashes of light. Earsplitting explosions. The metallic odor of blood.

"Daddy?"

Jackson broke from the nightmare and leaped to his feet in a crouching position. Body soaked in sweat. Heart pummeling into his ribs.

"Daddy?"

He blinked once.

Twice.

Ran the back of his hand across his eyes.

A sweet, petrified little face came into view, with big blue eyes wide and full of tears.

"Oh, Jesus." Jackson swallowed hard and grabbed for his little girl. He pulled her against his pounding heart and buried his face in her sweet-smelling baby-fine curls. "I'm sorry, Iz."

The nightmares came less often. But they were no less intense. Stress increased the instances, as did certain times of the year. Certain occasions.

He'd done the time in counseling.

Continued to fight the battle.

But his brother had paid the ultimate price.

He held Izzy close until the trembles in her tiny little body ceased. He kissed her hair. Kissed her cheek. "Daddy's so sorry."

He'd scared his little girl. Frightened her to tears. He was a horrible daddy.

Izzy moved from his embrace, leaned back, and looked at him with a little furrow between her eyes. "Bad dweam?"

He nodded. "Very bad."

She cupped his face in her chubby little hands. I wub you, Daddy. I pwotec you."

Ah, hell. His heart shattered. "I love you, baby girl. But it's Daddy's job to protect you."

And he would.

Even if it was from himself.

Chapter 6

When dawn broke, Abby woke feeling fresh.

Like a weight had been lifted from her nightmare.

She didn't know whether it was from the glass of wine she'd consumed before she'd gone to bed or that she'd opened up to Jackson and told him the truth of her sham marriage.

Whatever the reason, she'd slept the best she had since Mark Rich had put a ring on her finger, then taken it back. Her fears and apprehensions about returning to Sweet had dissipated like morning fog.

She felt new again and ready to take on anything.

She stepped from the shower, folded the towel around her body, and tucked the tail between her breasts. As she brushed her teeth, she looked in the mirror and didn't recognize herself. She had color in her face and brightness in her eyes, where for months she'd had dark circles and looked haggard and pale.

Her fault. She'd allowed herself to be a puppet. Allowed herself to be bought. Sold. And shipped off.

Well, she wasn't for sale anymore.

From now on, she'd write her own one-way ticket to happiness.

Any other day, she would have blow-dried her freshly washed hair, then forced it into submission with a flat iron. Today, freedom rang, and she let the natural curls take shape. They bounced up into loose ringlets like they were happy to be free.

Barefoot, she padded to the bedroom and kicked aside the expensive high heels lined up in front of the closet door. The closet itself was overflowing with the clothes she'd left behind and just yesterday pulled from boxes and rehung to sort through. There were dresses, and blouses, and boots, and an assortment of fun outfits that reflected the personality of her former self. Ignoring the outfit she'd first laid out on the bed, she pulled out a white cotton wrap dress she'd always loved and paired it with a wide brown leather belt.

Her initial thought looking at the ensemble was how—back in the day—Jackson had always appreciated the originality with which she'd dressed. Even if some of her former boyfriends hadn't been as appreciative.

She was glad she'd told him the truth about her marriage. She didn't feel he'd judged her. And though the words had danced at the tip of her tongue, she'd managed to keep the real reason she'd left Sweet and married Mark to herself. Only she knew the truth behind the reason she'd made such an error in judgment—she'd tried to find a replacement for Jackson.

From the floor of the closet, she pulled out her old blue-and-tan Tony Llama boots, shoved her feet inside, and wiggled her toes. They still fit. Still felt as comfortable as they had years ago. She traded her YSL clutch for a no-name Boho bag she found at the bottom of a storage box. Vanity, however, would not allow her to leave the house without at least a quick cover of foundation and some mascara.

Her boots made a tap-tap sound as she dashed downstairs and opened the front door to run some errands before she tackled more organizing. Surprise took her back when she discovered a calico kitten sitting on the doormat.

"Well, hello." She knelt. "Aren't you adorable?"

The multicolored kitten appeared to be only a couple months old. It looked up at her with big green eyes and gave her a squeaky little meow. Abby stroked her fingers across soft fur, which the kitten took as an invitation to climb up onto her lap. The more she petted, the more it purred.

Well, darn. Now she was in a bind. She didn't have the heart to push it aside and just leave. It was too little. Too helpless. Too cute. She needed to find out who it belonged to before she climbed into her car and took off.

The kitten used her arm as leverage and climbed up to her shoulder. It snuggled beneath her hair and purred in her ear.

"You sure know how to make friends quick." She extracted tiny needle claws and drew the kitten down into her arms. "Maybe I should ask the neighbors who you belong to. It should only take a minute, right?" She lifted the delightful little meower and touched its little pink nose to hers.

Decision made, she tossed her bag on a nearby chair, closed the door, and headed next door to Arlene Potter's little rock bungalow. A few days ago, the elderly woman's gossipy lifestyle would have terrified Abby into keeping her distance— like a twenty-mile radius. But with her new attitude, she wasn't about to let anything get in her way. And finding the kitten's home was important.

A quick rap on the door brought the elderly tattletale and her silvery blue hair running.

"Abby!" She leaned back and folded her arms across an ample bosom. "I was wondering when you'd make an appearance at my door."

I'll bet you were. Abby held out the arm that wasn't holding the kitten. "Here I am."

Arlene flashed a "gotcha" grin. Abby suddenly remembered that once Mrs. Potter got you inside her house, you were doomed to stay until either the chitchat or the coffeepot ran dry.

"Well, get on in here." Mrs. Potter stood back and waved her through. "I got a fresh pot brewing. The old-fashioned way." She gave Abby a nudge with a sharp elbow. "Don't have no use for those fancy schmantzy single-cup jobbers."

"I . . ." Abby scanned the living room and wondered just how many crocheted doilies one person really needed. "I really can't stay. I just came to ask if you knew whose kitten this is."

Arlene turned, and her hazel eyes widened as if she'd noticed the kitten for the first time. "Oh. That's probably one of the Cruise cats. Those people refuse to have their animals fixed, and they're always having litters they can't find homes for. I don't want to know what happens to those poor little things. Just ticks me off anyone is that irresponsible. They don't watch their kids, either. Let 'em run wild like coyotes."

Unbeknownst to her, Mrs. Potter had just delivered an answer embedded within a bit of gossip.

"Cute little thing." Mrs. Potter gave the kitten a gentle stroke. "Lucky too. Looks like it found a new home."

"Oh. No." Abby looked down into the big green eyes. "*I* can't keep it."

Mrs. Potter's pleasant expression turned into the big hairy eyeball. "So you'd just let that poor little innocent thing *disappear* with all the other Cruise cats?"

Horrors unimagined flew through Abby's mind, and she snuggled the kitten a little closer. "Of course not."

"Then she's yours."

"She?" Abby looked down into the kitten's sweet little face and melted just a little more. She'd make it a point to scour the neighborhood to see if the kitten belonged to anyone who would actually claim or want it, but she knew she'd already fallen in love. And anyone who wanted to treat it poorly could, well, they could just suck rotten eggs.

"Most calicos are female," Arlene informed her. "Something to do with the chromosomes. If it's a male, it's usually sterile."

"Wow. Aren't you a fountain of cat facts."

"Got that one from the Wiki." Mrs. Potter grinned as she pulled down two cups from a kitchen cupboard that could use a fresh coat of white paint and filled them with steaming coffee."

"The Wiki?"

"Pedia. I've got facts on just about everything in this town that walks on two legs or four. And even a few that slither around, like that George Crosby."

The residents of Sweet were on Wikipedia? Dear God, she'd better Google her own name.

"Did you know he was flirting out in public with Madge Peterson at church last Sunday?" Mrs. Potter huffed.

"Who?"

"George Crosby," she said, as though Abby was a wee bit on the dense side. "Imagine. Married to poor old Rose for fifty years and her barely being in the ground for a month before he starts flippin' his lashes at another woman. Yep. I got a lot of underground info on this town."

Frightening.

Arlene set a coffee cup in front of Abby, pushed the sugar and creamer closer, and gave a wink. "What I don't know yet is didja ever sneak into the Stallions locker room at naked time and what's going on with you and that hunkalicious Jackson Wilder."

*I*f he'd thought his days of running a shift at the hardware and feed store to cover his brother's missing ass were over, Jackson would have been wrong.

While Reno and his fiancée slept in and enjoyed an extended vacay, *he* was stuck restocking shelves and listening to Chester Banks complain about the lack of single ladies under sixty in the neighborhood. Jackson hated to disappoint the man and make him face the reality that he was past eighty and really, how well did the old equipment work when you got to that age?

Jackson shuddered.

Maybe he was just cranky from lack of sleep, but he'd almost pay the old cowboy to go complain to someone over at Bud's Diner. Or maybe he was worrying about how long his own equipment would function without a little workout once in a while. His dry spell had lasted way too long.

Which was *not* why he'd been thinking of Abby all night.

Last night, she'd filled his thoughts with concern—a need to take care of her the way he had when Jimmy Barton had thrown sand in her face, or when Levi Wittholm had spread rumors that he'd put some time between the sheets with her.

When she'd told him that her marriage had been a total sham, he'd been selfishly relieved. But when she'd revealed why her son of a bitch husband had treated her like trash and divorced her, his knees had nearly buckled. An overwhelming need to plant his fist in Mark Rich's face had kept him awake all night and made him wonder just how fast he could drive to Houston to deliver the punch.

When the little bell over the shop door ding-a-linged, he glanced up from refilling the barrel of Granny Vee's all-natural doggie donuts.

In walked the Abby he used to know.

Her hair fell in a cloud of soft curls over her shoulders. She'd wrapped her curvy body in a white dress that hugged her breasts, then fell slightly open only to be cinched in to her narrow waist by a wide brown belt. The dress drifted over her hips and thighs and came to a stop just above her knees. The boots on her feet she'd worn to school dances, and he'd watched her twirl around the floor, laughing until the dimples in her cheeks popped.

She looked amazing, and as she came toward him, a frisson of electricity tingled in his hands. Below his waist, there was a whole lot of *hell yeah* going on.

She smiled, and his gaze snapped to her full, glossy mouth.

He wanted to kiss her.

Wrap his arms around her and slide his tongue against hers.

He wanted to taste and tease.

Linger and play.

Stroke and promise.

He swallowed. Man, he had to get a handle on himself. "Wow. You look . . ."

"Awful?" Her top teeth sank into her supple bottom lip.

"No!" He gathered his wits and dumped them back into the bucket that was his head. "You look great. Really great. Different." His eyes took another slow cruise down the front of her revealing dress. "And you're holding a cat."

"Isn't she adorable?" Abby lifted the tiny kitten and rubbed noses.

"Did you steal that one too?"

Her eyes lit up and he knew she remembered the time they'd both nearly gone to jail. When they'd broken in and stolen the mistreated animals from the pet shop where she'd worked.

"Not this time." A laugh bubbled up. "This morning, I opened the front door, and there she was, looking up at me all helpless and scared."

"What are you going to do with it?"

"I'm going to keep her."

Jackson tilted his head. Keeping a pet showed signs of permanency. Of putting down roots. He wondered if Abby had thought that far ahead, or if she was just jumping in with both feet as usual. "Pets are a lot of responsibility, you know. They ground you so you can't just take off whenever the mood arises."

She looked up at him and hit him with a smile that took a tumble in his chest.

"Are you worried about *me* or the cat?"

"If *you're* taking care of the cat, I know it will be fine."

She came close enough to where he could hear the kitten's little motor running.

"So you're worried about me." Her hand came up, and her soft fingers gently touched his cheek.

"Don't be," she said. "I may not have everything figured out at the moment, but I'll get there."

And that's what worried him. She'd get things figured out, then she'd hightail it out of his life again before *he* had things figured out. "So what's her name?"

The multicolored kitten snuggled between her breasts.

Lucky cat.

"I thought maybe something like . . . Sweetums."

"What? That's a wussy name. She'd totally get her ass kicked by all the other neighborhood cats. You can't call her . . . *that*. See I can't even say it. It's too ridiculous."

Abby chuckled, and the sound drifted over him like a warm breeze.

"I suppose you want me to call her Rowdy, or Bullet, or *Chainsaw*," she said.

"Those aren't bad." He liked it when she teased him. "Maybe you could name her something like Flash, or Blaze, or Storm."

"Or maybe I could call her pooty pie."

"Oh my God." He slapped his forehead. "You're killing me. You'd be better off sticking with *Sweetums*."

"Ha!" She pointed her finger at him. "You said it."

Before he could wrap his hand around that finger and pull her against him, he gave the kitten—who purred contentedly between Abby's breasts—a rub between its ears.

Lucky damn cat.

"I'll think of something," she said. "And when I do, it will fit her as well as Jackson Wilder fits *you*."

He smiled at the cheerful animation that lit up her big blue eyes.

She fit him.

Whoa. Back the truck up. Where had *that* come from?

"So what brings you and . . . Fireball in today?"

"I'm not going to name her Fireball. But I do need supplies. Kitten food, litter, a cat box, some toys . . . you don't have a kitten starter kit do you?"

He chuckled. "No, but I'm pretty sure I've got everything you need." And with that innuendo left hanging, he escorted her to the pet-supplies aisle.

An hour later, he bagged up all her purchases and rang up the charges on her credit card. Lucky damn cat for showing up at Abby's door. She'd bought a little of everything, and everything had been top-of-the-line. She couldn't just have the apartment-sized cat condo. No, she had to have the multilevel palace, which included seven scratching posts, four punching bags, a tunnel, and a bed in the penthouse. He knew she was being careful about the money she spent, but apparently when it came to rescued cats, there was no limit.

"Would you mind carrying everything to my car?" she asked.

"I'm not sure it will all fit," he said, thinking about the small two-seater.

"It'll fit."

The paint cans hadn't fit, so what made her think a gigantic cat house would? "If you say so." He picked up her purchases and motioned for her to go first.

And yeah, she probably thought he was being a gentleman when all he really wanted was to watch her walk. He could watch her all damned day. The way she could look all casual and have such a sexy swagger at the same time just boggled his mind. But he was man enough to appreciate the hell out of it.

She held the door open while he maneuvered the cat condo through. When they stepped outside, he looked for her car. No silver Mercedes in sight.

"Where'd you park?"

"Right there." She pressed the button on her key fob and the locks of the black Escalade in front of them clicked open. Clutching the kitten to her chest, she opened the back door and stepped aside.

"Thought you had a Mercedes."

"I did."

"What happened to it?"

"I . . . dumped it."

The reference made to her ex-husband was not lost on him. "As in you pushed it off a cliff or sold it?"

She laughed. "Wish I would have thought of the cliff idea first, but no, I sold it and bought this. It's used, but I figured an SUV would be more suitable for my future."

He set the cat condo and bags in the back. "And that is?"

She reached for the door and leaned in close enough to bring with her an intoxicating floral scent. She smelled like heaven, and his imagination said she'd taste like it too.

"Y'all will just have to wait and see."

"Guess so." He gave her a small bow. "I thank you kindly for your business, Ms. . . ." He paused realizing he didn't know if she'd taken back her maiden name or retained the asshole's name.

"Morgan." Relief rippled through him as she playfully thrust her hand out. "Thank you for your assistance Mr. . . ."

"Wilder."

"Uh-uh." She slowly shook her head and looked up at him with those big blue eyes. Her head tilted. "Mr. *Hot Lips*."

Great. "Where'd you come up with that?" Like he didn't know.

The sultry gaze she dropped to his mouth left no question what was on her mind. He couldn't keep his lips off her. The smile tilting her luscious mouth said that maybe she didn't mind quite so much.

"Have a nice day." She gave him a wiggle of her fingers as she walked away.

While he stood in the street watching her toned legs and tight rear end sashay toward the driver's side, he realized he didn't have much patience with *wait and see*. "Hold up a minute."

She stopped and turned at the driver's door, thrusting out a hip to hold it open. His eyes stayed glued to that hip, and his imagination took off.

White panties, he guessed. Maybe even a thong. Definitely with lace. Abby had always been a girly girl. Silk and lace had always been her thing.

"What have you got planned for the rest of the day?" he asked.

"Why?" Her sexy Southern drawl dripped like honey.

He shrugged, doing his best to appear nonchalant and like he hadn't just been thinking about her underwear. "Thought if you were going to work on the house, I'd come over and help."

"You're not on duty?"

"Nope. I've got four glorious days off. Don't even have to work the store anymore. Reno will be back tomorrow."

"So . . ." She squinted at the bright sunshine and pulled the sunglasses from the top of her head down onto her nose. "You're saying you're available?"

"Pretty much."

That full pink mouth lifted into a smile. "Then stop by. We'll see what I can come up with." She gave him another little finger wave, then she and her pussycat got into the car and drove away.

We'll see what I can come up with.

Hell. If she couldn't come up with any ideas, he had a backlog.

When Abby had finally made up her mind to take action, she wondered what had taken her so long. After she'd gotten the kitten set up, and while the nameless little fur ball slept, Abby snuck out to check off the rest of the items on her *get 'er done* list. Not that she felt any less intimidated by the folks in town than she did a few days ago; she just figured if they were going to talk, then she couldn't stop them.

It would be cruel to do so anyway. The residents of Sweet did love their gossip. And while she'd never been much for the pastime herself, she did lean in now and again when the story was ultra juicy.

Now that she was back, she knew no place else would feel like home. She hoped she could stay. She wanted to stay. Heck, she never should have left in the first place. She knew that now. As far as what she wanted for her future, she might not have that all figured out.

Except for one thing.

Jackson.

She thought of him standing outside the hardware store and the look in his eyes when she'd called him hot lips. There had been laughter, but also intrigue. As if he thought maybe she *liked* his hot kisses.

He'd always been such a smart man.

Now, as her SUV tore down the gravel road, dust blew behind the tires like a storm rolling across the prairie. Abby glanced across the gently sloped hills, open meadows, and thick stands of oak trees. She'd spent a lot of time playing on this land. A lot of time swimming in the man-made pool in the creek. A lot of time riding horses and letting her hair fly in the wind.

The Wilder Ranch had always felt like home until a few nights ago, when she'd been thrust into an awkward situation that made her feel like she'd never belonged.

The tires rolled to a stop near the big rock-faced ranch house. As far as Abby could see, there were no extra trucks or cars to indicate anyone was home except Jana.

When Abby got out of the SUV, she heard bleating and looked down. A brown goat wearing a red satin ribbon around its neck trotted toward her.

"Well, hello there."

"Meh-eh-eh." The goat nodded.

"Aren't you looking fashionable today." Abby squatted and put herself face-to-face with the animal. She loved goats. And horses. And cows. Pretty much anything on four legs except skunks, thanks to Jackson's daring her to pet a baby once. He'd promised they didn't spray until they reached adulthood. Of course, she'd jumped in and taken his word for the truth. Two days later she was still trying to tomato-juice the stink out of her hair. Unfortunately, it had not been the last time Jackson or any of the other Wilder boys had fooled her.

She gave the goat a nice stroke on its long neck, then laughed when it butted her shoulder for more.

"Careful she doesn't get you dirty."

Abby looked up to find Jana coming out the door and walking toward her. "I'm not worried about getting dirty," she said.

"That's a pretty white dress. Miss Giddy will have it brown just like her in no time."

"Miss Giddy?" Abby stroked the animal's neck again, then stood. "Love that."

"I expect you came to see me." A smidge of guilt darkened the famous Wilder blue eyes.

Abby nodded. "You have time for a chat?"

"And an apology. How about I make us a pot of coffee?"

Between her regular morning brew and Mrs. Potter's full carafe, Abby was coffee'd out. "Sounds good." She followed Jackson's mother into the house, stopping to look at all the photos that lined the entry hall. The other night, she hadn't had a chance to really take note of all the changes that had recently been made. Today, she took a moment.

"I like the way you have the frames hanging from the antique wire fencing instead of just hanging on the wall," she said.

Jana's blue eyes—so much like her son's—brightened. "Thank you. I figured it was time to start making use of all those antiques I've got stored out in the barn. Joe was never interested in bringing them in. Figured a new vibe in the house would help me make a fresh start."

"That must be very difficult. You and Joe were . . ."

"Perfect for each other?"

"And together a long time."

"Ah." Jana sighed. "That we were. And now I'm trying to discover who I am. On my own."

Abby could relate. "I'm sure that's not easy."

"No one ever said life would be easy. You've just got to figure out what you really want and make it happen." Jana took Abby's arm and led her to the kitchen, which had not been changed.

The same big, worn table sat in the middle of the room with eight captain's chairs all pushed in just waiting for someone to drop by. With seven in the Wilder family, there had always been one left over for her, where she'd enjoyed many a meal between Jackson and Jake. Later, she discovered that Jana had always put her there to keep the two brothers from harassing each other at mealtime.

Abby pulled out *her* chair and sat down, while Jana flitted about the kitchen, scooping coffee into the coffeemaker and getting milk from the refrigerator.

"How do you figure out what you really want?"

With sugar bowl in hand, Jana turned, and her expression softened. "That's a tough one, isn't it?"

"I thought I knew. Until I didn't know. And by then . . ."

"Yeah." Jana set the sugar bowl down on the daisy-print tablecloth. "Sometimes things just snap your head around, don't they?"

Abby nodded. Folded her hands on top of the table. And took a breath. "You set me up the other night, didn't you?"

Jana's gaze was direct. "If you mean did I invite you over and purposefully forget to mention that the entire family plus neighbors, friends, and Jackson's ex-wife would be here, then yes. I set you up."

The truth stung. "Why?"

"Would you have come if I'd told you the truth?"

"Probably not."

"Then that's why I set you up." Jana cupped Abby's cheek in her hand. "It certainly wasn't out of spite or meanness."

"But I—"

"Walked out on my son when he was in harm's way?"

"Yes. And I know it was a horrible thing to do."

"Probably could have been handled better." Jana's shoulders lifted beneath her light pink cotton blouse. "But don't think I don't understand why you left. And don't think I'm mad at you or trying to seek revenge because of what you did. I invited you here the other night because I've always thought of you as the daughter I never had."

She reached across the table and took Abby's hands in her own. "Reno and Charli had come home—engaged. I got word that Jake will be coming home soon. Jackson's looking to step up in the fire department. It was a night to celebrate. And selfish as it might seem . . . I wanted you there. As a part of our family. Just like you've always been. I apologize for putting you in an uncomfortable position."

Abby's heart sunk so low in her chest, it stole her breath. "I've done some really stupid things. And I—"

"Will put them all behind you and move forward so you can find what you really want and make it happen."

"I'm not all that sure what *it* is."

Jana gave her a motherly smile. "Don't you?"

She could tell this woman who'd been like a second mother to her that what she'd wanted all along was her son, but Abby didn't know how she'd feel about that. She seemed very close to

Fiona, and she adored Izzy. Maybe Fiona had been her dream daughter-in-law. Maybe she was really unhappy about the divorce.

So how would she feel if Abby suddenly blurted out that she'd been in love with Jackson for as long as she could remember and that she truly believed her life would never be complete without him?

Whew.

No way could she spill those beans.

"I'm still trying to figure out who I am," she said instead. "Once I get that down, I guess I'll figure out what I want."

"You do that, sugarplum. And I'll tell y'all the same thing I told Reno when he was hemmin' and hawin' over what he was going to do about Charli. You can't reach the goal line with one step forward and two steps back. You have to keep moving."

"Sounds like reasonable advice."

"Of course, when we're talking about Jackson— who may well be the most hardheaded one of the bunch—you might need to put on the shoulder pads and tackle low." The coffeepot quit dripping, and Jana got up to pour two cups of coffee.

"I never said anything about Jackson."

"That's true. You didn't." Jana set the cups of steaming coffee on the table.

On autopilot, Abby splashed in sugar and cream and blew over the lip of the cup before she sipped and swallowed down the borderline-bitter liquid. Strong. Just as Jana had raised her sons.

Abby set her cup down and looked up. "I can't tell you how many times I wanted to call you."

"Oh?" Jana sipped without a blink.

"I actually did call once or twice," she admitted. "But when I heard your voice, I hung up."

"Ah. So that was you."

"You remember?"

Jana nodded. "Nobody calls the house phone anymore. It's all cell phones all the time. I figured the person calling either didn't have my cell phone number or—"

"Didn't have the courage to speak up."

"I was going to say or they were a very reserved obscene phone caller."

A motherly hand reached across the table and settled on top of Abby's fingers. "What stopped you from saying hello?"

"I figured I made my bed, and no one—especially anyone in this house—would want to talk to me or hear me complain. I thought it best to just cut ties with everyone."

"Well, that was silly."

"I left without saying good-bye." Abby tried not to cry, but if the big teardrop hanging from her bottom lashes was any indication, she'd failed. "Without telling anyone where I was going. Or why."

"And that was your business."

"I didn't mean to hurt anyone. I just . . ."

"You just love my son."

Abby nodded, and the teardrop splashed into her coffee.

"Then why did you leave?"

A sigh stuttered in her chest. "Because he made it clear he didn't feel the same." She glanced around the kitchen and soaked in the solace she'd always found there. "My mom and dad were so . . ."

"Wild?"

"Yeah. And as much as I tried to be a big sister for Annie, I ended up being more like her mother, and she resented that."

"Understandable."

"I always dreamed of being a part of all this." She waved her hand at the room, but the bigger picture was her intent. "The laughter, the fun, the closeness, the compassion . . ."

Jana gave her fingers a gentle, understanding squeeze.

"The night before Jackson left for Afghanistan I finally understood that was never going to happen. I left, so I wouldn't be reminded of what I could never have.

"Oh, sugarplum." Jana pulled Abby into her embrace. "Even without Jackson, you're a part of this family."

"Thank you."

"I promise not to use a football analogy like I did with Reno." She tucked a finger beneath Abby's chin and gently lifted so their eyes met. "But I can tell you that sometimes life is hard to understand. When I lost both my husband and my firstborn, I laid awake night after night asking why. I never did get an answer. I miss them both every single day. But the one thing I did learn was to never give up. Even when you feel like you're down on the ground and there are linebackers piled up on top of you and you can't breathe. You break through that dog pile and you get up.

You brush the dirt off your knees, get your butt back on that line of scrimmage, and you make it happen. It doesn't happen every play, but sooner or later, everyone scores a touchdown."

Abby grinned. Not just for the message but for the delivery.

"Oops." Jana grinned back. "I did it again."

In the Lone Star State, the only thing more important than the Lord was football. And big hair. Not necessarily in that order.

"So what you're saying is I should drop back into the pocket to make a pass?"

"Sugarplum, I'm saying that if you want to score that TD . . ." Jana gave her a saucy wink. "The best place to be is in the pocket."

Abby laughed. "Are we still talking about football?"

"Oh, hell no." Jana belted out a belly laugh.

Awkward, but good to know.

Chapter 7

When darkness fell in Sweet, the stars lit up the sky in a way that made it far too appealing to ignore. With autumn coming on, and winter not far behind, the pleasures of enjoying the great outdoors would diminish. Jackson didn't want the opportunity to pass.

As he knocked on the door of Abby's place, he figured he'd set himself up for a rejection. Or a snort of disbelief. Most certainly an eye roll. But that had never stopped him from getting what he wanted before.

The door opened, and Abby stood there with her kitten snuggled beneath her chin.

Once again he thought, *lucky damn cat*.

The sexy white dress had been replaced with a pair of jeans and a thin little camisole top. Her bare toenails were painted hot pink, and her hair was still fluffed out wild and curly—just the way he loved it most.

"Hi." Her full lips curled into a smile that kicked all his energy south of his belt. When she stepped back to let him in, he took a look around the room to see the progress she'd made.

Not much.

"What have you been up to?" he asked in a voice more casual than he actually felt inside.

She stroked the kitten's fur and glanced around the room. "Obviously, as little as possible. After I finished my errands, I came home and intended to start going through things in the kitchen. I ended up playing with the cat and baking some chocolate chip cookies. Want one?"

"Sure." He followed her into the kitchen. "You name that thing yet?"

"No." She handed him the kitten, who continued to purr as it climbed up the front of his shirt with its little razor claws and perched on his shoulder.

While Abby washed her hands, then handed him a couple of cookies, he watched the way she moved—a pleasant task he could engage in all day.

"But I like the sound of Pookie," she said.

"You are seriously setting your cat up for an ass whoopin'."

She laughed. "No I'm not. Don't you remember some of the names I came up with for my 4-H calves? Sweetie and Peach. Sugar and Baby."

"Yeah." He took a bite of cookie and found it warm and gooey, and he thought it would taste even better if he could spread that melted chocolate all over her. "And I remember hearing the other calves in the fair barn laughing too."

"You did not."

He loved that they had gotten back to teasing each other. Which was not to say everything flowed naturally between them. But it was a step in the right direction.

"So what's on your to-do list tonight?" He finished off cookie number one, chomped into cookie number two, and wished *he* was on her to-do list.

Okay, cowboy. Back off the inappropriate thoughts. They were barely finding their way back to being friends.

Still, he was a healthy guy, and she was a gorgeous woman. Sadly, maybe Hooch was right. Maybe it was impossible for men and women to just be friends.

He intended to give it a hell of a try. For a number of reasons.

"I don't know," she said. "One part of me says to get it in gear and get all this stuff divided up and—"

"What's your hurry?"

She shrugged and sank her teeth into a cookie. Her tongue darted out and licked away the melted chocolate on her lip. He tried not to groan.

"I need to get this work done, then figure out what to do with the rest of my life," she said.

"How about you start by taking a ride with me."

"Where to?"

It was a good sign she didn't immediately say no. "It's a surprise."

Her nose wrinkled. "If I remember right, your surprises are sometimes . . . icky."

"Icky?"

"Yeah, like the time you took me to the cave and I had to sit there watching millions of bats fly out and try not to freak out when the wind from their wings blew my hair around." She shuddered. "Icky."

"That was cool."

"You're such a guy."

"Well, you'll be happy to know this surprise has nothing to do with flying creatures."

She hesitated, but only momentarily. "Promise I won't have to crawl into anything dark and spooky or touch anything long and slimy?"

"I can't guarantee the long and slimy thing."

"Ummm."

"Kidding." He set the kitten down on the floor and watched it saunter off—tail flicking high in the air—toward the cat condo in the living room. "You have dinner yet?"

"Cookies."

"My favorite appetizer. Grab some shoes and a jacket. Unless you want me to carry you over my shoulder again."

Her eyes brightened. "You're taking me to dinner?"

"Among other places," he said.

"Good. I'm starving." She licked another drop of chocolate from her plump lip.

"Me too."

For him, understatements were becoming the new normal.

Abby watched through the windshield of Jackson's truck, surprised when he veered off the gravel road and onto a split in the grass that could barely be defined as a path. To be more accurate, it was a cattle trail. The truck bumped and jiggled along, and the motion tickled her stomach. Abby couldn't help but laugh. "Where are you taking me?"

He turned to look at her from across the cab. "You don't recognize this place?"

"Well, it is dark, and all I can see is what your headlights are hitting, so no. I'm clueless."

"Then you'll be surprised. Pleasantly I hope."

Moments later, the truck rolled to a stop, and the headlights lit up a wooden structure up in the trees.

"Oh! The tree house!" Built by the five Wilder Boys, the place was rustic, with rough-hewn timber and a deck railing made of branches. The corrugated tin roof protected the wood against the extreme Texas heat and finished off the look like the cherry on top of a sundae.

Opening her door, she jumped out and hurried up the ladder to the place they'd spent so many hours together—talking, laughing, dreaming, and working out problems. And like all teenagers, they had plenty. Mostly hers were questions of why certain boys wouldn't pay attention to her. His were why so many girls paid attention to him. Some things were never fair.

The tree house held other memories too—like prom night. She'd been going steady with Rick

Vanderhorn for six months. He'd asked her to prom, and she'd had a blast picking out her dress and dreaming of the biggest night of her junior year. The day before the big event, he dumped her for Cherry Carlisle—a sure thing.

Abby had been crushed and had cried for hours. Instead of putting on her pretty dress, she'd planned to throw herself a pity party with a tub of double chocolate caramel ice cream and frozen Snickers bars. But a knock on her door the night before the prom changed all that, and she'd ended up going with her best friend.

Jackson had been the perfect gentleman and the perfect date. Even afterward, when she'd snagged a bottle of sloe gin from her parents' liquor cabinet, and they drove out to the tree house, he'd helped her up the ladder because her heels kept getting caught in the hem of her dress. But more likely because she'd gotten a little tipsy.

Later, they'd both gotten pretty drunk. Between laughing at the way Toby Brent had dressed in a John Travolta white leisure suit and reprised dances from *Saturday Night Fever* to the huge rip under the arm of Misty Davenport's too-tight red satin hoochie-mama dress, they somehow ended up sitting closer and closer to each other. When the gin fizzed full throttle in their veins, they'd started to kiss. Then touch. And before they knew it, clothes came off, and they were in each other's arms.

They'd ended up making love. Throughout high school, she'd heard nightmare stories of girls giving it up to boys who were crude, careless, and selfish. Jackson had been sweet and tender. Careful and passionate.

At that time, Abby had always thought Jackson was a man of experience, but that night he'd confessed that she was his first. That he was her first also made it even more special. She'd been moved and happy. At least until they'd both passed out.

The following day, she'd been sick as a dog. Even so, she'd expected him to call. He hadn't until late that evening. They talked about their hangovers. They'd talked about the prom. They'd talked about his ranch chores and the biology test she had the following week. But he never mentioned what happened between the two of them. And neither did she.

Maybe he'd been too drunk to remember. Maybe he didn't want to remember. Maybe he regretted the whole thing.

She didn't want to know.

So, like a typical insecure seventeen-year-old, she'd played it off. Told him that Rick—the idiot who'd dumped her—had called her and begged her to come back to him. Though there'd been no way Abby would have gone back, she'd pretended to. Because really, a teenage girl did need to keep her wounded pride—and heart—intact.

With Jackson's lack of acknowledgment of their night together, that had been that.

To this day, *doing it* remained an unspoken topic.

But it was a night *she'd* never forget.

As nostalgia draped over her like a warm blanket, Abby stood on the little deck in the cool air listening to the water in the creek tumble over rocks and logs. The birds chirping in the trees. The sounds of night coming alive all around them.

"I always loved this place," she said, when Jackson climbed up and joined her.

"Yeah."

His warm palms settled over her shoulders and sent a tingle down her spine. Whether it was just from his touch or the memories of his touch that flooded her mind, she didn't know.

"It was a great hideaway."

"Can we go inside?" she asked.

"Hang on, let me get a light." He went back to the truck and came back holding the old Coleman lantern they'd used back in the day. The glow from the light spread golden warmth around the area. "We've made some improvements since you were here last. Raised the roof and made it more adult-size friendly."

"I always wondered why none of you became builders," she said. "Seems you always had a hammer and nails going."

"We did like to create. Reno and Jared planned to start a handcrafted furniture business, but . . ."

She heard the heartbreak in his tone, and as his sentence trailed off, she jumped in to fill the void. "I'm surprised you haven't built yourself a home yet. I know your parents gave all y'all portions of the ranch. So why are you living in an apartment above Reno's barn?"

He shrugged. "Time hasn't been right yet."

"What about when you were married?"

"We lived in San Antonio. Fiona and Izzy still live there."

"That's a long drive."

"We do our best to make it work. Although Fiona's been talking about moving to Sweet. I hope she does. Then I can see Izzy more often. You ready to see inside the tree house?"

"Absolutely."

His warm hand settled low on her spine as he reached around her, opened the door, and waited for her to step inside. He followed, and so did the light.

"Wow," she said. "Are you kidding me?"

Though the tree house couldn't have been bigger than eight feet by eight feet, a love seat and small pine table with two chairs had been placed inside. Warmth was created by a braided rug and several wildlife pictures on the walls.

"You like it?" he asked with just a touch of eagerness in his tone.

"It's much better than just a box with a wood floor."

"Jared took those photos the last time he was home on leave. He was always great with a camera."

Abby's heart twisted at the second mention of his brother and the sadness in his tone. She turned and hugged him. "He was a great guy. I know you really miss him."

"We all do," he said quietly.

As if it was second nature, his arms came around her, and he drew her in close. Against her cheek, she felt the beat of his heart. For a moment, while the crickets sang a melody, and the water tumbled down the creek, they stood in an embrace designed only for two friends to share the pain of a loss words could never define.

Slowly, they backed away.

"Are you hungry?" he asked.

"You actually have food? Or did your surprise include us going out into the forest and nailing Bambi?"

He laughed. "I can hardly see you—who wouldn't harm a hair on a bunny's head—doing that. So I brought dinner."

"That was nice of you. Did you stop by Bud's for Diablo burgers?"

"No." He sounded insulted. "I hit up the Wilder cafe."

"You cook?"

"Sugar, I'm a fireman." His grin turned her inside out. "We all turn on the heat in the kitchen."

No doubt.

"You figure out if you want to eat inside or out, and I'll go get the food."

The moment he left the room, it turned cold. Empty. Lackluster. She went outside and down the ladder. The night air was brisk, yet she had no qualms about sitting outside for a meal he'd cooked with his own two hands. She'd missed the great outdoors, but not nearly as much as she'd missed him. "As much as I love what you've done with the place," she called out, "I'd really like to sit out here. The weather is perfect tonight."

He reappeared with a big Dutch oven in his big hands. "Then I'll start a fire."

"Isn't that against fireman regulations?"

"Oh, you know me. Always trying to break the rules."

She knew many things about him. Breaking the rules—or at least bending them until they defied the laws of gravity—had always been his specialty. He'd never been a sit-around-and-let-it-happen kind of guy. He'd always taken a bull-by-the-horns full-tilt boogie approach to life.

Within minutes, he had a fire roaring in the ring surrounded with several layers of rock. They sat down on the sofa cover, and he handed her a paper bowl and plastic spoon.

"I figured something like this would be easiest. No dishes to wash, we can just throw the stuff in the fire." He lifted the lid on the Dutch oven, and a delicious aroma wafted up into the air.

"Mmmmm. Is that beef stew?"

"Yep."

"I've been planning to make some, which is why I came to your apartment that day—the apartment I didn't know existed until I barged in on you and Izzy. I still have the packages of beef in the freezer."

"Well, you can save that for a rainy day."

He filled her bowl, and she took a bite. A hint of spicy Southwestern flavor danced across her tongue. "This is delicious."

"I aim to please."

"We'll see about that."

The smile he flashed held a mischievous quality that said not only did he aim to please, but that he could knock her socks off in the process.

A quiver of desire danced through her belly and settled in next to the warm, delicious stew.

He reached into a bag and pulled out a bottle of red wine.

"You came prepared," she said, thinking this felt more like a date than just two old friends getting together for a meal. Then again, she'd been known to fantasize beyond her limits a time or two.

Jackson wouldn't need anything like that from her. With his devastating looks and hot body, she was sure he didn't spend many nights alone. At least not judging from the way the women in town looked at him. Okay, maybe salivated over him was a better description.

"It's local." He showed her the label. "There's a whole row of wineries on Highway 290 now. They're even calling it the Wine Road."

"I noticed that when I took a drive last week."

"There are some pretty good ones." He poured the wine into paper cups and handed her one. "Once in a while, I like to take the time and visit. Most places serve food and have nice areas outdoors to relax and enjoy a glass or two."

"Sounds like fun."

"Maybe I'll take you sometime."

She lifted her cup. "I'd like that."

The cabernet was smooth, and they sipped as they ate. While the fire snapped and crackled, the conversation flowed from his fire stories to her enthusiasm for some of the charity events she'd organized in Houston. He mentioned the upcoming Black Ties and Levi's charity auction to support the expansion of the Sweet Emergency Center, and she promised she'd attend.

Two things that seemed off-limits were delving any further into their prior marriages and subsequent divorces. For that, Abby felt relief. She didn't want to think of him with anyone else. And she certainly didn't want to spend any energy thinking about the man on whom she'd wasted so many years.

When they finished their meal, they tossed the bowls and utensils into the fire, then leaned back and continued to enjoy the wine.

Across the dancing flames, he watched her. And when the heat became too much to take, she got up and walked over to the creek to cool off. She was sure all those intense looks were just her imagination.

They were barely friends, she reminded herself.

"Are you okay?"

He'd come up behind her, and his breath brushed her cheek.

"I'm great." She released the lock of her hair that had been tucked behind her ear to ward off the tingles that skittered down her spine.

"You don't sound great." He came around to stand in front of her. "You sound . . . wistful."

She laughed. "I don't think I've ever heard you use that word before."

"Never had a reason to."

A canopy of live oaks filtered the moonlight, and, with the fire at their backs, it became difficult to see through the darkness. But Abby could feel the intensity in his eyes. She could smell the shower-clean scent of his skin. His irresistible masculinity.

"So tell me about this opportunity to move up in the ranks at the fire station," she said, searching for something to distract her attention from the awareness rising in her belly.

"Maybe later." He came closer. Tucked his hand beneath her chin and lifted her face. He moved in slowly, and she had plenty of time to turn away or run like hell.

She didn't.

Their eyes locked until his thick dark lashes swept down, and he focused on her mouth.

"I missed you, Abby," he whispered across her lips.

For a moment, while her heart hammered against her ribs, he just held her that way. Their breaths mingled, but their bodies did not touch. Until he lowered his head.

When his lips touched hers, they were gentle—for a single heartbeat. Then she was in his arms, and his hungry mouth moved over hers. With a deep, masculine groan of approval, he took possession, threaded his hands through her hair, and tilted her head so they melded together like hot and fudge.

Common sense said it was impossible for a human to melt, but Abby's bones suddenly went MIA.

Her arms wound around his neck. Aching for more, she leaned into him. While one of his hands held her close, the other slipped down her back, cupped her bottom, and drew her up against the long, hard length that said at the moment he wasn't thinking of *friendship*.

The intensity of the kiss shifted, deepened, and singed her as though she'd stepped through a wall of flames. His mouth left hers and traveled down the side of her neck. Her nipples tightened and ached as his warm breath brushed across her skin. Someone moaned. Him? Her? Hard to tell. Didn't matter.

She wanted more.

His grip on her bottom tightened, and all she could think—if she could think at all—was time had melted away, and she was right where she'd always wanted to be.

In the near distance, the roar of an engine approached, and, in a blink, her arms were empty.

"Goddammit."

"Who is it?" She hugged herself against the sudden chill.

"Kids." Absently, he tugged the zipper of her hoodie together. "A few of them from town discovered this place a while back and are trying to claim it for their own lover's lane. Pretty sure they don't know it's private property."

"They'll be surprised to see someone else has taken their spot," she said, trying to act like they hadn't just been locked in each other's arms.

His gaze came back to her, and she could see apology in his eyes.

Don't say it. Don't say it. Don't say it.

Yet even in the firelight as his gaze licked up and down her body he formed the words, "I'm sorry." His big hands went to his hips as he shook his head. "I don't know what happens to me when I get around you."

"Jackson, I . . . umm . . ." *Wait.* Maybe he really *didn't* know what made him grab her and kiss her every time they got close. Maybe she really was rowing the "Hey, I'm not just hot for you but I'm crazy about you" boat alone. Maybe all those signals she thought he'd been pitching her were lost in her own pathetic translation. Maybe all he really needed was a warm body.

She was a warm body.

And with the way he fired her up every time he kissed her, she was willing to help him ease that sexual frustration he kept denying.

Heavy rap music blaring, a Jeep pulled up, with a teenage couple and threw a bucket of water over anything Abby wanted to say or do.

"I've got to go take care of this," he said.

Dazed, Abby nodded.

What were they doing?

Where was this headed?

Were they friends as in friends who call once in a while to see how you were doing? Friends as in it's closing time, and you get a booty call because there was no one better at the bar?

She glanced across the space to where he animatedly explained to the young couple that they were trespassing, and her heart went all crazy in her chest.

She didn't want to be Jackson's booty call.

Not that she didn't like the booty. She just wanted something more.

When he came back, they definitely needed to talk.

They'd always been able to talk.

About everything.

Except how they might actually feel about each other deep down inside.

But when the couple drove off, and he came back, he was too frustrated to do anything more than pick up the remnants of their meal, put out the fire, and drive her home.

Chapter 8

$\mathcal{S}$unrise shot a streak of gold across the tree-tops. On horseback, Jackson raced his brothers across the meadow. It had been a couple months since they'd all been together and doing the one thing they all loved—riding the ranch and taking care of the animals and the land their father had entrusted in their care.

Jackson shifted his head and glanced at the men racing beside him. As boys, they might have beaten the shit out of each other at every turn and harassed each other at every opportunity, but he loved them. And if anyone ever caused them any harm, he'd take their heads off. Just one of the reasons it had been so hard to leave the Marines. He still felt like he had to even the score for what had happened to their big brother.

Jared had always been the one with the most heart. The most intelligence. The most to offer the world.

Not a day went by that Jackson didn't feel it should have been him to die instead of Jared. They all felt that way. But none more than him.

Beneath him, Ranger—the most stubborn horse on the planet—ate up the ground under his hooves. The gelding gave him nothing but a bad time unless it was time to race. The horse did love to compete. Something they both had in common.

In mere seconds, they reached the giant rock that had been the established finish line. Reno got there first and took glory in rubbing it in their faces.

"Ha!" Reno's grin split wide across his face. "I've been gone for months, and I can still beat you lightweights."

"What are you, five?" Jackson turned Ranger in a tight circle to calm him down. "The damn horse did all the work, not you."

"Sore loser." Jesse pushed his hat back on his head and looked at their older brother. "It's good to have you back."

"Good to be back. Although being on an extended vacation and having Charli all to myself?" His broad shoulders lifted. "Not going to complain."

"Even if you had to put up with her silly poodle?" Jackson asked.

"Even if."

While the horses settled, their riders relaxed.

"So how'd you pop the question?" Jesse wanted to know.

"She had a list of places in California she wanted to visit before she moved here, so we tried to hit up as many as possible in the length of time we had available."

"Didn't figure you for the amusement-park type," Jackson said.

"The only two on her list were Disneyland and Sea World, so I lucked out. I managed to talk her out of the whole Small World thing, although she did make me stand in line with her so she could get her picture taken with some chick named Rapunzel. Charli kept saying "Best day ever!" whatever the hell that meant."

"It's a part in the movie *Tangled*, where she finally gets out of her tower and—" Jackson noticed his brothers were staring at him as though he'd gone off the deep end. "Shit. TMI?"

Jesse scratched his head.

Reno laughed. "Now that you mention it, I do remember watching that movie with Izzy a time or two myself. So you're off the hook."

"Am I the only one who doesn't watch princess movies with her?" Jesse asked.

"Yeah, but your time is coming." Jackson swiveled his attention back to Reno. "And you proposed how?"

"In the garden at Hearst Castle. I'd been waiting for the right place and moment, then I just couldn't wait any longer. The tour moved ahead of us, and I think I said something totally dopey like "Will you be my queen? Or maybe it was, marry me, and I'll make you feel like a queen. I don't know. All I cared was that she said yes."

"Dude." Jesse laughed. "You are whipped."

"I know." Reno grinned again. "And I'm good

with that. Just don't forget, I can still whip *your* ass."

There were moments in life where you didn't have to work at feeling good, Jackson thought. This was one of them. "Big brother," he said. "It's good to see you smile again."

"And you're up to what, with Abby being back?"

Jackson never liked it when the focus drilled in on him. He shrugged. "Not much."

"I call bullshit," Jesse said with a grin as he lifted his hat and ran his fingers through his now-too-long hair. "I saw the way you were looking at each other at Mom's the other night."

"Sorry to disappoint you, but that was just a result of Mom's entrapment methods. Abby thought she was coming over to help go through the stuff in the barn. She had no idea she was about to be thrust into another situation to be judged or come face-to-face with the choices I've made in life."

"Yeah," Reno said. "I sensed her distress when she tried to escape. I kind of intimidated her into staying."

"She did kind of fly out of there pretty quick," Jesse said. "I noticed you followed her out the door."

"Hell, he ran," Reno said.

"Happy to know I can still entertain you two yahoos. But before you get any ideas, I followed her out to apologize for her being put on the spot. She's got a lot of crazy thoughts that everyone in town is talking behind her back and judging her about the divorce."

"They *are* talking about her divorce," Jesse said.

"People are curious as hell as to why she'd walk away from a sweet deal like that," Reno added.

The comment rubbed Jackson the wrong way because he knew the truth, and he'd defend her all day long. "Maybe *people* should mind their own damned business."

"Agreed." Reno glanced away, and when his dark eyes came back, they were filled with compassion. "My guess is there's a whole lot of story there nobody knows."

"Yep." Jackson's chest tightened. "So I'd appreciate it if y'all would go easy on her."

"I'm a little surprised to hear you defend her," Jesse said.

"We talked." Jackson shrugged. "We're cool."

"And that leaves you where with her now?" Jesse asked.

"Just friends."

"That's where all the trouble started to begin with," Reno reminded him.

"Ain't that the truth," Jesse added.

"Older and wiser now, boys." He gave his stubborn horse a nudge with his heels. "All that is past tense."

Unless he couldn't learn to keep his lips off hers.

Then he was in for a whole mess of trouble.

Abby stumbled from bed and walked down the hall to the bathroom. She did her business, then went to the sink to wash her face and hands. Unfortunately, she looked up into the mirror.

"Oh Lord."

Her reflection revealed every toss and every turn she'd taken in her little full-sized bed after Jackson had brought her home. Her hair stuck out at freakish angles, and she had pillow creases on both cheeks. She looked like ten miles of bad road and a hairpin turn.

When she came out of the bathroom she was greeted by her new little bundle of fur. "Well, hello, Miss Kitty." She reached down, picked up the kitten, and drew her close for a nose nuzzle. "And I guess that also means you now have a name."

The kitten gave a tiny meow, then she turned on her motor. Abby took that as an indication that the name set right with her.

"Yep. Miss Kitty, it is."

They went downstairs, and Abby opened the bag of kitten chow she'd bought from Jackson. Which brought her thoughts full circle to the dreams she'd had last night. If only life were as easy as falling asleep to get what you wanted.

Not since she'd been snuggled with Jackson beneath a blanket back in the day and they'd watched *Nightmare on Elm Street* had she ever known dreams to be so intense. But hers had been vivid—only in a nonnightmarish way. The color and images had been so clear and crisp and real, Abby woke in a sweat and thought she could still feel Jackson's strong hands on her skin. He'd held her. Caressed her. And she'd taken him into her body—gasping at the memory of what all those hard muscles felt like. So much so that when she woke, she burned for his touch.

Last night he'd kissed her.

Again.

And she still had no idea why.

Other than the brief moments when his lips were on hers, he seemed cool and definitely reserved. But when he kissed her, the lid blew off the passion meter.

Not that she minded.

The only thing she did mind was that he'd apologized. And *that* left her in a whole state of confusion she'd be happy to never visit again.

While Miss Kitty nibbled her grilled-chicken-flavored kitten cuisine, Abby fixed herself an egg and piece of toast. While she sipped her cup of coffee, she made a to-do list and had to force herself not to put Jackson's name at the top.

In the past, when she'd been organizing charity events, she'd start with a mile-long list of what must be done and a mini wish list of what she'd also like to accomplish to up the game. She wasn't always successful, but when she hit a home run, the joy that spread through her had been incomparable.

So she'd become a list maker if only to stay focused and feel like—in a world she couldn't control—she had at least one foot on solid ground.

Today's number one to-do was to take Miss Kitty to see the vet, who also happened to be Jackson's older brother. So after a shower, a splash of makeup, and a sweep through her closet for something to wear that fit her old personality and not the uptight Junior Leaguer she'd become, she put the kitten in the cat carrier and off they went.

As pet clinics went, Sweet's version was nothing fancy. Just an old converted house off Main Street. The stucco was light pink, and the trim was mint green. It was an old-time combination that reminded Abby of something you'd see in an episode of *The Andy Griffith Show*. Outside the building a hanging sign announced DR. JESSE WILDER, DVM. On the lawn another sign read DOG AREA. YOU POOP. YOU SCOOP. Attached to the post was a box that contained plastic disposal bags.

Genius.

She grabbed the cat carrier from the passenger seat and went inside for the appointment she'd made yesterday. The waiting area was small, with a linoleum floor and spotless. Near the door sat a woman Abby didn't recognize holding a quivering Chihuahua in a pink sweater with sparkly silver pom-poms. Abby gave her a smile as she came through the door, went to the reception desk, and waited for someone who worked there to appear.

Moments later Mrs. Orville, a high-school friend's mother, came out from the back room, where various barks and meows could be heard echoing loudly.

"Abby! When I saw *Morgan* on the appointment books, I wondered if that could be you."

Abby smiled. "How are you, Mrs. Orville?"

"Oh, fine and dandy." For several minutes the older woman told her exactly how she was from the corns on her toes to the arthritis creepin' up her spine to the fact the Mr. Orville had taken to wearing a CPAP so she could get some reprieve from all the snoring. Except now she had to tolerate the hum of the machine. She quickly moved onto how Abby's old friend, Lila Sue, had just had her second set of twins and how Abby should give her a call. When the woman sailed into explaining that she was there helping the handsome doctor out because he just couldn't seem to keep his pretty assistants for more than a month or two, Abby had to interrupt before her ears started to bleed.

"I have an appointment at eleven."

Mrs. Orville didn't even bother to look at the appointment book. She grabbed some paperwork and escorted Abby into one of the exam rooms.

"Looks like you've got a cute little kitten there," she said. "You can take her out of the carrier. Dr. Wilder will be here in just a few minutes. While you wait, go ahead and fill out the forms and give them to the doc when he comes in."

"Thank you."

Abby filled out the forms and was nuzzling Miss Kitty when Jesse walked into the room, wearing a white doctor's coat over jeans and a light blue shirt. With his longish blond hair, dark blue eyes, and killer smile, he looked more like a Hollywood god than a man who took care of pets.

"Hey there, sparkplug." He flashed the smile that no doubt brought women to their knees—for various reasons. "Who's your friend?"

"She showed up at my door. Arlene Potter says the neighbors won't get their cats fixed, and, from what I could find out, nobody wants to claim her."

She gave the kitten a stroke down her back, to which two little paws came up ready to box and play. "So I did."

Jesse lifted the bundle of fur in his capable hands and Abby had to admit she was surprised at the gentleness with which he held and talked to the kitten. "Then she's a lucky cat." He looked at Abby and nailed her with laser focus. "Thought you were putting the house up for sale and moving on."

She shrugged. "I don't really have an exact plan."

"So does that mean there's a possibility you might stay in Sweet?"

"Maybe. When I first thought of it, I pretty much shot the idea down as soon as it flew through my head."

"Why?" His head tilted as he set Miss Kitty down on the exam table and took her temperature, to which the kitten voiced her disapproval with a loud meow. "This is your home."

"It *was*. But everything changes. And sometimes you just find you need to move on."

"How'd that work for you last time?"

"Wow." His bluntness shocked her down to the bone. Not that it wasn't warranted. "That was harsh."

"We grew up together, Abby. You were at our house as much as you were at your own. And you had a very close relationship with my brother. So I'm not saying anything to you that I wouldn't say to Reno, Jack, or Jake if they were in your situation." He inspected Miss Kitty's eyes, ears, and teeth. "I'm not trying to be mean, just trying to figure out where you're coming from and where you're going."

If she were pushed to tell the truth, the whole truth, and nothing but the truth, she'd admit that she had two lists of where she was going. A reality list. And a wish list. She'd give him extra points for guessing who was at the top of the latter.

"And how it involves my brother," he added.

Bingo.

"Your brother and I are trying to find a way to be friends again. That's all."

"Uh-huh."

The kitten batted at the stethoscope as he pressed it to her little body.

"I'm not saying it will be easy," she said. "After all, I did . . ."

"Pull a pretty shitty stunt cutting him off like that?"

She cringed. "Yes."

"Then why'd you do it?"

Hoo boy. "I couldn't even begin to tell you why, Jesse. It would take hours."

He looked up. "I've got time."

"Well . . ." She scratched her head. "I don't really . . ."

"Don't sweat it, sparkplug. We all know why you ran."

"We?" She took a breath, hoping it would slow her racing heart. "Who's *we*?"

He grinned. "Everybody except Jack."

She folded her arms, trying to play it cool. "Exactly what is it you all think you know?"

"That you've probably been in love with him since you learned to tie your shoes. I just don't know why you two never got together."

Because Jackson didn't feel the same way. Apparently, he just liked to kiss her without knowing why.

"We all figured you got tired of waiting for him to make his move."

"You're too pretty to be so smart, Dr. Wilder."

He laughed. Gave the kitten a stroke down her back and she arched in pleasure. "You got poop?"

"Excuse me?"

"Poop." He pointed at the cat. "To see if she has worms."

"Oh. No. I didn't know I was supposed to bring any in. I'm not even sure she's done that in the cat box yet."

"When she does, bring in a sample, and we'll check it out. You squeamish?"

"For?"

He reached around and held up a hypodermic needle.

"Oh. No. That stuff doesn't bother me."

"Great." He gave the kitten the injection so fast and smooth she didn't even flinch. "You looking for a job?"

"A job?"

"Yeah. I can't seem to keep the vet-assistant position filled. Thus the reason for Mrs. Orville. She used to work for old Doc Michaels back in the day. She agreed to help me out until I found a replacement for Sherrie. Or Lana. Or Lisa. Or whatever her name was. But only if I kept my hands to myself."

Abby laughed. "Well, Mrs. Orville *is* pretty hot with those pink camo Crocs and polyester pants."

"Yeah. That's what I was thinking."

"Word on the street is the reason you can't keep an assistant is because you sleep with them all and break their fragile little hearts because you won't commit."

"Yeah." He shook his head. "I've heard that too."

"You know what I think?"

"What's that?"

"I think it's all B.S."

He looked up from inspecting Miss Kitty's ears, grinned, and used her own line against her. "You're too pretty to be so smart."

"So why do you let everyone believe you're some kind of man-whore?"

He shrugged. "Easier than trying to deny. I'm not saying I'm an angel by any means, but who am I to spoil people's fun. For some reason, folks like to either have something to gossip about or someone to live vicariously through. Doesn't bother me. I know the truth."

"Which is?"

"I can't keep assistants because the pay is low, the hours are long, and with an area as small as Sweet to find job candidates, the selection is slim. So I have to go outside the area, and after a few months, they realize the commute is too long and the pay is too low so . . ."

"The cycle repeats itself."

"Exactly."

"So I was right, you're not some big ego-driven heartbreaker."

He laughed. "I'm like anyone else. Someday I'd like to find the right woman and settle down. But by the time I get there, I could be settling into my golden years."

"So you're in no hurry."

That Wilder grin came back. "Like I said, I'm no angel. So . . . about that job." He handed Miss Kitty back to her. "You interested?"

"I don't know anything about being a vet assistant."

"You did 4-H and FFA. You've been around animals your whole life. Well, maybe except for the time you were in Houston. And I'm not sure professional football players don't fit into that category."

She had to agree.

"You're a quick learner," he said. "I can teach you what you need to know."

She'd been looking for what she wanted to do with her life. Did that include working with animals? She didn't know. But she was willing to give it a try.

"I might be interested."

"Great. Show up here tomorrow at nine and let's see how it goes. The pay won't buy you a new Mercedes, but it'll cover your cat-food bill."

"Sounds good." She eased Miss Kitty back into her carrier.

"Besides, the longer I can keep you here in town"—he gave her a knowing look—"the more time you and that jackass brother of mine have to figure out that you two belong together."

She lifted her head to protest, but the grin on his face was so genuine, she didn't have the heart to argue.

Besides, she agreed.

He showed her out to the reception area with a wave and a "See you tomorrow." Abby set the cat carrier down on the floor and stood at the counter while she paid Mrs. Orville the fees for the visit.

"Surprised to see you back in town."

Abby turned to find Pauline Purdy sitting in the chair directly behind her holding a fur explosion Abby guessed to be a Pomeranian or one of those puffball yappy kind of dogs. The large and in-charge woman was decked out in one of her stretched to the max polyester suits and a lacquered hairdo that closely resembled the dog on her lap.

Abby had briefly worked for the woman and her husband at the Touch and Go Market before she moved to Houston. Paul Purdy was a lecherous old dude who liked to cop a feel every chance he got. And Pauline was . . . well, there was no other way to say it than she was the town beeotch who believed that Abby had been luring her hefty and lewd husband into having an affair.

Abby had done everything possible not to put herself in the position to give Mr. Purdy's wandering hands any opportunities or the missus any room for speculation. Didn't matter, she'd become number one on Mrs. Purdy's hate list. The day she quit, she'd been beyond relieved.

"Hello, Mrs. Purdy." She put on her best smile. "How are you?"

"Probably better than you are."

Annnnnd here it came. The exact reason Abby had tried to be invisible when she'd come back to Sweet. There weren't many who were as judgmental, openly opinionated, and mean-spirited as the Purdys. But Abby didn't want to give anyone a reason to paint a target on her back. Or her character. So she took the high road.

"You mind your own business, Pauline." Mrs. Orville came to her defense, and Abby wanted to give her a great big hug.

"I'm just sittin' here, aren't I?" Mrs. Purdy snarled. "Doesn't a person have a right to speak these days?"

Abby turned her back. The spiteful woman could say what she wanted, but it didn't mean Abby had to hold the door open.

"I hope you're not wanting your old job back," Mrs. Purdy continued. "Because we don't have any openings. Not that I'd rehire you anyway, with you leaving us in the lurch like that."

Abby bit her tongue and kept her head down as she reached into her wallet for her credit card.

"Plus you getting dumped by that husband of yours? Says something, don't you think?"

"I've got to go get your receipt." Mrs. Orville patted her hand, and whispered, "Don't you let her get the best of you."

And there lay the problem.

Abby suddenly felt as though she didn't have any *best* left. It had drained from her like dirty bathwater.

"If you weren't even reliable enough to keep a job at a grocery store . . . well, it just makes a soul wonder why someone as successful and wealthy as Mark Rich would—"

"That's enough."

Abby turned at the deep growl of a voice behind her.

Arms folded, Jackson stood in front of her former employer. He looked down at her as though he could squish her like a bug. Abby kind of hoped he would.

"Everyone has a reason for doing things," he said. "Just like the way you and the mister jack up the prices so you can afford your fur coats and diamonds. Even when you know there's not a soul in Sweet who gives an honest shit about how you look."

Pauline Purdy's mouth dropped open, and her gasp sucked up half the air in the room. "Well, I never."

"Probably a big part of your problem," he said.

The woman stood, and the top of her head barely came to the center of his chest. Eyes glinting with anger, she looked up at him, and said, "I'm sure your mother will be quite disappointed to know how you've spoken to me."

"And I'm sure if my mother heard you talking to someone she cares about like that, she'd take you to task herself."

While Abby stood there frozen, Mrs. Purdy grabbed her purse and her pooch and stormed out the door.

When the door slammed, Mrs. Orville came back into the room, receipt in hand. "What was that?"

"I think you can scratch Mrs. Purdy off the books," Jackson said.

The older woman's head tilted. "For just today or for good?"

Jackson grinned.

Mrs. Orville grabbed a red pen. "Got it."

"What are you doing here?" Abby asked him.

"Came to take my brother to lunch." Eyes narrowed, his gaze moved up and down her body as if searching for war wounds. "You okay?"

"Yes. And thank you."

He shrugged. "Always happy to help a lady in distress."

She knew he hadn't meant to push her thoughts in any certain direction, but the comment led her to think of the way he'd met Fiona. "You can't rescue everybody you know."

That gaze licked over her again. "That your cat?" He pointed to the plastic carrier at her feet.

"Miss Kitty."

"*That's* the name you came up with?"

She nodded, keeping the variety of mixed emotions inside her heart anchored.

"Well, it's better than *Sweetums*." He picked up the carrier and the kitten inside squeaked a meow. "If you're done, I'll help you to your car."

She could argue that she was perfectly capable of carrying the little plastic box herself, but she couldn't get over the fact that he'd jumped to her defense so quickly. And what damsel wouldn't want to spend just a few more minutes with such a handsome knight? At least she'd have enough fuel to conjure up more nighttime fantasies.

"I'll see you tomorrow, Mrs. Orville." The woman gave her a wave and a smile.

Jackson followed her outside to her SUV and waited while she opened the door. He leaned in and set the carrier on the passenger seat. Somehow in the process, she became trapped between him and the door.

He was crowding her.

Purposely?

She looked up into those dream-inspiring eyes. Hard to tell.

Until he braced his arm on the top of the door and trailed the backs of his fingers with the other hand down her arm.

"I'm sorry about Mrs. Purdy and her big mouth."

"She's only saying what everyone else is thinking. Most people don't understand that just because someone is one of the richest men in the state doesn't make him a good person."

"The Rich family made most of their money in oil. To some, that's the equivalent of being a divine being. But you're right, that doesn't qualify someone as being good. And it doesn't mean you have to put up with people's bad behavior."

She wondered if he realized that the more he talked, the more he touched her. The backs of his fingers had changed to his fingertips. And each slow, methodical caress sent all kinds of crazy signals to parts of her that had been long, long denied. She'd gone beyond chills to shivers, and now to an all-out sweat.

Trying to keep things at a friendly level—or

at least to keep her from embarrassing herself by grabbing his head and yanking his lips down to hers—she smiled up at him, and said, "Thanks for the rescue, but I've gotta go."

He took her hand. Held it for more than a moment. And searched her face as if he was waiting for . . . what. She had no idea.

"Anytime."

With a move as smooth as she could muster, she escaped to the driver's side.

"Hey," he called just before she got inside the SUV. "Why did you tell Mrs. Orville you'd see her tomorrow? Is your cat sick?"

"She's fine. Your brother offered me a job as his assistant. I start work tomorrow."

"You what?"

She gave him a finger wave and was gone before the *holy fuck* look on his face exploded into verbal judo.

"Are you kidding me?"

Jackson exploded into his brother's tiny office. The framed diplomas on the wall shuddered with the bang of the door.

Jesse looked up from behind the desk; a smirk in full volume tilted his mouth. "I haven't even said a word yet, little brother."

"Tell me you did *not* just hire Abby as your next assistant."

"No can do."

"What the fuck, Jess? If you think she's going to be your next conquest, you'd better think again."

"Why?"

"Why?" Jackson jammed his hands on his hips.

"That's what I said. Why do you care who I choose to see."

"Because you don't *see* women. You don't *date* women. You go to bed with them, then, when you won't commit, they take off for the hills."

"And the problem with that is?"

"We're talking about Abby, Jess. Not some new girl in town."

"I like Abby."

The blood in his veins sweltered. "I am so going to kick your ass if you even think of touching her."

"Why, Jack? Why do you care?" Jesse got up out of his chair and came around the desk until they stood toe to toe. "You told me and Reno that you and her were just friends. *Your* exact words. *Just friends.* I think she's beautiful. And smart. And nice. So why shouldn't I be interested in her? Why shouldn't I want a relationship with her?"

"Because you don't have relationships. And because . . ."

"Because what?" His brother smiled, and the urge to rearrange his pretty face died.

Jackson dropped his chin and shook his head. "I don't know."

"Oh, brother." Jesse grasped his shoulder. "You know, for a guy who runs into burning buildings and stands up to terrorists like they're flies on a wall, you sure can be a pussy about some stuff."

"I'm *not* a pussy."

"Really?"

"Sometimes things are just complicated."

"Only because you make them that way." Jesse punched him in the chest.

Jackson rubbed the ache above his heart.

"It's you or me, little bro," Jesse said in a taunting tone.

"You stay the fuck away from her."

Another grin verified that his brother had been playing him all along.

"If you're so damned interested in her for yourself, then why the hell are you still standing here messing up my day with that ugly face?"

Jackson shook his head. Maybe Jesse was right. Maybe it was time to own up to the facts.

He loved Abby. But what were the risks if he allowed himself to completely fall *in* love with her?

Colossal.

In the past, he'd refused to go there because her friendship had been too important. The two times they'd been together—in the carnal sense—he'd pretended like it hadn't been any big deal. But both times had rocked him to the core. In the moment, it had seemed better to dismiss it than to get too involved and watch the friendship disintegrate.

He hadn't even realized the impact of how he really felt about her until he'd gone off to Afghanistan. By then, she'd cut him out of her life, and, somehow, he convinced himself that he'd been right to let things slide.

But afterward, each day that passed, he found he wanted to be with her more. Each day he rediscovered the bits and pieces of what had brought them together as friends in the first place. Now?

He worried that if he gave in to his increasing need for her—for more—the results would be disastrous.

He didn't want to lose her again.

He couldn't lose her again.

Not when he felt as though he was just getting a part of himself back.

Why couldn't life be as simple as putting out a fire?

Chapter 9

$\mathcal{L}$ater that afternoon, a knock on the door surprised Abby. She hadn't expected anyone and, covered from head to toe with dust and grime, she certainly wasn't prepared to receive company. Whereas a year ago she'd have had the housekeeper answer the door while she made herself presentable, today she brushed her hands down the legs of her jeans, blew the strand of hair away from her eye, and opened the door.

"Hi. Wow, you look busy."

Jana, Charli, Fiona, and Izzy stood on her front porch. Charli held a rectangular plastic container in her hands. Jana held a wicker basket. And Fiona held the most adorable little girl in the world.

"Hi," Abby said. "What a surprise."

"I know we should have called ahead, but we figured that would just give you a reason to make excuses not to see us. So we decided to barge in." Jana stepped inside, gave her a kiss on the cheek, and held up the basket. "But we brought treats."

Charli leaned in and kissed her on the cheek too. "I made her leave the blender at home. Woman is notorious for making alcoholic slushies."

"Margaritas," Jana said. "I even make them for Izzy."

When Abby's eyebrows shot upward, Jana said, "Virgin style. Come on. What kind of grandma do you think I am?"

"The best," Fiona said, following them inside.

With that, Jana and Charli disappeared into the kitchen.

Abby didn't expect Fiona to follow suit with a buss on the cheek. They hadn't even formally met. Not to mention they both had a past with the same man.

Closing the door, Abby pushed aside the awkwardness and extended her hand. "It's so nice to meet you."

Fiona's gorgeous face lifted with a smile, and their hands met.

"It's nice to finally meet you too."

Her words sounded genuine, which helped calm the jumping beans in Abby's stomach. But not by much.

Dressed in pink stretch pants and a flouncy black-and-white zebra top, Izzy held out her chubby little arms.

Abby looked at Fiona. "Is it okay?"

"If you hold her?" Fiona smiled. "Of course." She gave her daughter a kiss on the forehead and handed her over. "Is this uncomfortable for you? My being here?"

"Probably no more than it is for you," Abby confessed.

"Then let's not let it be," Fiona said. "There's no reason we can't be friends just because we love the same man."

We *love*, she'd said.

Not we *loved*.

Jackson spoke very highly of his ex-wife, and Abby knew he cared very much for her. As a family, they looked perfect together. They seemed to get along well. And because they had a child, everyone—including Abby—knew it would be best for them to get back together. To be a family again.

If that were to happen, or if Abby sensed there was interest on both parties to do so, she would back far out of the picture. Even as she wished she could be in Fiona's shoes. Which today happened to be a really cute pair of turquoise wedge flip-flops with rhinestone straps.

"I agree." Hoping they could indeed be friends—or at least friendly—she gave Fiona a sincere smile.

When the gesture was returned, Abby relaxed and took pleasure in the baby weight in her arms and the sweet-little-girl smell. Baby shampoo and strawberry Chapstick if Abby was correct. Something hit her heart, and she couldn't stop the longing that hit her like a brick.

When Jana and Charli came back into the room, Izzy giggled and pointed at her grandma, who was making a funny face. The moment Miss Kitty strutted in behind them—orange-and-black tail flicking high in the air—Izzy said "Keke." Then she squirmed to get down.

"She has the attention of a gnat," Fiona apologized, as Izzy toddled off for a little one-on-one with the kitten, who'd decided to show off by doing a somersault, then chasing her tail.

"Just like her father," Jana added. "The only time he's got any focus is when he's got a weapon in his hands."

"That's a scary thought," Charli said.

"Only if you're a fire or a terrorist," Jana said.

When it came to Jackson's hands, all Abby could think was how they felt on her body.

She gave everyone a smile. "I hope you'll excuse my appearance. I've been going through boxes. Or I should say memorabilia." She held up another of her mother's slogan T-shirts. This one a tye-dyed catastrophe. "Because nothing says the 1960s any better than DRAFT BEER, NOT BOYS."

Jana chuckled. "You look fine. And if you find one that says MAKE LOVE, NOT WAR, I call dibs."

"So what brings you all here today?"

"We were sitting around Jana's kitchen table tossing around wedding ideas and snacking on cheese doodles," Charli said, giving Abby the same easy smile she'd used when she'd hosted the television show. "And it just seemed like a good time to get to know you better."

"And bring cupcakes," Fiona said.

Abby's stomach gurgled. "You brought cupcakes?"

"And chicken salad sandwiches," Charli chimed in. "I used a recipe from my friend Suzanne in L.A., who hosts a local cooking show. The cranberries and toasted almonds make it out of this world. Hope you're hungry."

Abby nodded. "Starving." She'd probably eaten more in the past week than she had in an entire month when she'd been married. But who could resist?

In the kitchen, Jana began taking things out of the basket. She held up a plastic container and a loaf of country-style bread. "Sandwiches first or cupcakes?"

"If I keep this up, my pants won't fit," Abby said. "Still, I vote for cupcakes."

"Real women have real curves," Charli said. "I think we're all too obsessed with what we think the ideal woman looks like. And since Reno likes curves, I vote cupcakes first."

"There are days I don't even bother to look in the mirror," Fiona added. "So count me in for dessert first."

When Izzy ran into the room holding her little hands up for a sugary treat, the decision was made.

"Majority rules," Jana said. "Dessert first."

Gathered around her parents' midcentury kitchen set that bore the scratches and dents from many a poker night, Charli lifted the lid off the plastic carrier to reveal a dozen delicately decorated treats. The cupcakes had been capped with a fine dusting of snowy coconut and accented with an edible lilac and small mint leaf.

"Those are too beautiful to eat," Abby said, even though her mouth watered.

"Thank you." Fiona beamed with pride. "But if you don't devour them all, you'll hurt my feelings."

"You made these?"

While Fiona nodded, Jana handed one to Izzy, who immediately picked off the mint leaf with an "Eeeew." Apparently to a three-year-old, green and leafy equaled gross.

"Fiona's been working really hard at perfecting her craft. The cupcake competition's tight in San Antonio, so she's thinking about moving and opening up a small shop here."

"That would be great," Charli said. "Then you and Izzy would be closer to Jackson."

"That's the idea." Fiona grabbed a cupcake for herself. "The thirty miles to San Antonio doesn't seem like much unless you have to drive it all the time. Usually, when his shift ends, he's exhausted and can barely make it home. Let alone stop by our place to visit after work."

"Then maybe he should move back to San Antonio," Abby dared to suggest.

Fiona shook her head. "Sweet feels more like home."

"That's exactly what I thought when I first came here," Charli said. "And exactly why it wasn't difficult to walk away from the TV show. Well, that and the fact that I found the most incredible man on earth to spend the rest of my life with."

Jana glowed. "Having raised him, I'll take that as a compliment."

Over cupcakes, chicken salad, and homemade bread, Abby bonded with the women gathered around her table. They united over wedding talk of roses vs. daisies. Satin vs. chiffon. White cake vs. chocolate. As hard as she'd tried, she'd never been able to achieve that type of camaraderie with the women in the Junior League or any of the other organizations she'd become a part of in Houston. This was not to say there weren't nice ladies in the groups. Maybe it had just been her, knowing that with every step she took she lived a lie that most could probably recognize, so didn't want to get too close.

Fiona had said it best.

Sweet felt like home.

Abby wasn't exactly sure what her dance card held for the future, but like a person deprived of life's simple pleasures, she planned to enjoy everything to the max. Especially if it was as sinfully delicious as the lavender-laced cupcakes she and the others had devoured.

Hours later, they'd put some old Motown albums on the record player. Izzy had been fascinated by the spinning disk and thought it would be fun to put Miss Kitty on for a disastrous whirl. They talked more about Charli and Reno's wedding plans, possible honeymoon locations, and the news that Jana—who'd now been a widow for several years—had started dating again. The lucky man mentioned was Martin Lane, the silver-haired gentleman Abby had seen at Jana's side at the welcome-home celebration.

To know that the woman Abby had respected and admired her whole life might be finding love again made her heart warm and happy.

When the chitchat and laughter waned, they began to help Abby sort through her parents' assortment of junk. When Abby thought to put several items in the donate pile, Charli and Jana snatched them up for the soon-to-exist antiques-and-design shop they planned to name after Jana's goat.

In the midst of a breakout boogie to Martha Reeves and the Vandellas going full blast on the stereo, someone knocked on the door. With Izzy—her dancing partner—in her arms, Abby opened the door to find Jackson standing there. The look of surprise on his face made Abby laugh. The snug fit of the dark blue SAFD T-shirt stretched across his broad chest made her heart do a quick "How ya doin'?"

"Perfect timing," Abby told him.

He glanced inside the living room, where the other women continued to dance while sorting through boxes.

"Dance, Daddy!" Izzy opened up her arms and lunged for him.

Without missing a beat, he came inside the house and led Izzy into a silly, exaggerated tango. Izzy's giggles filled the room even after the song had ended. Clearly, she adored her daddy. Then again, Abby had known that from the first moment she'd seen them together.

Abby fell just a little more in love. If that was even possible.

When Jackson set Izzy down, she went back to playing on the floor with Miss Kitty and a teaser wand. Each time the kitten sat up on her back haunches and batted at the dangling feather, Izzy giggled. The delightful sound couldn't help but make a person smile.

"What's going on here?" he asked, looking around at the stacked boxes and array of household goods scattered everywhere.

"We came over to enlist Abby's help in wedding planning and stayed to help her get things moving," Jana said. "She's got a lot to do before she can get on with her life."

He gave Abby a strange look that turned his blue eyes darker. "Really."

A statement, Abby noticed. Not a question.

"All these boxes have to go in the storage unit parked in the driveway," Charli said, closing the lid of a large box.

"Maybe you can give her a hand, Jackson?" Fiona added.

Before Abby could blink, her friends had grabbed up their purses and a protesting Izzy, and headed out the door.

When the two of them were alone, Jackson put his hands on his hips and glanced around at the barely restrained chaos in the room.

"You need help?" he asked on a long breath of air that signaled exhaustion and, if she was correct, a snip of irritation as well.

She shrugged. "It can wait. I'm sure you're tired."

"If you throw in dinner and a cup of coffee, I'm good."

Yes. He *was* good.

But that was another subject for another day.

"Deal." When she put out her hand he just looked at it. "Or not." Embarrassed, she tucked her hand behind her back.

Without an explanation, he began to pick up boxes and stack them against his chest. "Is the unit unlocked?"

She nodded. Something had obviously darkened his mood. Whether it was work-related or something personal, it was really none of her business. She picked up a box and followed him out the door. Several wordless trips later, they had the boxes cleared from the living room and the storage unit locked.

When Jackson closed the front door behind him, he finally asked, "So what was my ex-wife doing here?"

Ah. So *that* was what had his boxers in a twist?

"She came over with your mom and Charli."

"And?"

If Abby thought she'd imagined the full-on glower he'd nailed in her direction, she'd be wrong.

"And . . . she's really nice."

He had the nerve to do an eye roll. "What did she say?"

Holy cow. What did he expect she would say? Fiona was one of the nicest people she'd ever met. And even if she had said anything, Abby wasn't the type to step in the middle of a situation and make it worse. If there was something going on between Jackson and Fiona, they needed to work it out for themselves.

Then again, since he'd walked in with an obvious chip on his shoulder, it wouldn't hurt to try to tease him out of it.

"Well . . . she said that you had some real issues."

"Issues?" His brows shot up his forehead. "What the hell kind of issues?"

"Kidding." She touched his arm, and he stepped back as though he'd been burned. Wow. Okay. WTH? "Get over yourself, Jackson. Fiona said nothing other than it was nice to meet me and that maybe we could be friends. Honestly, we were more focused on cupcakes, chicken salad, and wedding plans than *you*."

She crossed her arms. "Why? What do you *think* she'd say? What dirty little secrets are you hiding?"

"Nothing."

The frown wrinkling his forehead in deep horizontal grooves rejected that single-word statement all to hell.

"Uh-huh." She leaned in. "I'm not buying it. But if you still want dinner, pack those record albums in boxes while I run up and take a quick shower." She tugged at her stained T-shirt. "I've been working all day, and I just need a moment to cool off."

Without waiting for a response from Mr. Grumpy Pants, Abby marched upstairs, wondering what, exactly, had jammed such an enormous stick up his butt.

Water rushed through the pipes in Abby's house, and Jackson could barely keep his mind on the menial task he'd been given. Most of the record albums were classics he hadn't heard in a long time. As he thumbed through several, he couldn't resist putting on the *Very Best of Marvin Gaye*. Without much thought, he dropped the needle on track three. Immediately, he recognized he'd made a huge mistake. When Marvin started singing about sexual healing, Jackson couldn't get his mind off Abby.

Upstairs in the shower.

Warm, wet, and naked.

He hadn't meant to walk into her house with a leftover attitude from his conversation with Jesse. But the moment she'd opened the door, and he saw his mother and his ex there, he couldn't help but wonder exactly what they'd told her about the dissolution of his marriage to Fiona. Though he and Abby were working on their friendship, and though he'd obviously been doing his best to thwart their alliance all to hell by kissing her every time she came within arm's reach, he didn't need her to know that the depth of his feelings for her had possibly been a huge obstacle in his marriage.

She didn't need that burden on her shoulders.

It was all him.

All his fault.

All his own weakness.

He dropped down on the sofa, laid his head back, closed his eyes, and took a deep breath. The day had been long. His work shift had gone from a quiet morning to an afternoon filled with three-alarm responses and a fatal accident in which an elderly woman had gotten on the freeway going the wrong way. To top it off, the captain had pulled him into his office and questioned him about the progress he'd made on his study materials and whether he'd made any further decisions.

Jackson loved being a fireman. He couldn't imagine himself doing anything else. But stepping up into bigger shoes meant less time for his family. The study hours would most likely jeopardize his time with Izzy. Plus there was a chance he could be sent to another station or even a different area in order to progress with the promotion.

He didn't mind being low man on the totem pole. Just like when he'd been in the Marines. He hadn't minded taking orders. He'd regretted moving up because it had put him at an equal level with Jared—in charge of his own group of men. If he'd stayed low man, he'd have had a better chance to protect his brother that day.

Or taken the bullet himself.

He scrubbed a hand over his face and took another deep breath to clear away the images of what he hadn't been able to control. The loss he hadn't been able to stop.

With a loud purr, the kitten crawled up his chest and settled on his shoulder. The sound was soothing, and while Marvin Gaye and Diana Ross eased into "You Are Everything" he closed his eyes and let all thoughts—except those of Abby— warm, wet, and naked—slip from his mind.

When Abby reentered the living room feeling fresh from the shower and in a better frame of mind, her heart rolled over in her chest and went legs up.

On the sofa, Jackson had his head back, his eyes closed. His broad chest moved up and down with a slow, steady pace that let Abby know he was sound asleep. On his shoulder, Miss Kitty had curled up into a ball, and her little motor was running a satisfied purr.

From the stubborn set of his jaw to the long, muscular legs stretched out, she took the opportunity to look him over. While she did, she fought the desire to curl up beside him and snuggle in too. But she'd promised him dinner, and she figured the best thing would be to let him sleep while she put everything together.

As silently as she could, she pulled out the grilling pan and grabbed a couple chicken breasts and some zucchini from the fridge. As she sliced the vegetable and sprinkled it with olive oil, she realized how much she'd missed being able to cook a meal. When she'd been married, she'd never been allowed. There had been a full-time chef in place before Abby had even moved in.

Mark had controlled the meal planning and the proportions that had been served. If Abby had wanted a peanut butter and jelly sandwich, Consuela the cook would lower her thick black brows, and say "Mr. Rich no want you to snack."

In the beginning, when Abby had been out on errands, she'd treated herself to an occasional bag of chips or her favorite candy bar. But when her own personal funds had run out, and Mark had given her an allowance, he'd made her hand over receipts. And when she realized that she'd be chastised for the occasional snack, or heaven forbid, a venti hazelnut macchiato from Starbucks, she'd given them up.

Much as she had everything else.

From the cupboard, she grabbed a box of rice pilaf and dusted the chicken breasts with garlic salt and pepper, then put them alongside the zucchini slices on the hot grill. Moments later, the food began to sizzle, and a wonderful aroma rose and tickled her appetite. The water for the rice had begun to boil, and she stirred in the margarine. A sense of well-being surrounded her as she went about doing a mundane task most people did every day.

It didn't feel mundane to her.

Not with the sexy man asleep on her sofa.

Not with all the hot desires and risqué images that floated through her head while she stirred a box of instant rice mix into a pot of boiling water.

Without warning, he was behind her, a big hand to the small of her back and his body heat turning all those racy images inside out.

"Mmm. That smells good," he said in a low voice made deeper from his little catnap.

"Thanks."

He leaned in closer. Brought with him that warm, sleepy, masculine scent. "*You* smell good."

Her heart did a flip and drove all those naughty thoughts downward through her belly and straight into her lacy white underwear. His breath against her cheek made it difficult to focus on the chicken and vegetable sizzling on the pan.

"Need help?" he asked.

She shook her head, afraid to move even a fraction. Afraid to look into his eyes. Afraid of being able to keep her hands to herself. "This will be ready in just a few more minutes." Her words rushed on—almost on their own. "I appreciate your getting the boxes stored. Tomorrow, after I'm done at your brother's clinic, I should be able to start painting and—"

He turned her to face him. "What's your hurry?" His eyes searched her face, fell to her mouth. Lingered.

"Hurry?"

"My mom said you had a lot to do, so you could get on with your life. Not the first time I've heard that." His gaze came back up to hers. "So what's on the list? What's driving you?"

His gaze fell to her mouth again.

Nervous, she licked her lips.

"What do you need?" he asked.

Wrong question to ask when he stood so close. Smelled so good. Felt so warm.

Before she could answer, he slid one big hand to her waist. The other around to her back. He pulled her against him so that all that separated them was a layer of clothes.

She felt a rush. A shiver. A flush spread through her chest as her heart kicked into overdrive.

"I know what I need," he murmured. Lowered his head. And then he was kissing her.

As much as her mind told her to back away, she melted into him. His mouth grew more urgent, and she opened to him, reveled in the deliciousness of his kiss. His arms went around her, and he held her tight. Her arms snaked around his neck, her back arched, and the heat between them exploded.

Fire flashed deep in her belly and all the way down to her toes. The kiss ignited into something more than just a meeting of lips and tongues and breath. It fueled her every wish, desire, and yes, her own need. The kiss touched her everywhere— across her skin, through her heart, and straight down to her soul.

"I need you," he whispered when his lips left her mouth to sear a scorching trail along her jaw and down the side of her neck.

Don't analyze, she told herself. Don't think about what he means. Don't think about what he really needs.

Don't think.

In a moment of complete weakness, she gave herself permission to give in to the desire. She wanted to fall into him. To feel the weight of him slide along her body. To touch him. To feel his fire.

She wanted him to sink into her and never ever leave.

His hand moved to her butt, lifted her against him and the long, hard erection pressing against the fly of his jeans. While the sizzle in the grilling pan died out, the passion between them heated up. He backed her against the refrigerator, then his mouth was back on her lips. His tongue tangled with hers, teased, probed. Promised. His hands were everywhere—pressing into her back, sliding down her waist, cupping her breasts through the thin cotton shirt she'd put on after her shower.

From somewhere in the universe, a phone rang. Abby flinched at the harsh interruption.

"Ssssh," he murmured. "Ignore it."

His kisses grew feverish. Desperate. He clutched her tighter. But the ringing didn't stop. When they finally broke apart they realized the ringtone came from his back pocket.

"Damn it."

Yeah.

He backed away, pulled the phone out, looked at the screen, and cursed again. He pushed the button and looked at her with apology in his eyes.

Hopefully, this time *not* because he'd kissed her.

"Yeah?" he said into the receiver.

An awkward moment passed, and she slipped away, going to the stove and kicking the burner back on.

"I'll be right there." He pushed the button on the phone again and looked at her. "Gotta go. Fire at the Lloyds' barn."

For lack of something fairly intelligent to say and to cover up her humiliation, disappointment, and concern for the Lloyds, she said, "Do you want to take the food with you? I can put it in a microwave bowl."

"I'll take a rain check." He headed toward the door, and she prayed that he would just go without apology.

No such luck.

They reached the door. Before he opened it, he turned toward her and cupped her face between his hands.

"It's obvious I'm confused about some things," he said. "Until I figure it out, don't let me do that again. I don't care what I say. I don't care how bad I beg. Do *not* let me touch you. Okay?"

"Ummm." How could she explain that she'd *wanted* him to touch her? That she feared she'd want him to touch her again.

And again.

And again.

And that any resolve or responsibility on her part was pretty much hopeless.

"Promise, Abby."

"Okay."

His gaze dropped to her lips and held. Almost invisibly he moved closer. Close enough to feel his breath on her face.

Yes. Yes. Yes.

His eyes were eating her up.

His lips twitched just slightly, as if they were having a hard time keeping their distance. As if they weren't going to be happy anywhere except on hers.

And because she obviously and totally sucked at keeping a promise she never wanted to make in the first place, she lifted her chin to give him and his sensuous lips a better angle.

She closed her eyes.

"Damn it."

Her eyes popped open to watch him turn on the heel of his boots, pull a quick Houdini, and disappear.

Chapter 10

The weekend passed with no sign of Jackson, and Abby fell into the pattern of waking each morning with Miss Kitty purring at her side. At the start of a new week she got up, got dressed, made a quick breakfast, and went into the pet clinic to help Jesse Wilder keep his little animal kingdom to a dull roar.

Like the rest of his brothers, Jesse was a born flirt. He had the face of a fallen angel and dark blue eyes with long lashes that could sweep a girl right off her feet. Yet when it came to the animals in his care and the oath he'd taken to keep and make them healthy, he took his business very seriously.

As he tossed a folder on the desk, he gave her a shaky smile that said he was both exhausted and also eager to move on to other things for the day. He leaned the elbows of those strong arms on the counter and peered over her shoulder at the supply list she was filling out.

"Biscuit needs to come back for a follow-up," he told her as Madge Farmer carried the newly neutered pug to the counter. Biscuit panted heavily, as though Mrs. Farmer was either squishing his fat tummy and making it hard to breathe, or the lower portion of his stout body was in dire need of some heavy pain meds.

Since Jesse wouldn't let an animal suffer, Abby guessed it was the former.

By the time she got Biscuit checked out, the waiting room was empty, and Abby had all appointments for the following day confirmed. Plus she'd updated most of the patient records and taken a medication inventory. She was feeling quite good about her accomplishments.

"The back end is clear of patients, and you're free for the rest of the day," she told him as he looked over a chart.

"You're doing a great job here, Abby. If you quit, I'm not sure how I'll survive." He grinned. "Marry me. That way you can never leave."

She laughed. "I'm flattered. But you still have too many tongues to set wagging."

"Well, there is that. Of course, I could always leave the romance rumors up to Chester."

"Heaven help us all."

He pulled off his white jacket and hung it on a peg near the office door. "Mom called earlier, and we've got a couple heifers and calves missing. Jack and Reno are going to meet me at the ranch." He gave her a quick once-over. "Since you're already in jeans and boots, you want to come help?"

"Sure." Why the idea sounded so appealing

was anyone's guess. Maybe it was the chance to get up on a horse again. Or maybe it was the chance to see Jackson in action—a sexy cowboy in full control, looking hot in jeans, a T-shirt, and straw hat. She held back a sigh. "Just let me lock the drawer, and I'm good to go."

She handed him the business cell phone in case of emergencies or if anyone needed to make an appointment.

Though Abby had her own car, Jesse gave her a ride out to the ranch. They were met by Jana's ever-amorous goat, who today wore a light blue ribbon, and the other Wilder boys, who were saddling up the horses.

The look Jackson gave them when they drove up was total *WTF?*

"Oh boy." Jesse gave a slightly demented laugh. "Time to have a little fun."

"Fun? I thought you were worried about the cattle."

"Come on, sparkplug. You've been around this ranch long enough to know that chances are we'll find those heifers safe and sound. On the other hand, rarely do I get an opportunity to ruffle my little brother's feathers and watch him explode."

"I'm not sure I understand."

"Really?" His turned his head to look at her. "Guess that stubborn streak goes both ways."

"I beg your pardon?"

"Do me a favor." He flashed a familiar smile. One she'd seen too many times before.

"The last time I agreed to that," she said, "you conned me into cleaning up the house when your parents went on vacation, and you boys had a party to which I do believe the sheriff *and* the fire department were called." She remembered the bottle rocket someone had accidentally shot off inside the house. Luckily, Jackson had proven his early skills as a firefighter, which fell short when it came to the aftermath.

"Good times." Jesse nodded. "Look. I'll give you a raise if you'll just go along with everything I say."

"If you listen to gossip, thanks to my divorce, I'm independently wealthy. And according to Pauline Purdy, I don't even need the paycheck you're giving me."

"Pauline Purdy's a prune."

Abby laughed.

"So you'll work for free?"

She grinned. "I didn't say that."

He settled his long arm across the back of the seat, leaned in, and gave her an unexpected hug. Jesse was a huge flirt, but the hug held no passion. Only friendship. And maybe a little mischief.

"Is he watching?" he asked.

"He?"

"My little brother."

She peered over his shoulder to find a blue-eyed glare that could cut steel looking back.

"Yes."

He pulled her closer and tucked her beneath his muscular arm. "How long has it been since you've been on a horse?"

The conversation didn't match the body language, but, obviously, Jesse had something going on in his mind, and she was pretty danged sure it didn't involve actually hitting on her.

"A while," she answered, trying not to laugh at the naughty gleam in his eyes.

"Still know how to ride?"

"Does a bat fly in the dark?"

"Too bad I won't be able to give you a refresher." He caressed his large hand over her shoulder. "Can you fake it?"

"That's a loaded question."

He laughed, leaned closer still.

His truck door was flung open.

"What the hell, Jess?"

Jackson didn't look happy. He didn't look amused. And Abby couldn't say why that gave her such a big thrill right in the pit of her stomach.

"Hey, little bro." Jesse grinned and tapped the bill of Jackson's straw hat in an "I'm the bigger, badder brother" manner.

Guessing by his lethal scowl, Jackson was about to pull Jesse out of the truck and stomp his arrogant ass.

"How about you saddle up Magic for Abby," Jesse continued without missing a beat, then got out of the truck, pushing Jackson aside. "She's going to help us look for the cattle."

After a long, heated glare, Jackson turned on his heel and walked away.

Near the barn, Reno tightened the cinch on Cisco's saddle and lifted his chin at Jesse. Jesse returned the gesture.

Ah, so the older Wilder boys were in cahoots.

Jackson didn't stand a chance with whatever

they were up to. She wondered if she should intervene.

Jesse reached into the cab of the truck and helped her slide across the seat. When her feet were on the ground he remained standing close.

"He doesn't look happy," she said, watching Jackson lead Magic to the hitching post.

"Nope. He'd probably like to kick my ass right now."

"I don't want to cause trouble between you two."

"Now don't go trying to take away all the fun. Trouble's our middle name." Jesse glanced away, then back to her. "A minute ago, I asked if you could fake it. Bad choice of words. What I meant was can you follow my lead?"

Even not knowing exactly where this was headed, she trusted him. She'd always trusted the Wilders. Though a time or two she'd regretted her decision.

She shrugged. "Sure."

When Jackson turned around to take a look, Jesse smiled and kissed her forehead. "Come on." He draped his arm over her shoulders. "This is going to be fun."

$\mathcal{F}$or almost half an hour, they rode as a foursome across flat meadows and rocky hills. Past clusters of prickly pears and beneath the canopies of live oaks. In the distance, a small herd of whitetail bounded off to safety, and at least half a dozen turkey vultures circled overhead.

Abby had forgotten how peaceful to the soul riding the range could be. In the past, she'd done it hundreds of times. But she'd never had the displeasure to ride behind Jackson's stiff, broad shoulders. Nor had she been the subject of his icy ire.

Could he be jealous?

No way.

Although Jesse was certainly putting on a convincing performance. And she—as he had asked—was doing her part to follow his lead.

Most likely straight to hell.

She watched the way Jackson sat tall and straight in the saddle like he'd been born to it. There had been many horses on the ranch over the years, but whether they were wild or tame mattered not to him. And as he glanced toward a large stand of canopied oaks searching for the lost cattle, he looked in full control.

Was he?

He'd told her he was confused. She took it that he meant he was confused about *her*. She'd learned from the past not to put too much into words, but the way he kept kissing her added a lot more meaning. Was it too much to hope he felt the same as she?

Probably.

While Reno and Jackson rode ahead, Jesse held out his arm to halt her progress. He sidestepped his horse close, leaned in, and laid his hand on her shoulder.

"Reno and I can search for the cattle on our own," he said in a quiet voice. "It's time you put little brother out of his misery."

Unsure of exactly what misery she was supposed to relieve him of, she glanced ahead at the two men riding away. "Awww. I was having so much fun."

"I like your style." Jesse grinned. "But it's long past time you two got off this not so merry-go-round you're on."

She didn't need to ask for clarification.

"My little brother has been through some troubling times. He's got this incredibly misplaced sense of honor he's trying to live with. It's killing him. And you." He tucked his knuckles beneath her chin. "It's time for you to strip him down and take the lead."

A laugh bubbled from her throat. "Are you telling me to have sex with him?"

"That might be a good start. But you and I and Reno and everyone else in this damned town know it's about more than that with you two. Even if Jack hasn't a clue." He gave her shoulder a squeeze. "Time to grab for the brass ring or let it go."

A huge lump stuck in the center of her chest. "Why are you doing this, Jesse, when you know how much I hurt him?"

"Because you've always been like a little sister, and we know *why* you hurt him. Doesn't make it right. But since you were both too stubborn back then to admit things and work them out, we tried to understand. But you do need to take a little of the blame for never telling him how you feel."

"You're right."

"I might be making assumptions but, darlin',

it's time." He shrugged his broad shoulders. "Stop dancin' around the truth. Talk. Make love. Work it out. Find your damn happily ever after. His too."

She glanced across the wide meadow. Blinked away the moisture in her eyes. "I don't know what to say."

"Say you love my brother."

"I love your brother." She nodded. "I always have."

"Then kick that pony into gear. Jack might be up there acting like he doesn't give a shit, but I guarandamntee if you take off, he'll follow."

"I hope you find your happily ever after too, Jesse."

"One Wilder at a time, sparkplug." He grinned. "Now get out of here."

She leaned over, kissed him on the cheek, and kicked the gelding into a gallop with a "Yah."

With the sun on her face and the wind in her hair, Abby and Magic raced across the meadow. For the first time in longer than she could remember, she felt absolutely free.

At the sound of Abby's shout, Jackson spun his horse around in time to see her take off. "What the hell did you say to her, Jess?"

Beside him, Reno chuckled, then rode on ahead.

"Didn't say anything," Jesse said beneath a grin Jackson wanted to wipe off.

"Then what did she take off like that for?"

Jesse shrugged. "Don't know."

Jackson turned and watched Abby and Magic disappear into the darkness of a grove of trees. "Shit." He kicked Ranger into gear, and, for once in his stubborn life, the horse didn't hesitate.

She'd gotten a decent head start, but Ranger—when he decided to move—was fast. Still, he followed nothing but a dust trail.

In those miles and minutes, his concern turned to anger. His anger to frustration. Somehow, he ended up back at concerned.

When it came to Abby, his feelings were a complete muddle.

He wanted her.

Loved her.

Resented her because she'd cut him off. Yet he couldn't blame her for doing so.

She'd had a right to find happiness when he hadn't been willing to give it to her. Hell, when he hadn't even known he'd *wanted* to give it to her.

Over time, things change, yet here he was, still stuck in the middle of did he or didn't he?

She'd been a part of his life for so long, and when she wasn't in it, he felt empty and lost. He'd tried to live his life without her, and he'd done a shitty job. The joke was on him. He'd always been a risk-taker—yet when it came to her and either making his move or letting her go, he froze.

Selfishly, he figured she'd always be around, and he could have the best of both worlds.

She'd proven him wrong.

When she came back, and their friendship picked up again, he'd tried to convince himself he'd be okay without her.

But could he?

At full speed, the horse beneath him raced alongside the creek, but he had no time to pay attention to the water tumbling over rocks and tree roots. The dust trail had died, and his concern for Abby's well-being kicked in to full panic mode.

What if she'd fallen?

What if she was hurt?

What if he couldn't find her?

What if? What if? What if?

The endless possibilities made him cringe.

The horse slowed when he came to the small rock formation that created a natural waterfall. When Jackson saw Magic standing beneath an oak and tied to a low branch, he released the breath he'd been holding.

The tree house.

He should have known she'd come here.

Something must be on her mind for her to have taken off like that. Hopefully, it didn't involve the sudden attention Jesse had been paying her.

Ranger had barely come to a halt before Jackson was out of the saddle and climbing the wooden ladder.

"Abby!"

When he reached the deck, the door was closed. He turned the handle. Pushed it open. "Abby, what the hell—"

His words died on complete and utter surprise.

In the center of the room, with the late-afternoon sunshine pouring through the windows and bathing her in a golden glow, Abby stood with her hair down and the long, loose curls draped over her shoulders in a wild, sexy tangle. Her cheeks were flushed from the ride. Her boots were gone, and bare, pink-painted toenails peeked out from beneath her jeans.

Her hands slowly unbuttoned her cotton blouse and inch by inch revealed a lacy white bra with scalloped edges that looked like flower petals. His fingers itched to pluck those soft edges away and expose the satiny skin beneath.

Maintaining direct eye contact with him, she shrugged the blouse from her shoulders and let it sail to the floor while he stood there motionless. Afraid to move for fear the fantasy would evaporate.

"What are you doing?" Yeah, probably the lamest question he'd ever asked in his life. Especially since he really didn't care *what* she was doing as long as she *kept* doing it.

"Taking my clothes off."

"I can see that."

She tilted her head and smiled. "Then why'd you ask?"

He shrugged. "Seemed the right thing to do."

Her hands skimmed down the tight, flat plane of her belly to her zipper. On a slow slide, the jeans that fit snug to her hips and thighs slipped to the floor. She stepped out of them and kicked them off. While his tongue practically unfurled from his mouth, she stood in front of him wearing a pair of see-thru panties where only a little patch of heart-shaped lace covered her crotch.

She looked like a Victoria's Secret angel minus the wings.

And still, he remained motionless.

Frozen.

Turned on to the point where he felt the need to reach down and grab hold of himself to relieve the ache.

Somehow, by the love of God or some other sane deity flying around the universe, he managed to drag his gaze back up to her face. "You going swimming or something?"

"No."

"So you're what, just going to stand around looking fantastic in your underwear?"

She chuckled and the sound sent a tickle through his chest. She came closer, reached out, and settled her hand on his chest.

Her touch sent a shiver down his back that wrapped around his waist and reached down into his loins. He clenched his fists, wanting to reach for her and give his damned racing heart a real reason to pound. Instead, he closed his eyes and tried to remember the damned vow to keep his hands, lips, and all other body parts to himself. Tried to evoke the promise he'd coaxed from *her* to never allow him to touch her again.

Wait.

She was the one currently doing the touching.

He opened his eyes and found a smile lifting the corners of her luscious lips.

Had she actually made the promise?

He couldn't remember. He'd been so tied up in his need for her, his ears must have gone deaf.

All he wanted right now was for that soft hand with the pretty pink fingernails to slide south until it eased the erection straining against the zipper of his jeans. He'd told her not to let him touch her again. So how wrong of him was it to stand there and just . . . let *her* do the touching?

"I was afraid you wouldn't follow me," she said.

"You knew I would." To his own ears, his voice sounded rough. Strained. Barely contained.

"Did I?" Her head tilted, and somehow her eyes turned a deeper shade of blue. Flecks of silver danced through their centers. "Other than you've been teasing and taunting me, I really don't know much about you anymore. It's been such a long time."

Both her hands were on his chest now, flattened against his pounding heart. She moved closer, leaned in, and brought her sweet scent with her. His damned foolish heart kicked up another notch.

"Maybe it's time we really got reacquainted," she whispered. Kissed his beard-stubbled jaw. And let those magical hands roam over his chest. "No more quick, confusing kisses."

"I don't know if that's a good idea." He managed not to groan when her soft lips trailed kisses down one side of his neck, and her fingertips caressed the other.

"Don't you?"

What the hell was with all the questions he couldn't seem to answer?

"Abby, I—"

She shushed him with little more than a breath of air. Then she lifted to her toes and looked into his eyes. "Rhetorical question."

Damn, he couldn't focus. Not when her breasts were pressed against his chest, and all his normal thinking had shot into his pants.

She brushed her lips over his again, and the heady shock of it sent pleasure pinging through his body like the steel ball in an arcade game. He was trying to be good. Trying to stick to the rules. Trying so hard that he felt like he would shatter in millions of unfulfilled fragments.

He should tell her to put her clothes back on, get on her horse, and head home.

Good thing he didn't consider himself a stupid man.

"You smell so good," she murmured while she nuzzled his collarbone. "Taste even better." Her fingers threaded through his hair and drew his head down. She looked into his eyes.

"And don't worry. *You* don't have to break the promise. I don't mind doing *all* the touching." Her lips brushed the corners of his mouth in agonizing slow motion, then came full center. Her teeth skimmed his lower lip, gently nipped, and she slid her tongue across to soothe the flesh. That delicate taste did nothing to ease the feral need clawing him from the inside out.

To his utter amazement, he managed to stand still while she slipped her tongue between his lips and with slow, tantalizing measures, played a wicked game of hide-and-seek inside his mouth. He maintained control when her hands roamed his back, and even when they cupped his ass and drew him closer. But when she leaned in more and sighed into the kiss, the sound traveled through every cell, along every nerve ending, and lit him up like a three-alarm blaze.

His control snapped.

He kicked the door closed.

Reached for her.

Pulled her hard against him so that her erect nipples pressed into his chest.

"Game over, sugar."

$\mathcal{A}$bby lost her breath as he backed her toward the wall and took complete control. She lost herself in the frenzy of his touch. His taste. His scent. His powerful, primitive maleness.

As they kissed, he explored—sliding his palms down her sides to her waist and the curve of her hips. One hand came back up to cup the weight of her breast. Above the lace fabric, his strong fingers rolled and tested her hardened nipple.

"I tried to be good," he rasped against her mouth.

"Mmmm." She nipped his bottom lip, then gently sucked it into her mouth. "I like you better when you're bad."

He flashed a devilish smile. "How bad?"

She lowered her hand to the front of his zipper and pressed her palm against his long, thick erection. "Breaking-all-the-rules bad."

"Every single one of them?" He kissed the side of her neck just beneath her ear. A responding chill tickled low in her abdomen.

She gave him a squeeze, and beneath her fingers, his cock jumped. Then she reached for the top button on his shirt. Pop.

"Every." Pop.

"Single." Pop.

"One." The remaining buttons popped open in quick succession, and she pushed the shirt down his arms. Let her gaze slide over his smooth, tanned shoulders and broad chest. Let her fingers play over the mouthwatering ripples of muscle down his stomach. Her fingers trailed over to the tattoo encircling his left biceps. "Nice."

He tore his gaze from her mouth and glanced down at his arm. "Crossed fireman axes."

"Mmmm. Makes me want to lick you all over." She smoothed her hands over his chest. Liquid heat flooded her veins—opened up the emotions and desires she'd tried to keep tamed.

"How about if I start here." Leaning in, she gave a lazy lick across his flat nipple and smiled as it hardened against her tongue. His long moan encouraged her, and she moved to the other side. Just when she thought she'd regained control of the situation, he curved his big hands beneath her bottom and lifted her. While he kissed her, sliding his slick tongue against her own, she wrapped her legs around his hips. With her back against the wall, the heat and pressure of his erection against her core sent a dart of urgency through her blood.

He drew his head back and looked at her.

"What?" she asked.

"Just thought you should know that I plan to touch you . . ." With her wrapped in his arms, he turned, knelt, and gently laid her on the rug. As he leaned over her, she trailed her hand down his smooth chest to his buckle. Before she could make progress, he drew her hands away, pinned them beside her head, and lowered his forehead to hers. "All over."

Yes. Please. "I thought *I* was going to do all the touching."

Gaze intense, he slowly shook his head. "My turn."

As promised, he ran the backs of his fingers down her bare stomach. Goose bumps pebbled on her flesh. He braced himself on his elbows, leaned in, and used his warm, slick tongue to discover those places that made her shiver and moan.

Outside, the woods were alive with the sounds of wildlife, water spilling over rocks and sand. The rustle of a breeze whispered through the tall grass. Inside, there were only moans, sighs, and an occasional "Oh my God."

In the heat of soft touches and tender strokes, he unhooked her bra and tossed it over his shoulder. His eager hands and his work-roughened fingertips made her come alive. As he circled the pads of his fingers over her nipples, his touch was almost a tease—until he leaned in for a taste.

Then things got serious.

With the tips of his fingers, he traced a gentle path across her pubic bone, down the crease of her thigh, back up and down the other side. With each pass, he came closer to her core until his fingers teased right over the surface of the lace, now soaked with desire. Then his fingers slipped beneath the elastic, gently parted her, and skimmed over her throbbing bud.

Her fingers dug into his arms, and she arched

against his hand, trying to intensify the pleasure. He'd always been a man of action, and he acted then, smiling at her gasp as he slid first one, then two fingers deep into her core.

She was on fire. Hot. Needy. And wet.

"Clothes off," she panted when those clever fingers began a deliberate in-and-out, swirling stroke that heightened her pleasure.

Obliging, he hooked his fingers into the lace band holding her panties together and slid the fabric down her legs. Unfortunately, that meant he left all the tingling nerves in her clitoris raw and swollen and aching for his return.

"Now yours," she said in a voice that sounded a little intense and a whole lot desperate.

A foil packet appeared, was torn open, and his pants and boxer briefs sailed to the floor. He moved over her. Slid his hands up her thighs, her belly, and over her breasts. She arched, and desire dripped like lava through her veins as he sucked one swollen nipple into his mouth, glided his tongue along the crest, and gave it a gentle pull with his lips.

And then they were face-to-face.

Skin to skin.

He settled between her thighs. Rubbed the thick swollen head of his penis between her slick folds. Against her tingling core. Teasing. Tempting.

"Don't make me beg," she moaned, but knew she would if he wanted.

They locked eyes.

"Never."

He kissed her. His tongue danced over hers, then he took control by smoothly sucking her tongue into his mouth and sending an electrical shock down through her heart and between her legs. He positioned his hands beneath her butt and tilted her hips. Then he slid inside her, hard and deep.

She sighed. Felt the power of their unity all the way to her soul. Nothing had ever felt this good.

Once he was fully inside, he pulled her tight against him, rotated his hips, then paused. He lowered his forehead to hers, closed his eyes, and moaned.

The satisfaction on his face told her everything she needed to know.

He was savoring it.

Taking pleasure in the moment.

The union.

For a man known for his rush to respond in emergency situations, when it came to making love, he took his time. Let it seep into his soul. And he would make sure she left his arms fully sated and with a smile on her face.

When he began to move again, it started like the slow climb to the peak of a roller-coaster ride. His hands gripped her butt, his strong fingers claimed control and added an extra surge of pleasure. They took their time and celebrated each other's bodies. They moved together with increased hunger. Tension wound low and tight as his hips moved faster, his thrusts sank deeper.

"God, Abby. You feel so damned good."

"I can feel even better."

"I honestly don't know how."

His next thrust came hard and deep. She constricted her core muscles, gripped him tight, and swirled her hips.

"Oh, damn." He groaned.

While she thanked *Cosmo* magazine for that slick move, he lowered his face into the crook of her neck and shifted into an out-of-control pounding pleasure until they came together in a breath-stealing explosion that left both of them gasping for air.

*B*eneath the rafters and the long, sweeping branches of the live oaks surrounding the tree house, Abby lay nestled into the crook of Jackson's shoulder, her hand on his chest, feeling his heartbeat return to normal. His arms were wrapped tightly around her, and he held her close.

At that moment or any other in time, there was no place else she'd rather be. He let go a long sigh, drew her in closer, and kissed the top of her head. She allowed contentment to settle into her soul.

Somehow, they'd found each other again. In those quiet moments of listening to the birds chirp outside and the rush of the water flow through the creek, she allowed herself to be hopeful. She closed her eyes and took a deep breath.

Beneath her palm his heartbeat tripped, then charged into overdrive.

"I'm glad we got that out of our systems," he said.

What?

Her eyes popped open. Every ounce of calm, harmony, and hope she'd felt just moments before, shattered. Air propelled through her lungs sharp as razors.

"Did we?" She angled her head to look up at him. She didn't know about him, but to her what they'd just shared had been phenomenal, and she'd be damned willing to do it again. Right now.

Eyes closed, he gave an almost imperceptible nod.

Disappointment sank deep into her heart.

He was pushing her away.

Again.

Just as he had after their junior prom. Just as he had the night before he'd gone off to war.

A case of old habits die hard? Or just the way he expected—wanted—things to be between them?

Didn't matter. It hurt like hell.

"So . . . what," she said. "Now we just go back to being *friends*? No kissing? No touching?"

"Sure."

Sure?

What the hell kind of response was *that*?

"That didn't work very well before," she reminded him as she sat up and reached for her clothes.

"That was then. This is now."

Buttoning her blouse, she turned to find him now standing as well, with his unzipped jeans hanging low over his lean hips. He bent and snapped his shirt up off the floor.

"So this meant . . . *nothing*?" God, she sounded pathetic.

His silence spoke louder than words. Add that
to the fact that he couldn't look her in the eye, and
you had what added up to be a monumental lie he
couldn't even voice.

"Just to clarify. *This* . . ." Her hands waved
through the air between them. "Was just *us* using
each other to get *it* out of our systems?"

For a man who exuded alpha, he seemed aw-
fully interested in zipping up his pants.

"Maybe."

She called bullshit. But apparently he wasn't
going to back down. And she certainly wasn't
going to beg. So really, he left her with only one
thing she could do.

Prove him wrong.

Call his bluff.

"Well," she said, pulling on her boots and con-
juring up some acting skills she'd hoped *never* to
use again, "that's a relief."

Pants zipped, his head snapped up. "What?"

"Because now you're out of *my* system too." She
forced a smile.

"I am?"

Obviously, he missed the part about the street
traveling in two directions. She could be wrong
about his feelings, but it was worth the risk to
push that proverbial envelope.

He was worth the risk.

She'd walked away once without giving everything her best effort. She wouldn't make that mistake again.

They might not be having the conversation
she'd expected to have, but sometimes actions

spoke louder. And she planned to take a full-on "I am woman, hear me roar" approach.

"Sure." She zinged him with his own lame response. "Isn't that great? With all that drama off my chest and you out of my system, I can really start living my new life."

Dark brows pulled together over narrowed blue eyes. He looked so befuddled, she wanted to pinch his cheeks.

"Which means what exactly?"

"What almost every thirty-one-year-old woman is looking for—a new career, new man, new . . . everything." She leaned in and kissed his cheek. "Thanks, Jackson."

As she climbed down the ladder and headed toward her horse, an F-bomb raised the treehouse roof.

She smiled.

Game on, bucko.

*M*oron.

There were times in his life when Jackson thought he was a pretty *with-it* guy. Chasing down wayward steers. Fighting fires. Taking down the enemy.

Other times, he had to admit to being a complete idiot.

He was glad they got that out of their systems?

Fuck.

He'd been so locked on autopilot, so used to denying his feelings, that when the most idiotic words he'd ever uttered had spilled from his mouth, he'd been stunned. But then, Abby had jumped in and agreed, and it had been too damned late to grab the words back.

With all that drama off my chest and you out of my system, I can really start living my new life.

He didn't want her living a new life.

Especially without him.

Now what the hell was he supposed to do?

Chapter 11

While nobody minded jumping on board Engine One and racing off to protect those in danger, the SAFD did mind when some twisted individual in an office building threw the fire alarm to buy them time for a late project.

Even if it was funny as hell.

Jackson hiked himself up into the cab, eased into the seat, and stretched out his legs. "That's gotta be a first," he said to Mike, who'd planted himself in the opposite rear-facing seat.

Hooch grinned. "I actually pulled that stunt in high school when I needed to finish a term paper so I didn't fail a class."

"No shit?"

"Let's just say back in those days, I wasn't the fine upstanding citizen I am now."

Jackson laughed. "Whoever said you fit *that* description?"

"Trying to be." Mike looked out the window

as the truck rolled out of the parking lot at BAR Computronics. "Isn't easy, though."

"I hear you." As of two days ago, Jackson had dived into the *what the fuck had he been thinking* category.

While the engine rumbled beneath him, he closed his eyes, and his mind immediately rushed back to two amazing hours spent with Abby in the tree house.

Two amazing hours he'd take back in a second if he could.

Most days, he could blame his exhaustion on his work shift, or the ranch work, or any number of physical-labor jobs he did throughout the week. Today, as the engine rolled back to the station, he could only blame his own stupidity for the lack of sleep and mental overtime he'd been putting in.

The moment Jesse had pulled up to the ranch with Abby at his side, Jackson had smelled trouble. And he'd ignored it.

Blatantly.

As usual, he'd allowed himself to get tangled up in the bullshit his brothers deemed entertainment. When he'd been a kid, they'd gone about torturing him and Jake—the youngest—in ways that were surely illegal in most states. Oh, he didn't doubt they loved him and would cut off an arm to protect him, but that didn't mean they didn't enjoy the hell out of sticking their damn noses in where they didn't belong.

He'd been set up, and he should have sensed the danger. But he'd taken one look at Abby sitting next to his brother, with Jesse's arm slung over her shoulder like he was claiming her, and Jackson's senses went on full-impact implode.

There wasn't a damn reason in hell he should have felt that sharp bite of jealousy stab him in the heart. He had no right. But the fact remained that he was a selfish son of a bitch, and even though he couldn't—or wouldn't—claim her, he didn't want anyone else to have that right either.

Did that mean he expected her to live her life in misery? Alone? With a cat?

Jury was still out.

Yeah, he could be a selfish prick at times.

He'd only made the situation worse by giving in to his body's needs. By letting all those fantasies he'd had of her for a million nights come alive in his head and transfer down into the rest of him, which wouldn't listen to reason.

Damn, it had been so good to hold her. To realize that all those things he'd wondered about the two of them together were fact, not fiction.

Still, he'd take those hours with her all back if he could.

Only to repeat them all over again.

"Troubles?"

Jackson jerked his attention back to Mike. "You could call it that."

"You've got to get over yourself, my man." Mike's dark brows were pulled together over eyes focused and unrelenting.

"What the hell are you talking about?"

"I'm talking about your being such a stubborn ass that you're going to let her slip through your fingers—again—because you won't tell her how you feel."

"I can't risk it." He shook his head. "I can't explain it but . . . I need her. She's the only person outside my family I've ever trusted enough to completely let down my guard. Her friendship means more than . . . well, it just does. If I tell her, I risk losing everything. And I've already lost enough."

"How do you know she doesn't want to be with you and feel the same way?"

"Come on. You know me. I'm a scrambled, fucked-up mess. Who'd want to deal with that day after day?"

"True. But you are *hot*, according to Mighty Mouse and Lil Bit, and just might be worth the effort."

"Okay, that just sounds wrong coming out of your mouth in too many ways to count."

Mike shrugged. "The females in the station said it, not me."

Jackson shook his head. "Besides, Abby made her feelings pretty clear when she thanked me for opening the door for her to find someone else."

Mike's dark eyebrows shot upward. "When the hell did that happen?"

"After we—"

"Holy shit. Are you kidding me?"

"What?" Jackson's shoulders stiffened. "I didn't even say anything."

"You don't have to. That mushy look you just got on your face said it all."

"I did *not* get a mushy look."

"Yeah." Mike laughed. "You did. And unless you do something about it, you are so screwed."

"Tell me something I don't already know."

Who knew that puppies could get themselves into such precarious situations as stuck in a drainage ditch? Abby certainly had no idea. But when Buster Crompton and his wife Sylvia came into the pet clinic with a shivering, scared little pup with dirty black-and-tan fur and eyebrows that made it look like it was wearing a brown mask, Abby, once again, found out the hard way that people could be cruel and heartless.

"Oh, the poor little thing." She got up from the reception desk and went into the waiting room to take the information from the Cromptons on what had happened.

Mrs. Crompton handed the puppy over to Abby, and her heart clenched at the violent trembling in her arms. Instinctually, she held it close to her heart, stroked its thin little body, and spoke to it in a low, comforting tone.

"Somebody dumped a whole litter into the drainage ditch by the side of the road," Mrs. Crompton said, anger clearly etched in her tone. "Most of them got stuck in the grate. This was the only one to survive."

"My God." Abby couldn't believe anyone would want to hurt puppies. They were just help-less little babies. "Who would be so cruel?"

"You'd be surprised," Mr. Crompton said. "People won't get their animals fixed, and next thing they know they're overrun with unwanted cats and dogs."

"I understand. I found a kitten at my front door, and Mrs. Potter said the same thing about a family in the area. So the kitten belongs to me now."

Sylvia Crompton nodded. "This little one deserves a good home after what she's been through. 'Course, there's nowhere to take these animals without driving all the way into San Antonio. Guess that's why people just dump them off somewhere."

"It's not right," Abby said, trying to keep the anger harnessed.

"No. It's not." Mr. Crompton stroked the puppy's little head with one gentle finger. "We'd take her, but we already have three dogs and two cats at home. But we're more than willing to pay for her medical needs, and we can be surrogate parents until a home can be found."

"That's so nice of you." Abby's chilled heart warmed with the Cromptons' kindness. "I'll let Dr. Wilder know you're here."

Abby carried the puppy into the small office at the back of the converted house that made up the clinic. When she opened Jesse's office door, he looked up from the files spread across his desk.

"Whatcha got there?"

Quickly she explained the situation, and Jesse elaborated on the same issue the Cromptons had touched on. Too many animals. Nowhere close by or convenient to take them. Some people couldn't be bothered to do the right thing. He got up from behind the desk and held out his hands. "I'll take her and check her out."

Abby didn't want to let go. "Can I hold her while you do the exam?"

A smiled lifted his mouth. "Sure."

She kissed the top of the pup's dirty black head. "It's going to be okay, sweetie," she said to the pup, who looked up with sad eyes and licked her chin with a swipe of its little pink tongue. Abby followed Jesse down the hall to the exam room and, as always, was impressed by the gentle way he handled the animal. If she wasn't already head-over-common-sense in love with his brother, she could fall really hard for a man with such a big heart.

When the exam was done, and Jesse had given the pup her required vaccinations, Abby tucked the still-quivering little bundle of fur back up against her chest and beneath her chin. After a moment, the quivering stopped. The puppy let out a snuffling little sigh. And Abby fell in love.

"Abby?"

"Hmm?" She looked up to find Jesse studying her with a huge grin.

"Did that pup just find a new home?"

"Yes." She sighed. "I think I'm destined to be a crazy cat *and* dog lady."

"Not the worst thing a person could be."

True. But add that designation to the one she already wore as a woman who loved a man who wouldn't or couldn't love her back, and that just made her plain-ass pathetic.

As afternoons went, Abby's wasn't meant to be busier than any other. But with her new family member, she needed supplies. And there was only one place in town to get those supplies. So at the end of her already jam-packed day, she and the pup headed toward Wilder and Sons Hardware & Feed. Jesse said that Reno would take care of all that she needed for her new addition. She was glad to know Reno was back at the store and that she wouldn't have to face Jackson.

At least not while her defenses were paper-thin.

After she and Jesse had given the pup some water and a little nourishment, she wrapped the sweet little thing up in a borrowed blanket and headed to the hardware store.

The bell over the door jingled, and she waited for Reno to come to the front. Instead, Jackson walked in from the back room. She hadn't seen him or talked to him since that afternoon last week at the tree house. Needless to say, she felt a smidge awkward. But he'd never know that.

No way in hell.

She still had her *roar* on.

"Hey." At a leisurely pace, his gaze cruised up and down her body as if he was remembering all the places his hands, mouth, and other parts of his body had touched and explored.

She remembered too.

Especially at night, when she went to bed.

She could still feel his hands on her skin, caressing, loving. Afterward, she knew with a sinking heart that once hadn't been enough.

She wanted more.

She wanted it all.

She wanted *him*.

Yeah, tag her and bag her for a ride on the crazy train.

"What are you doing here?" she asked.

"Reno and Charli had an appointment for some wedding stuff, so I told him I'd close up shop."

"Well, that was nice. I'm sure they appreciate it."

He shrugged. "Actually, I did it for selfish reasons. We're adding another girl to the family, so I don't have to just look at my ugly brothers all the time."

"Liar." She laughed. "You did it because you love your brother, and you're happy for him."

"Guilty." He rocked back on his heels. "So who've you got there?"

"This is . . ." She looked down at the sleeping pup and knew that though she'd had a hard time finding a name to fit Miss Kitty, this little one came with a story. "Liberty."

Jackson crossed the store in a long, casual stride. He reached out and stroked the pup's little black head between the ears. "Cute. Who's it belong to?"

"Me."

"You?"

"Yeah."

One brow lifted. "Think you might be heading into crazy cat and dog lady territory?"

She chuckled. "That's what I told your brother."

"And he said?"

"There are worse things." Like possibly substituting unwanted pets for the baby she'd so badly desired.

"Very true." He reached down and took her hand into his warm palm. "You okay?"

"About?"

"Last week. At the tree house. I should have called, but—"

"No worries." Ha! "I've been too busy to notice."

The frown darkening his face said he didn't like that comment.

She wrinkled her nose and set her heels. She aimed to prove him wrong about them. *He* was wrong. But he had to come to that realization himself. And so she had to stick with her plan. "This doesn't have to be awkward, you know," she said. "We've been here before. Right?"

His shoulders lifted. "Guess so."

"And you made it really clear that you'd gotten me out of your system." She eased her hand away. "So . . ."

"Daddy." Izzy toddled in from the back room, rubbing her eyes as if she'd just woken from a nap. Abby's heart clenched at how adorable she looked in her sparkly T-shirt, sparkle-toed tennis shoes, jeans, and sparkly pink tutu.

"Hey, sugar bear."

Abby's heart tumbled as Jackson swung his little girl up into his arms and gave her a kiss on her forehead. She giggled and patted his cheeks with her chubby little hands.

"Hi, Izzy."

Izzy turned and gave Abby a shy hello. Then she looked down and discovered the bundle in Abby's arms. "Pwetty puppy."

"Do you want to hold her?" Abby asked.

Izzy nodded, and her golden curls bounced.

"Do you mind?" Abby asked Jackson.

"That's a very young pup. Looks fragile. Izzy's not—"

Abby got the message that a three-year-old might not be gentle. "How about we sit on the floor together," she said to Izzy. "You can put the puppy in your lap."

Izzy nodded. Problem solved.

Jackson set Izzy down. "You know the floor's not really—"

"Clean?" Abby chuckled. "So what? You think I live in fear of dust bunnies or something?"

"I just—"

"No worries." Abby gave that broad chest a couple of reassuring pats, then pulled her hand away when it wanted to linger. "I got this, big guy."

She sank to the ground, and Izzy immediately crawled into her lap, bringing with her a sweet-little-girl scent and a warmth that curled around Abby's heart.

During the day, she seemed able to put aside that desire for a particular man to love and a family of her own. But at night, when she wandered through the empty house, she couldn't help but feel the loneliness. Miss Kitty helped. The puppy would help. They were a wonderful complement to her life. Maybe it was wrong of her to want it all. But she did.

As she positioned the puppy in Izzy's lap, Abby looked up at the big man looking down at them. In a blink, he joined them on the floor and took Izzy's little hand to show her how to gently stroke the puppy's fur.

A huge sigh caught in Abby's chest.

She didn't just want it all; she wanted it all with *him*.

"Sheth thoft," Izzy said, wide-eyed and smiling.

"Izzy loves puppies," Jackson said, leaning in and kissing the top of his little girl's head. "And kitties. And bunnies."

"And mouthies, Daddy."

"Mousies," he translated with a smile of absolute adoration.

Abby brushed back Izzy's golden curls. "You can come visit Miss Kitty and Liberty anytime you want."

Izzy looked up and grinned, and Abby's heart swelled.

For a few moments, they all sat there together in a little circle. And while Abby wanted to sink into the fantasy that tickled the back of her mind, she'd learned to be a realist. Plus someone in the picture was missing. "Does your mommy like puppies and kitties too?"

Izzy buried her nose in dirty puppy fur and nodded. "But not mouthies."

"Fiona always had dogs growing up, but they live in an apartment that doesn't allow them," Jackson said in a tone that was a bit unsure as to where the conversation was headed.

"All the more reason for them to move to Sweet." Abby smiled. "Maybe you and your mommy can come by my house after she picks you up. I know Miss Kitty would be really happy because she loves the way you play with her little feather toy."

"You don't have to do that." Jackson's brows ere pulled tight.

Abby looked up. "Why wouldn't I?"

"I just . . ."

"You think it's awkward between Fiona and me?"

"Maybe."

"Don't be silly. We moved past awkward in the first five minutes." Abby stroked her fingers through Izzy's soft curls. "She's a really nice woman."

"She is."

"So what's the big deal?" Abby shrugged. Time for a change of subject. "Maybe while Izzy and I stay here with the puppy, you could gather up all the dog stuff I need to take home?"

His eyebrows came up, and a grin replaced the tightness around his mouth. "I don't have any dog condos."

"Oh." A laugh slipped past her lips. "Yeah. That was a big waste of money. Miss Kitty usually ends up sleeping on top of my shoulder at night. I've even woken up with her sleeping between the girls."

"The girls?"

She pointed to the front of her shirt.

His gaze dropped to her breasts and held. "Smart cat." He dragged his eyes back up to her face. "Guess I'd better go gather up your supplies."

"Thanks." Before he stood, she said, "Hey. Do you know how a person would go about starting a business?"

"What kind of business are we talking about?"

"A nonprofit."

"What kind of nonprofit?"

She stroked the puppy's head. "Oh, maybe one that supports rescuing animals."

"Well, all I know how to do is put out fires," he said.

Or start them in some pathetically needy heart.

"So I'm not really sure," he said. "But if it's something you're really interested in, I'd be glad to help you find out."

Snuggled in and happy with all the attention, the puppy released a big sigh that made Izzy go "Awwwww" and kiss the top of its head.

"Yeah. I'm serious. I was thinking maybe a secondhand shop with all the proceeds going to a no-kill shelter."

"We sure could use one around here." Jackson looked at her with what foolishly to her appeared to be hope. "Does that mean you plan on staying in Sweet?"

"Maybe," she said, sounding a lot more casual than she felt. "Maybe not."

Then again, where on earth would she go when there was nowhere else she'd rather be?

When Sweet put on a party, it usually rocked the house, or barn, or whatever four walls it claimed. The following Friday night, when Abby walked into the Black Ties and Levi's Charity Auction to raise funds for Sweet's Emergency Center she thought it safe to put a red X next to a big *hell yeah*.

As a rule, not much went on in the small town. Oh sure, there was the renowned Sweet Apple Butter Festival, which benefited the American Cancer Society. And no one missed the Turkey Trot on Thanksgiving morning—an event that paled in comparison to Macy's big to-do but did wonders for the coffers of the Make-A-Wish Foundation.

When it came to opening their hearts and wallets, the community was nearly unstoppable. Abby took a look around and imagined no place better to start a nonprofit to support the rescue of abandoned and abused animals.

The interior of the Community Hall had been transformed into a wonderland of red satin and twinkling lights. White linen tablecloths covered the folding tables, and red rose centerpieces with votive lights took the harshness away from the white cinder-block walls. The curtains onstage were awash with red and purple that set a rather passionate mood.

According to the announcements, there was to be a dinner, a silent and live auction, and a dance afterward. With the number of attendees already milling about the room, Abby had no doubt the event would be a huge success.

That did not stop the nerves at the back of her neck from pricking her with sharp reminders that there were still those present, like Pauline and Paul Purdy—her former employers—who would see her and wonder who, what, when, and why. With a bonus thought of "Oh gawd, how awful."

To ease the apprehension of what the night might bring, Abby grabbed a glass of champagne as a waiter passed by and downed it.

"Hey. There you are."

Abby set the empty glass on a nearby table and looked up to find Charli and Fiona coming toward her. While the men in the room were decked out in crisp Levi's—or as was the standard in a ranching town—Wranglers, black ties, and tuxedo jackets, the women had dressed for the occasion in everything from frothy prom dresses to flamboyant sequined affairs. Apparently, she and the two women coming her way had all taken the same LBD approach to their evening wear. She, however, had chosen her curve-hugging dress for one reason and one man.

Sometimes, a woman knew when she looked good because she felt good in what she was wearing. Tonight, she had her roar on, and—win or lose—planned to put Phase II of opening Jackson's eyes to the test.

"Hey," she said back.

"Can you believe this?" Charli asked with a toothy grin. "I mean, who'dve thunk little old Sweet could make such a flashy statement?"

"Apparently, you haven't seen them hit the streets with their rubber poultry hats for the Turkey Trot," Abby said.

"I have." Fiona raised her hand. "And it isn't pretty."

"The boys look good, though," Charli commented, with a glance over her shoulder.

"I just got here, so I haven't had a chance to take a gander yet," Abby admitted.

"Well, it's a must. I even made Reno put his name in the hat."

"But you're engaged," Fiona reminded Charli. "This is kind of a bachelor auction."

"He's still unmarried." Charli grinned. "And I

don't mind paying high dollar for some hard . . . labor."

"Oh. I get it." Abby laughed. "This is where you bid on someone to wash your car."

"Naked," Charli said.

"Or check the shower tiles."

"Also naked."

Abby laughed. "I'm guessing that as long as there's wet and naked, we're all good."

Fiona let out a long sigh.

"What was that?" Charli asked with a lift to her perfect brows. "Have you got a victim—I mean a participant in mind?"

Fiona glanced across the hall. "Have you seen Jackson's fireman buddy?"

"No." Charli looked across the room. "Should we?"

"Too late," Fiona said. "I've got first dibs."

At that moment, Abby noticed the Wilder boys walk across the front of the room near the stage. Individually, they were stunning. As a group, they looked as appetizing as a decadent box of chocolates. Abby couldn't tear her eyes away from Jackson. Put him in a fireman suit, a tux jacket and jeans, or a simple T-shirt and cargo shorts, and he took her breath away.

Truthfully, she liked him best in nothing at all.

"Holy guacamole." Charli gestured to a tall, dark, and devastating man walking with the group. "Is *that* who you're talking about?"

Fiona nodded. "I want to lick him up one side and down the other like a cherry Popsicle."

"Honey, you bid as high as you can go," Charli

said. "And if you run out of money, you just let me know. I'd be happy to chip in."

"Me too," Abby added. Not that she was trying to pawn Jackson's ex-wife off on someone to get her out of the picture but because everyone deserved to be happy. And the dark-haired, dark-eyed hunk looked like he could give Fiona a whole lot of happy.

"Thanks, you guys." Fiona smiled. "I haven't been with anyone since Jackson and I split. I hate to act like such a hoochie mama, but—"

"Hey. There's a little hoochie in all of us," Charli said. "Didn't I tell you how I finally got Reno to make the big move?"

"No."

"The famous Wilder barbecue party? While we were dancing, I conveniently told him I'd forgotten to put panties on under my dress. He could barely keep his hands to himself. Then I told him if he was interested, I'd meet him back at his house."

"Oooh, devious." Abby laughed. "Was there any rubber left on his tires?"

"Nope." Charli grinned. "But that was one hoochie-mama move I'll never regret."

"I call it brilliant," Fiona said. "Reno needed yanking out of that dark place he'd put himself into."

"Agreed." Charli glanced across the room and got a sudden hunger in her eye. "This totally feels like high school, with us on one side of the room and the boys on the other. I'll talk to you girls later. I've still got a hoochie move or two up my sleeve." With the flash of a grin, she was gone.

Fiona lingered. "Can we talk for a minute?"

Uh-oh. "Sure."

"I just wanted to thank you for being so nice to Izzy."

"I adore her. She's a wonderful little girl."

"I think so. But then I'm the mom, so I'm prejudiced. But you're the girlfriend, and sometimes—"

"Whoa." Abby grabbed another flute of champagne for herself and one for Fiona as a waiter passed by. She was definitely going to need liquid courage for this convo. "I'm *not* the girlfriend. Who told you that?"

Fiona gave her a direct look. One of the many things Abby liked about her. "If you aren't, you should be."

"Okay, now I feel awkward." She took a drink and let the bubbles fizz over her tongue.

"Let's face it, Abby. Some things are meant to be together. The moon and stars. French fries and ketchup. You and Jackson."

"I don't think he sees it that way."

"Are you sure?" Fiona tilted her head, and a cascade of thick blond curls fell over her shoulder.

"Pretty sure." She couldn't believe they were having this discussion.

"Can we be honest? Woman to woman," Fiona asked.

"Absolutely."

"Because I really like you," Fiona said. "And I'd really like for us to be friends."

"Me too."

"And what I'm going to say might sound really . . . blunt? But I don't mean it in a nasty way."

"Okay. I'm effectively braced. Hit me."

"During our marriage, you were always there."

"I'm not sure what you mean."

"I love Jackson from the bottom of my heart. I always will. But we were never *in* love. We met under an unusual circumstance. He felt guilt. I felt hero worship—not to mention he looks really hot in that fireman's uniform. And we fell in lust. I never fooled myself for a minute that we were in love. But when I got pregnant, we tried to do the right thing. He tried really hard."

Fiona sighed. "God, I give him a ton of credit for that. But *you* were always there, in the back of his mind. And even if I'd fallen crazy in love with him, I'd never have stood a chance."

"I . . . ummm . . . crap." Abby took a drink. Washed away the emotion clogging her throat.

"Whether he knows it or will acknowledge it or not, Jackson is and always has been in love with you, Abby. It hurt him really bad when you cut him out of your life. But I think I might understand why you felt the need to do that. For a man who will willingly rush into a burning building and risk his life, he's not so willing to risk his heart. I really hope you can change that."

A ribbon of affection curled through Abby. When girls were young, it was easy to make friends. Once you reached high school, not so much. She was going to count herself in the lucky bunch having met up with Fiona. "Has anyone ever told you you're an amazing person?"

Fiona smiled. "Not for a long time."

Abby glanced across the room, where Jackson stood talking to the dark-haired man Fiona wanted to lick like a Popsicle. Abby tilted her head in his direction. "Maybe *he'll* be the one?"

Fiona's bright blue eyes traveled across the room. At that moment, the man looked at her too and Abby could swear she saw sparks collide.

"One can only hope. I just have to be careful from now on, you know? I have Izzy, and I need to set a good example for her. Plus, I've already gone the lust-not-love route. I don't want to make a return trip."

"I get that." Abby finished off her champagne. "The whole friends-with-benefits thing can be exceedingly unappealing."

"Then kick him off that train," Fiona said, even though Abby hadn't mentioned anyone in particular. "Force him to see your relationship for what it really is. He's stubborn, but he's not stupid."

"There are some things you think a man could do for himself."

"Well, there's a lot they *can* do, but there's also a lot they *refuse* to do," Fiona said. "That's why they need us. To help them strip away that barrier— along with their clothes."

Abby laughed. "But that's the best part."

Fiona's expression turned serious. "I know you love him. Everyone but he can probably see that. And I really want that man to be happy. He's an amazing dad, and he's also just a really good guy. Everyone deserves to find happiness." She hugged Abby. "So go get him. And don't let him talk himself out of it."

Abby returned the embrace.

Go get him.
Don't let him talk himself out of it.
Force him to see your relationship for what it really is.
Great advice from a very smart woman that Abby fully intended to take.

"Who's the blonde?" Mike Halsey asked.

While George Strait sang over the rent-a-DJ's sound system, Jackson's gaze followed the direction of his buddy's attention, which seemed to be focused right on Abby, who looked amazing in a little black dress that clung like a black satin sheet to her curvy body. Her wild curls had been pulled up into a messy tumble atop her head. And she wore only a simple pair of dangly earrings as an accent.

The way that dress fit, he wondered what was underneath.

If anything was underneath.

And what would it take for him to convince her to let him take a look?

Not telling her that he'd gotten her out of his system. That was for damned sure.

The black tie around his neck tightened, and his fingers curled into his palms. Then he noticed Fiona standing beside her. "*Which* blonde?"

Mike lifted his chin. "The one with her hair down."

"Oh." Whew. "That's my ex-wife."

Mike's head snapped around "No shit?"

"No shit."

"Huh." Mike's grin widened. "So who's the blonde next to her?"

"That, my friend, is Abby Morgan."

"Ah. Now I get why you're all twisted up like a pretzel."

For whatever reason, Mike couldn't pull his eyes back into his head, and Jackson hoped he wasn't going to have to warn his friend to back off.

"You okay with your ex and Abby being so friendly?"

"Hadn't thought about it." Well, he had, but he wasn't about to admit that particular weakness to anyone. "Why?"

"With the way she's looking at you, you might want to put some effort in that direction." Mike clamped a hand over Jackson's shoulder. "Because either she wants to jump your bones or skin you alive. Hard to tell in this low light."

Jackson snapped his head back around to find the two women looking directly at him. Yep. They were talking about him.

"You think I should be worried?"

"What?" Hooch laughed. "Like you think they're over there talking about the size of your dick?"

He frowned. "Women do compare notes."

"Then you'd better get your ass over there before they get out the tape measure."

"I'm on it."

Though he'd tried to be a good husband, and though he and Fiona were great friends, she had a cannonload of ammo stocked up should he decide to piss her off. Abby didn't need any more reasons to think he was an ass. He'd already provided her with her own handful of bullets. Like telling her he'd gotten her out of his system after they'd made love.

Stupidest comment he'd ever made.

And in his lifetime he'd made plenty.

Once he'd touched her, he knew it would never be enough. Not in a million lifetimes. The minute he'd held her in his arms, he felt as if he'd come home. Yeah, they'd had a great friendship when they were kids, and it grew into something special when they'd gotten older. But now he was just plain afraid to let himself believe that it could all work out the way it went inside his head.

Why couldn't he just let himself go?

Why couldn't he just allow himself to take hold of all the feelings she raised inside him and run with them?

Things had changed since she went away. Not just that they'd both married other people but that those relationships had made them act different. React different. The war had changed him. The violent death of his brother and the untimely loss of his father had changed him. Being a father and learning it wasn't all about him and his needs anymore had changed him.

Though there were times he'd failed, he tried to be there for others. Just one of the many reasons he'd chosen to be a firefighter. And when push came to shove, he hoped someone would always be there for him too.

Why couldn't he just let himself go?

Because he was a pro at stepping in his own mistakes. Open mouth, insert foot—that was him all over the place. And also because there was that part of himself that feared they wouldn't be there and that he'd be left again.

Of course, that particular paranoia didn't stop him from wanting Abby in his arms, in his bed, and in his life. His mother had always told him he was a glutton for punishment. Maybe that was true.

On second thought, there was no *maybe* about it.

As the waiters began to serve the dinner, folks stopped mingling and sat down to enjoy the catered meal. When Fiona and Abby went their separate ways, he headed in Abby's direction, determined to be her dinner partner.

When he got to the table, Jesse was already there.

Figured.

Just as Jesse lifted the cloth napkin from the table to hand to Abby, Jackson clamped a hand over his shoulder. His brother looked up and had the audacity to grin.

"What's up, little brother?"

I'm thinking about kicking your ass.

"Mom wants you," Jackson said, knowing the statement was a bald-faced lie and that he didn't care. Especially when Abby looked up and gave him a smile that made him melt.

"Really?" Jesse's brows pulled together, and Jackson refrained from a "Gotcha."

"Yeah. She's over there alone. Martin couldn't make it tonight. Something about his daughter in Seattle making waves about something or other. Mom wants you to sit with her."

At least there was some truth to that.

"Why can't *you* sit with her?"

Jackson gave him a "You really want to go there?" glare.

A heartbeat later, Jesse excused himself from the table. Jackson was only too happy to take his place.

He gave a nod to the others at the round table, knowing the music was too loud for conversation other than with the person next to him. Which was really the only person he had any interest in anyway. So it worked out great for him.

"You look beautiful." He took a sip of the Jameson in his hand, set the short tumbler down on the table, and leaned in to inhale Abby's delicious scent. "Smell even better."

That garnered him another smile.

"Thanks. I wasn't sure this dress would fit anymore. I haven't exactly been saying no to things that are really bad for me."

Though he hoped that comment wasn't directed at him, he *knew* he was bad for her. But for some reason, his head, his body, and his heart weren't in sync.

"I don't think I've ever seen you look more amazing."

"You're just saying that so I'll bid on you tonight." She lifted her champagne and sipped. Looked at him over the rim of the glass flute and drew him into that blue gaze like she'd said "abracadabra."

He laughed. "I hope someone does, or I'll be embarrassed as hell. Speaking of the auction, did you get a chance to look at the silent bid items?"

"Not yet. I ran into Charli and Fiona as soon as I got here, then Jesse pulled a chair out for me."

He glanced around the room. "Looks like it's going to take a while for this table to get served. Want to go take a look now?"

"Sure."

They stood, and he pulled out her chair. Together, they went into the lounge, where several rows of tables had been set up. Each one displayed a slew of items from handmade jewelry to day-spa certificates to a basket of smoked meat and sauces from Sweet Pickens. If he were honest, he'd admit that he couldn't care less about the items on the tables, that he'd only wanted a moment alone with her. To find some way to touch her no matter how briefly.

But then she was rushing down the aisle, picking up a basket.

"I *have* to get this for Izzy," she said with a huge grin.

When he reached her side he discovered the white wicker basket held a stuffed dog, cat, and bunny—all wearing rhinestone tiaras.

"The only thing missing is a mousie," Abby said, stealing his heart even more. If that were possible. That she remembered his daughter's passion for all things cute and fluffy meant a lot.

She grabbed the pencil on the table and wrote her name and an amount on the bid sheet. His eyes bugged out.

"Abby. Those stuffed animals and that basket are *not* worth that much money."

"I said I wanted to *get* it for Izzy—*not* bid on it."

She shrugged her shoulders beneath the long sleeves of that clingy black dress that hit her about midthigh. "I don't feel like coming back every five minutes to check on the bids," she said through lips wet with a sheer red gloss that made his jeans tighten. "Besides, I love doing charity."

He was willing to be charity.

"Abby?" She looked up at him and gave him a smile he wanted to see every day for the rest of his life. He cupped his hand beneath her arm, ready to draw her in close. "Can I—"

"There you are."

He and Abby both turned to find Arlene Potter and Gladys Lewis marching toward them in bold satin gowns and orthopedic shoes. Their blue hair clashed with the fuchsia and pistachio colors wrapped around their elderly girths that swooshed as they walked. Both women wore several strands of pearls around their crepey necks.

"Hello, ladies." Jackson extended his hand, in response to which, Gladys took it and pulled him in for a zealous kiss on the cheek with her lipstick-smeared mouth.

"My God, you look handsome," Gladys proclaimed.

"Oh. Here we go," Arlene countered. "You think this young man is going to be interested in an old biddy like you?"

"No." Gladys wrinkled her nose, which pushed her glasses farther up on her nose. "But you know how I love a man in uniform."

"He's not wearing a uniform, you crazy old broad."

If one didn't know Arlene and Gladys had been best friends for over a quarter of a century, they might think a chick fight was about to erupt. Jackson knew them, and he still wasn't willing to risk seeing a jumble of elastic hose and orthopedic shoes.

"You were looking for us?" he asked.

"We were looking for *you*," Arlene said, placing her hand on his arm and smiling up at him. "If you have a moment, we'd like to go over the program with all the participants."

"You don't mind if we steal him away, do you, dearie? We promise to give him back in reasonable condition." This delivered from Gladys to Abby with a wink.

"Have at it." Abby laughed and said to him, "Good luck. I'll see you later *if* there's anything left after you tangle with these two."

He caught her hand before she could turn. "Save a dance for me?"

A slow smile spread across her glossy mouth. "We'll see."

He watched her walk away. He had no choice. Turning his head would take an act of God. Because Abby didn't just walk. Every sway of her hips played like a soulful, sexy, rhythm-and-blues tune that danced through his head.

Chapter 12

From the audience, Abby sat in the dark, paddle in hand, waiting for the live auction to begin. Jackson hadn't returned to the table, which had worked out fine because Charli came over to join her. While they'd picked at the rubbery chicken breast and undercooked green beans, they talked wedding plans, and babies, and the impossible good looks and banging physiques of the Wilder boys.

"Every one of them is the devil," Abby said, lifting her glass for a sip of champagne that was going straight to her head and her hormones every time she caught a glimpse of Jackson in those snug jeans and black tuxedo jacket.

"Obviously, I haven't met Jake yet because he hasn't been home," Charli said. "But I've seen his picture and—"

"He's the worst," Abby said with a laugh. "It doesn't matter if he's even taller than the rest of them, he's the little brother who's always trying to prove himself. Of course, I guess that describes Jackson too. My kid sister was always a little in love with Jake. I don't know why they never got together."

"Where's your sister now?"

"Living with some grunge musician in Seattle. I have yet to see a picture of him when he isn't wearing a flannel shirt and slouch beanie."

"Sounds like you don't approve."

"I try not to judge. But she's my sister, and I love her. And . . . now she's expecting a baby."

"Is he going to be a good dad?"

A long sigh pushed from Abby's lungs. "He might if he actually got out and got a job to provide for his family. But he keeps telling her that he needs to suffer for his art. Annie works as a waitress, so they don't starve."

"How's she going to do that job when she's nine months pregnant?"

"I'm sure a lot of women manage. But I'm guessing it's not easy."

Charli placed her hand over Abby's arm and gave a squeeze. "Well, at least the baby will have a rock-star auntie."

It would be easy to launch into a rant about how worried she was about Annie's well-being. She smiled instead. Once their parents had taken on the life style of full-time party animals, Abby had instantly become a surrogate mother. She'd pretty much sucked, but somehow her baby sister had managed to escape bodily harm. For that, Abby was grateful as hell.

When the music died down, and the emcee

stepped up on the stage, nervous energy zapped her spine. "So you're bidding on Reno?"

"Hell yeah." Charli's dark eyes widened. "I plan to make him my personal love slave."

Abby laughed. "I'm not sure I get this whole auction thing. I mean, you pay for a guy, but what are you really supposed to do with them? I'm not sure it's legal to sell sex in the state of Texas. But if so, heaven forbid one of the golden girls is the highest bidder."

"Now there's something I don't even want to think about." Charli set her wadded-up napkin on the table and grabbed her paddle. "I think you're supposed to either go out on a date or use them for some kind of chore around your house. But the only heavy lifting I expect Reno to do is when he puts chocolate-dipped strawberries in my mouth and takes his clothes off."

Abby had to laugh at Charli's enthusiasm for the man she loved. She also couldn't help wonder if Reno had put her through her paces before he caved. She didn't know what it was about the Wilder boys that made them so difficult and so sexy all at the same time.

The auction opened with a couple of men Abby didn't recognize. It quickly became apparent that the contestants were going to come in *all* shapes and sizes. When one of the men who'd probably seen his way around an all-you-can-eat buffet a time too many sold for fifty bucks to a woman wearing a hot pink satin dress and a purple boa, Abby thought there might be a very interesting evening ahead.

Several minutes into the program, the very handsome Deputy Brady Bennett was put up on the stage and the bidding quickly soared to five hundred dollars. Abby had to wonder how high the bid might have skyrocketed if Brady had been allowed to take off his shirt. Judging by the smile on his face, Brady seemed mighty happy with the redhead who'd won.

Next came Jackson's hunky friend, who they now discovered was Mike "Hooch" Halsey from the San Antonio Fire Department. He was a long, tall, muscular man with dark bedroom eyes that seemed to seek out someone in the audience.

Wasn't that interesting.

"At the rate the bidding's going, Fiona won't be able to afford him," Charli whispered.

"I don't think some silly auction is going to matter." Abby watched his dark gaze wander out over the crowd. "He's looking for her. If she doesn't bid, he's going to zero in anyway."

Much to Abby and Charli's disappointment, Fiona didn't even raise her paddle. Magic Mike and his dreamy brown eyes sold to Jana Wilder, who stood and made it clear she was just buying another son to do some extra work around the ranch. That got a laugh, and Fireman Halsey seemed totally okay with it. Even if his eyes did manage to stray to the gorgeous Fiona, who was sitting right beside Jana.

Onstage, Jesse stepped out, looking like he should be on a Hollywood red carpet and not on a dilapidated stage in a run-down community hall. The chatter in the audience picked up, and, as soon as the bids began, the paddles flew with such frequency they created a breeze. Jesse—who strutted his stuff to get the bids higher—went for a thousand to Jillian Hough, Sweet's newest and most notably horny divorcee.

"I think we can safely assume Jillian won't be having him take out the trash," Charli said. "Unless they need to get rid of evidence."

Next up came Reno—who looked utterly uncomfortable in the spotlight—and the bidding began. Before Charli could even raise her paddle, another woman in the audience held hers up. Charli eased up out of her chair to see who'd bid. A frown spoiled her gorgeous face. "Oh, no, she didn't."

"Who didn't?"

"Lila Ridenbaugh just bid on Reno."

"I take it you two have a past?"

Charli nodded. "She wants to make Reno her next baby daddy. Over my dead body." Charli stood, held her paddle high, and shouted, "Two thousand." The *take that* grin she flashed at Lila went beyond victorious. Plain and simple it hollered, "Keep your desperate baby-daddy-seeking claws out of my man."

As soon as the gasp heard round the room cleared, Abby felt daggers hit their table from Lila's obviously enraged glare. No one else in the room was dumb enough to bid on an engaged man, but Charli squealed with delight as soon as she heard "Sold."

"You're funny," Abby said.

"And hot for him." She gave Abby a quick buss on the cheek. "See you later."

With the distraction gone, Abby sat there in the dark, paddle waiting, nerves spiraling in her heart like a corkscrew. Her knees shook, and when she reached for her champagne, Jackson stepped onto the stage.

Tall.

Virile.

Mouthwateringly hot.

The nerves in her heart gelled into a frenzy of elbow-shoving hormones and shot through the pit of her stomach and between her legs. It took everything she had to act cool. Like she was just any other participant waiting to spend a chunk of change for charity and not a woman with a very specific goal in mind.

Her plan was risky. But she'd spend every dollar she had to make it happen.

After the auction, Jackson looked around for Abby, who'd paid a ridiculous amount of money to snag him for a night when she could have him for free.

Anytime.

Anywhere.

But by the time he'd gotten off the stage and unsuccessfully dodged a few *attaboys*, she'd disappeared.

After saying his good-byes, he walked out into the cool night air and down the block, where he'd parked his truck. As he headed toward her house, he wondered why she hadn't stuck around for the dancing afterward or to find out if she'd been awarded the stuffed animal basket for Izzy. She had. And he'd set it on the seat next to him, ready to deliver.

At a red light, he yanked off the black coat and bow tie and tossed them to the floor. When he glanced beside him at the wicker basket, six plastic googly eyes stared back.

Abby had paid hundreds more than the stuffed ensemble was worth. Hell, she'd paid thousands for a date with him.

On some level, he supposed he should be offended that she felt she'd had to pay for his . . . attention. Or even that should their positions be reversed, he'd never be able to afford to pay such a lavish sum for her *attention.* But tonight her generosity would go great lengths for the much-needed expansion of the emergency center. In that sense, he didn't mind being a bought man.

Especially by a woman who rocked a curve-hugging little black dress and red skyscraper high heels that almost made him call 9–1–1 to put out the fire in his blood.

With only a single light glowing behind the curtains of Abby's house, Jackson's finger hovered over the doorbell. Maybe she'd already gone to bed. When thoughts of her curled up in next to nothing beneath cool sheets swirled through his mind, his finger put steady pressure on that little button that would gain him access.

Moments later, the door opened and Abby stood there still wearing the clingy dress with a low-cut back that revealed smooth skin and the fact that she wore no bra. From the looks of things, no panties, either. Her feet were bare. And in her hand she held a glass of white wine.

"Jackson?" Surprise filled her eyes as she looked up at him. "What are you doing here?"

He held up the wicker basket. "Thought I should deliver this since you took off so fast."

"Oh. Thank you." She took it and set it on a table near the door. "I could have picked it up at a later time, but I appreciate your thoughtfulness."

Thoughtfulness?

Right now, he was only grateful to be standing there enjoying the sensual rush that spread through his body while she rubbed one sexy bare foot over the other. Red-painted toenails were a double turn-on.

"No problem," he managed, without sounding like a strangled cat.

She smiled. Parted her plump, moist lips, and took a sip of wine. His sensual rush whipped into full-blown sexual desire.

"Mind if I come in?" he asked.

"Why?"

"Why?" Was she kidding?

"Yes." She set her glass down on the table next to the basket. "Why?"

"Well . . ." A million hot, lusty thoughts ran through his head, and he was ready to get down to business. "You just paid a whole lot of money for me, and—"

"It's a little late to start painting walls, don't you think?"

"Walls?"

"That's why I bid on you," she said in a very businesslike tone. "I need to get this house done. And now that I'm working for your brother, I have less time. So I paid to have you do the work for me. Or at least as much as my donation would allow."

"You paid thousands of dollars for me to be a . . . handyman?"

Her slim shoulders lifted.

"That's not what I—"

She gave a little laugh that raised the hair on the back of his neck.

"You thought what? That I was paying for sex?" Her delicately arched brows came together. "I don't think the charity was set up as a prostitution ring. Besides, *you* were the one who said you were glad you'd gotten me out of your system. So why would I expect you'd ever want to do *that* with *me* again?"

Damn it.

She was totally throwing his own words back in his face.

Words he regretted from the moment he'd spoken them.

"I wouldn't go so far as to say that," he said.

She braced her hand on the doorframe. Which thrust out one splendidly curvaceous hip. Which realigned the slinky, clingy little black dress just enough to give him an eyeful of sweet, soft cleavage. Which sent everything in his heart spinning and everything below his belt jumping to attention.

Which proved he was just a complete dog.

"Then what *would* you say to that?" she asked.

Now she folded her arms across her chest, completely hiding that sweet, soft cleavage from view. And though he much preferred her in the more provocative pose, at least the change gave him time to roll his tongue back up in his mouth enough to speak the English language.

"I probably misspoke."

One delicate eyebrow in that expressive face lifted. "Misspoke?"

"Okay." He pushed out a lungful of air. "I probably lied."

"Probably?"

"Jesus, Abby." His patience hit the red line. And all because he was too chicken-shit to tell her how he really felt because he was too paranoid he'd lose her. Again. She'd always been the only person outside of his family to really *get* him. To really listen to what he had to say. To care about him even if he made a stupendous ass of himself. "I didn't come over here to get the third degree." Which he seemed to be doing right now.

"Oh. That's right." She pursed her lips. "You came over here for sex."

A rebuttal died on his lips when she stepped out of the doorway and came toward him, bringing her sweet scent and luscious curves.

"Listen, *Jack*." She curled her fingers into the front of his shirt.

He swallowed hard when she brought her face close to his and looked directly into his eyes. He'd completely forgotten the side of Abby that he loved the most—the side that was done putting up with his shit and was about to bring the hammer down on his stubborn head. He loved it when she was assertive. Just like that day in the tree house when she'd made it clear that she wanted him. Or at least certain parts of him.

His heart pounded beneath her fist.

"I'm done playing games," she said, then continued before he could respond. "*That's* the reason for my disappearing act six years ago *and* tonight. You left for the war without any promises. Without any hope. You left me here worrying that I'd never see you again. And that even if you did come back, you'd never come back for *me*. You made that perfectly clear the night before you left. We made love—beautiful, wonderful, soul-fulfilling love. And afterward? You pushed me away. Acted like it had never happened. Just like the night of the prom. Just like the day at the tree house."

Jackson swallowed. Hard.

She sucked in a stuttered breath like she was reaching for courage or just trying to keep from slamming her fist into his face. "The problem is there was one thing I didn't have the courage to tell you before you left," she said. "It's the same thing I didn't have the nerve to tell you when you showed up at my door when I came back. Well . . . like it or not, I'm telling you now."

Her pause lingered a lifetime. "I don't want to be your *friend* anymore."

The words delivered a sucker punch that stole his breath.

"I don't want to be your *friend with benefits*," she

continued. "And unless you're willing to admit there's more between us than just friendship . . . I don't ever want to see you again."

"What?"

Moisture glimmered in her eyes. "I love you, Jackson. I've been in love with you almost my whole life. Maybe it's been unreasonable to expect you to feel the same way." Her slim shoulders lifted and dropped. "I don't know. But I can't ignore the way I feel. And I can't keep pretending to be *just* your friend anymore. So how do you feel about that?"

How did he feel?

Damn. He couldn't *feel* or think of anything past the shock and surprise of her words. Why hadn't he gotten a clue sooner? Why hadn't she said something a long time ago? Oh. Yeah. Because he'd pushed her away.

He was such a stupid ass.

"Abby . . . I . . ."

A painful pause hung between them while a million thoughts and emotions ran laps through his head and heart and tangled the words on his tongue.

"Yeah." The hopeful light in her eyes extinguished. She sighed as her fingers uncurled from his shirt, and she stepped back into the house. "That's what I thought."

"Abby."

"Good-bye, Jackson."

"Abby, don't do this."

She closed the door in his face.

Frustration twisted in his gut as he raised his

knuckles to pound on the door. To force her to retract the finality of her words.

What the hell?

She'd denied him the opportunity to respond.

And he had a *lot* to say.

Finally.

He knocked on the door and got no response.

Rang the doorbell to no gain.

When it became clear she wasn't about to open the door, he dropped his hand to his side and walked back to his truck. He pulled open the door and climbed inside. Started the engine. Pressed his foot down on the brake and put it in gear. His hands trembled on the steering wheel. He lifted them and looked at them like they belonged to someone else.

He didn't get nervous.

Hell, he'd always been the first to charge into battle, a three-alarm blaze, or a car teetering over the edge of a bridge.

He didn't fucking get nervous.

But it wasn't nerves. It was words that had him trembling like a kid on a scary ride.

She'd loved him her whole life?

Holy. Shit.

How could he push that little nugget of valuable information aside? It's what he'd always wanted but never imagined. Never dared to hope for because the fear of the loss of her had always outweighed the reward.

She'd loved him her whole life.

So why was he sitting in his truck like a big dumb-ass with his heart running a marathon and the woman he'd loved practically *his* whole life inside that house, locking him out?

 $\mathcal{A}$ bby ignored the pounding on the door and the ring of the bell as she grabbed her glass off the table and downed the remains of the Moscato. Her heart did a slow roll in her chest, then tightened and sucked the breath from her lungs like she'd dived off a thousand-foot cliff.

She'd taken a chance.

Played her cards.

And lost.

When she'd made her declaration, the shuttered look on his face, his closed-off body language, and his lack of a response hadn't been a surprise.

But it had been devastating.

All she'd ever wanted was Jackson Wilder.

He didn't want her.

End of story.

She didn't want to hear his explanations or excuses, so there was no point in prolonging the inevitable. She let the doorbell go unanswered. Eventually, he gave up, and she heard the engine of his truck roll over.

Her heart ached as she padded barefoot through the living room and peered inside the cat condo, where Liberty and Miss Kitty were curled up together. She picked up the various balls, chews, and yarn mice that were scattered about and tucked them inside a different compartment for another day of play. Then she gave each of them a soft stroke over their little heads.

"Sleep tight little guys." Yeah, maybe they were actually girls. And maybe they would only sleep for an hour or two, then they'd be bouncing around the house in a game of tag and tumble. But she loved them, and they all belonged to each other.

Exhaustion washed over her, and all she could think to do was to get to bed before she crumbled into a heap of blubbering misery.

As she headed toward the stairs, she passed by the wicker basket she'd bought for Izzy. She picked it up and looked at the sweet faces on the stuffed animals and their shiny little tiaras. Hopefully, the gift would bring Izzy some joy. Just because Jackson didn't want anything more from her than a buddy hug or quick sexual release, she didn't intend to end the new friendships she'd started or the older ones she valued.

She'd come back to Sweet to face her demons. To find the courage either to move forward or walk away. To be honest with herself about what—and who—she truly wanted.

She might have lost the man she loved, but she wouldn't stop breathing.

Chapter 13

When she was halfway up the stairs, the sudden pounding on the door made her jump. In case it was a neighbor in need, she didn't hesitate to open it.

In a rush, Jackson pulled her into his arms and was kissing her mouth, her cheeks, everywhere his lips could land. Then he cupped her face in his hands, touched his forehead to hers, and looked down into her eyes.

"Yes," he said.

Her heart took off in a dead run, and hope pumped through her blood. "Yes, what?"

He pressed his mouth to hers. Fed her a kiss that told her everything she wanted—needed to know.

Still, she craved the words.

Needed to hear him say them if only to make it real to himself.

"Yes," he said again. "I want *more* than a friendship with you. I want to be *more* than friends with benefits, Abby. I want *you*."

"Are you sure?"

He nodded. "I just don't want to disappoint you."

"How could you disappoint me?" She caressed his face. "I've known you practically forever. I know who you are."

"I've failed too many times. You deserve someone special."

"*You're* special to me."

He bent his head and kissed her again. Backed her into the house and kicked the door closed behind him.

"To be perfectly clear. I operate on two levels," he said between kisses. "Act first. And think later. *You* are like a fire in my blood. And everyone knows that I'm the first one to rush in, guns blazing. I have no control. And that's what it's like with you. No. Control."

"You say that like it's a bad thing," she said.

"For you? For us? It might be. I want more. But that doesn't mean I'm not scared to death to go after it or that I won't totally screw it up."

She smiled. "I'll protect you."

"Yeah, but who's going to protect my damned heart once you figure out I'm—"

"Sssh." She pressed her finger to his lips. "You're the man I always knew you'd be. The man I've always wanted. I know you're not perfect. No one is. All I have to do to prove that theory is look in the mirror."

His eyes darkened. Searched hers. "Then if neither of us is perfect, maybe we're perfect for each other."

The weight in her heart lifted. "I can't tell you how long I've waited to hear you say that."

"What?" He grinned. "You didn't know the day I kicked Jimmy Barton's ass back in kindergarten when he threw sand in your face?"

"Well . . ." She lifted to her toes and pressed her lips to his. "There was that."

"Do that again."

"What?" She noted the seriousness in his eyes. "Kiss you?"

"Yes."

She cupped the back of his strong neck, wove her fingers up into the soft hair at his nape, and drew his head down. "Gladly."

The kiss they shared robbed her of thought. It was hot and tingly, with carnal implications and whispers of need and love. His greedy hands slid down her arms and back, gripped her bottom, and brought her body against his. Her back arched, and his long, thick erection pressed into her from behind the fabric of his jeans.

She loved knowing she excited him.

Made him lose control.

She slipped her hand down the front of his pants, gave him a firm squeeze, and caressed him through the denim.

He pushed into her hand even while he said, "You might want to stop that."

"Why?"

"You got plans for the rest of the night?" he asked.

"No."

He lowered his face to the curve of her neck. "I do. And I'll be damned if I'll let it end too soon." He grasped the bottom of her dress, drew it up over her head, and tossed it to the chair.

"Jesus, Abby." Air rushed from his lungs. "Have you been naked under there all night?"

"I'm wearing a thong."

"And a nice one it is too." His big hand trailed down her stomach, then covered the skimpy scrap of black lace with a gentle squeeze. "If I'd known this was all you had on beneath that dress, I would never have made it up on that stage without embarrassing the hell out of myself."

He kissed her. Played a sensual game of give-and-take with her tongue. Then, while he rubbed her sex and made her throb, he skated those moist kisses down the side of her neck. Continued lower, where he paid careful attention to each breast by licking. Sucking. And gently blowing warm air across her peaked nipples.

"If I'd have known you'd do this," she said, threading her fingers through his hair, "I might have mentioned it sooner."

Much to her delight, his kisses didn't stop at her breasts. He sank to his knees, and those incredible lips traveled down her belly. Warm and slick, his tongue licked and teased along the outline of her thong. Strong hands slid up the backs of her legs, gently grasped her behind, and brought her to his mouth. He pressed his lips to the apex of her thighs, kissed and blew his hot breath against the black lace, and set fire to her blood.

"That feels amazing," she murmured, arching against him. "But . . ."

He looked up. "But?"

"I really need to touch you."

"Be my guest." He held his arms open wide.

She grabbed hold of his shirt and dragged him up to his full height. She popped the buttons free, and an appreciative sigh slipped past her lips when her fingertips met the warmth of that strong chest. Short, soft blond hairs lightly spread across the tanned skin between flat brown nipples, then narrowed and dipped to a trail that swirled around his belly button and disappeared below his zipper.

She pushed the shirt from his shoulders and grabbed for his belt, laughing when their hands tangled in the process of velvety strokes and quick touches. Boots, denim, and boxer briefs were tossed aside.

"Now, we're talking." She took her time to look him over and admire the sizeable erection that jutted from his hard-muscled body. She cupped his testicles in her hands and tested their weight while he smiled. When she caressed and stroked him with determined fingers, his eyes drifted closed, and he gave a groan that was all male.

"Don't you dare take off that thong while I'm not looking," he warned.

She squeezed him again. "Wouldn't dream of it."

With his eyes closed and his head tipped back, she bent at the knees and took what she wanted. She stroked the length of him, took the smooth, swollen crest of his cock between her lips, and received another low, deep groan for her efforts. His hands dove into her hair, but instead of forcing her head to stay in place, he ran his fingers through like he was playing with water. Just as she was getting into a rhythm, his hands paused and his body tensed.

"Sugar, you need to stop," he growled. "Or this will be over before we even get started." He reached down, slipped his hands beneath her arms, and lifted her to her feet. He glanced over at the sofa piled high with boxes of her parents' cast-offs. "Guess the sofa's out of the question."

She chuckled. "If you think you can make it upstairs, I've got a full-sized bed that your feet will probably hang off."

He gave her a hot, lingering kiss. "Lead the way."

She took him by the hand and headed up the stairs. Midway up, he tugged her hand and forced her to a halt on the step above him. She turned and found him looking up at her with heavy eyelids and desire darkening his face.

"If I have to watch your fine ass and that little string thong one more second . . . Nope." He gripped both her arms and set her down on the step. "Not going to make it."

He positioned himself down a couple of stairs, braced his hands on either side of her hips, and leaned into her. While her blood and heart pounded in her ears, and her lady parts jumped up and down for attention, he kissed her like he meant business. And then he sank. Broke the kiss with a smacking sound, tugged the triangle of black lace off, and threw it over his shoulder. Where it landed she didn't care.

A second later, he was back, easing her legs apart. Covering her with his moist mouth.

Sensation whipped through her abdomen as he used his fingers to part her, then pressed his warm tongue up and down her clit and slid into her core.

"Mmmm," he murmured against her slick, eager flesh. "Much better."

She braced her elbows on the stairs, dropped her head back, and with a long, drawn-out moan that matched the long, slow slide of his tongue, agreed.

This was much, much better.

Out of all her favorite things in the world, having Jackson naked between her thighs ranked right up there at the number one spot.

*H*er skin was so soft, Jackson thought as he pressed kisses to the inside of her thighs. He couldn't imagine a better place to be than between those sweet, firm thighs, and hearing her moan his name. At least until she sank her fingers into his hair and lifted his head.

He looked up at the dreamy tilt to her eyes and the little smile that curled her mouth.

"You need to stop," she whispered, mimicking his earlier words. "Or it'll be over before we even get started."

He moved up her body, kissed her breasts, her shoulders, her mouth. Rubbed his erection in that slick spot between her thighs. "You have something else in mind?"

She nodded. Wrapped her legs around his hips and drew him down.

He wanted to take his time.

To make slow, passionate love to her.

She deserved that. She deserved more. But when the head of his cock nudged the entrance of her hot, moist, tight body, he lost all focus.

Something raw and primal cut through him like a diamond-tipped saw. When she wrapped her hand around his cock and gave him a long, firm stroke, he was gone. Lost in the intense pleasure of her touch.

She guided him in and dropped her head back to the step with a long sigh as he fully pushed into her. He felt her stretch to accept all of him. Felt the liquid warmth surround him like nothing he'd ever known.

It *was* nothing he'd ever known.

Urgency pumped through his veins. His lungs squeezed, and his gut tightened when he stopped moving his hips.

Embedded deep inside her, his dick throbbed.

Begged for him to continue.

"Sugar." He eased from her wet heat. "I left the condoms in my pants downstairs."

"It's okay. I'm good." She nodded fast and furious. "Clean. On birth control." She lifted her head and looked at him through a lust-filled haze. "You good?"

"I'm good," he panted. "Clean. Not on birth control."

She gripped his hips tighter with her legs, effectively trapping him and sending a clear message. "Then if you stop now and go back down these stairs, I may have to kill you."

Even if she hadn't been on birth control, he wouldn't have stopped unless she'd told him to.

Abby wanted a baby. And he'd be happy to give her a dozen.

Starting right now.

He pushed in deeper until the head of his penis touched her cervix. He retreated and pushed in again, almost losing his mind and control over the absolute pleasure and sensation of being inside her without a layer of latex between them.

His arms shook as he thrust into her over and over. First slow. Steady. Gentle. Then faster. Harder. Deeper. All the while he watched her beautiful face. When her hands came up, and she caressed her own breasts, it was like watching the best kind of porn up close and personal. She made him want to last forever just to please her and keep that smile on her lips.

When their eyes met, she arched up to meet his thrust. And when her breaths came quicker—a little harsher—he knew she was close. He braced himself with one arm and, with the pad of his thumb, found the button within her slick folds. A few light swirls and teasing strokes had her inner muscles clenching around him. Pulling him in tighter.

"Oh. God." A lusty moan slipped past her lips. She pinched her nipples between her thumb and finger. "Don't stop. Don't stop. Don't—"

Her words died out on a long moan.

The vibration and visceral tug of her core muscles started down deep, radiated along his shaft, and squeezed him tight. His balls tightened. The intensity of his pleasure curled inside his gut and swept across his flesh. Her orgasm gripped him hard. Milked him. Stripped him of thought and left him raw and exposed. He let go with a final push and a deep groan that was ripped from his soul.

As he pulsed into her, he knew he'd never experienced such complete surrender.

She curled her arms around him and sighed with contentment against his cheek.

"My, God," he panted. "All these years we've just been running up and down these stairs without giving them a second thought. I am so building a two-story house."

Chapter 14

*A*fter several more lovemaking sessions that extended from the kitchen, where they'd gone looking for a snack and ended up feasting on each other, to the bathroom, where they'd gone to wash off the pancake syrup and ended up playing scrub-a-dub-dub, they finally collapsed in her small bed. To keep from falling off, they had to lie close to each other, which initiated another passionate, unhurried mating. Not that she minded.

Sometime during the middle of the night, Abby woke to the bed's shaking. Since Texas was hardly the earthquake capital of the world, she pushed aside panic and opened her eyes.

Fully awake, she became aware of harsh breathing and moist heat rising from Jackson, who now lay curled up on his side, facing away from her. It didn't take a genius to recognize he was in the grip of a nightmare.

She touched his shoulder. Gently brushed her

fingers down the muscled length of his arm. "Jackson?" she whispered so as not to startle him. While he trembled beneath her touch she continued to stroke his arm and call to him in a low, soothing tone.

He came awake with a gasp. Bolted upright in the bed and threw off the sheet. In the faint moonlight that big, strong, hard-muscled, naked body dropped to a crouch. Face buried in his hands he sucked in deep, ragged breaths.

She didn't stop to question, just surrendered to the need to comfort. Slipping the covers from her legs, she slid from bed, hunkered down beside him, and eased her hand to his back. "Jackson? It's okay." She gave him a reassuring caress. *"You're* okay."

"Damn it."

"Sssh. It's okay," she repeated.

Several seconds passed with him breathing harshly and her soothing him. Finally, he took a deep breath and moved his hands away from his face. For a moment he just looked at her, almost as if he was trying to figure out who she was. Then he stood and pulled her into his arms.

"I'm sorry," he said, his voice thick with emotion.

"Don't be." She wrapped her arms around him and held him close. "PTSD?"

He nodded against her shoulder.

"Want to talk about it?"

"No."

"Please?"

"And give you another reason to run like hell?"

He leaned back. Brows pulled tight over those blue eyes, he looked down at her. "I don't think so."

She lifted her hand to smooth that deep furrow in his forehead. "I'm not going anywhere."

An almost imperceptible nod tilted his chin. "God, I need a shower to shake this off." Then Mr. Charming was back with a devilish grin. "Care to join me?"

She kissed him. "Are you trying to divert my attention away from the real problem?"

"Definitely." He lowered his head and fed her a hot, needy kiss. "But also because I really need you right now."

"Sex doesn't resolve everything, Jackson."

"Ninety-nine and a half percent of the time it does."

She smoothed her hands over his strong back muscles. "I want to be more than that for you."

"You've always been more than that for me, Abby. But right now, I just need to . . . lose myself in you." He let go a heavy sigh. "Is that okay?"

She wanted him—heart, soul, demons, baggage, past, present, future—whatever made up the man in her arms. "It's always okay."

While the cicadas did their thing outside, and Liberty and Miss Kitty romped like a pair of wild things downstairs, Abby walked into the bedroom and handed Jackson a glass of Chivas neat.

"For medicinal purposes," she said.

"You should have been a nurse." He smiled up at her, patted the bed beside him, then took a drink. When she slid in next to him, he curled his arm around her and drew her close. "Maybe I should buy you one of those cute little outfits."

"I thought we already logged in enough hours playing doctor when we were kids."

He sipped the whiskey and smiled. "If you're wearing white stockings—the lace-edged ones that only go up to your thighs—I'm never too old."

Though she chuckled at his comment, she knew it—like their lovemaking in the shower just now—was just a diversion from the real matter. So while he lay propped up with pillows and his back against the headboard, she snuggled down and laid her cheek against his warm chest. While he sipped the whiskey in silence she listened to his heartbeat, which periodically seemed to skip.

She waited for him to step through the door she'd opened and tell her about the nightmare that had twisted him inside out.

For the longest time she listened to the night sounds outside. To the pup and kitten downstairs bumping into things as they played. To the fragility in the silence of the events that brought Jackson so much pain.

When he drained the drink, he set the empty glass on the nightstand. "Thank you," he said, with a kiss to the top of her head.

She nodded against his chest.

And waited.

"The nightmares aren't as bad as they used to be," he finally said, his words vibrating against her ear. "But there are certain times when they come back with as much force as ever."

She sat up, changing their positions so that she was now the one holding him. "Tell me."

"It was around this time of year . . ." He glided his fingertips down her arm. "When Jared was killed."

"Oh." Her chest cramped and stole her breath. "God. I'm so sorry."

"I was there that day," he admitted in a strangled whisper. "When the Taliban launched an attack. And I couldn't stop it. I couldn't stop my brother from taking fire. I couldn't stop him from dying."

"Oh, Jackson." The idea that he'd seen his brother die was unfathomable. If Jared's death set a fire in her blood, she couldn't imagine how Jackson must have felt that day. Or how he felt now.

"A tactical vest protects you from front to back," he said. "But not side to side. Not when your arms are raised, and you're engaged in a full-on battle. The bullet caught him in the armpit. The damage was . . . unsurvivable."

"I'm so sorry." Her words sounded weak, but the sincerity behind them was strong.

"Reno blamed himself. Jesse blamed himself. But I was there. And I couldn't do a damn thing to stop it."

"Oh, baby." She caressed the side of his face. "You can't blame yourself. Jared wouldn't want that. Your brother was a hero. All of you are."

Eyes dark with sorrow, he ran a hand through his hair. "None of us joined the Marines to be heroes. We all joined to fight for our country. To kick the asses of those who brought down those planes and those towers. To protect our loved ones from it ever happening again. Some gave all. And the rest of us came home to battle the nightmares of what happens over there to good men and women who only want to do what's right. Who fight with honor against an enemy who doesn't even wear a recognizable uniform."

He paused. Closed his eyes and flinched, as if he were seeing the ugliness of that war—that day—all over again.

"I did the counseling, but I refused the medication," he admitted. "They told me the nightmares may never go away. Most of the time I think I have a handle on them, but once in a while they sneak up on me when I'm not looking and . . . Izzy's seen the results. I scare her."

"*You* don't scare her, Jackson. She loves you so much. She's little right now. Someday she'll understand. And when she does, she'll be so proud."

"I don't want her to understand. I want to protect her from being forced to understand. But she's sharp. Nothing gets past her." He pulled air into his lungs. "A couple nights ago, I had an overnight. And I had a nightmare. She woke me up. And even though she was scared and had tears in her eyes, do you know what she did?"

"What?"

Moisture floated in his eyes, and a grim smile pulled at his mouth. "She put her little hands on my cheeks and she told me she'd protect me."

"She's an amazing little girl."

"She is. But how effed up is it that a three-year-old has to deal with her father's demons? I battle with that all the time, Abby. Sometimes . . . I wonder if she'd be better off without me."

Abby drew back. "What the hell do you mean by that?"

"I don't mean *that.*" His lips flattened, and his brows pulled together tight. "I mean if I had walked away. Prayed Fiona would find a nice man who'd be a good father to Izzy. A father who didn't have a million pounds of baggage strapped to his back."

"Stop that. Your daughter loves you, Jackson. There is no such thing as a perfect life. Would we like there to be? Of course. We would like our children to never know heartache and misery. But a life like that doesn't exist. So you give them all the love you can. You keep trying to do all the right things. And you pray, Jackson. You pray really hard that life will hand you a bouquet of roses instead of the thorns. That's all you can do."

While he studied her face as though trying to believe what she'd said, she drew in a measured breath. Bit her bottom lip to keep from crying.

She'd always had love, respect, and admiration for the U.S. military and coalition forces. She'd never understood their kind of bravery and probably never would. But as she held this man in her arms, she knew she'd do whatever she had to do to protect him. To make him happy. To keep him happy. And to make it clear that her love was unconditional.

"With all my heart and soul, I love you, Jackson. But the next time you start talking nonsense like that—about not being good enough or about walking away I will—"

Suddenly she was beneath him—his big, strong body covered hers like a ceiling of concrete.

He grinned down at her like they hadn't just had a soul-baring conversation. "I love it when you go all fierce and assertive on me."

She tried not to laugh. "I mean it. I will . . ." Ah, God, it was hard to think with him sucking on her neck like that and her nipples going all wild and crazy.

"You'll what?" He chuckled. Obviously preferring levity over gravity. "I'm a big bad-ass Marine slash fireman, sugar. What are you going to do to me?"

Somehow—and she had to believe it was only because he'd allowed it—she rolled him to his back and straddled his hips with her thighs. She intertwined their fingers and slid his hands up above his head.

Laughter danced in his eyes as he smiled up at her.

Then his face turned serious.

Slowly, he unlaced their fingers and lifted his hands to her face. His eyes met hers as his thumb swept a slow caress across her bottom lip. And then his smile was back.

"I love you, Abby."

They were only four little words.

Four little words that sent her heart soaring.

Four little words she'd waited so long to hear.

And all she could think was . . . wow.

*J*ackson woke spooned with Abby's fine naked behind nestled up against his morning erection. Anyone in their right mind would figure he was drained dry, but he'd waited so long to have her—especially in this new and fully recognized relationship, he didn't figure he'd dry up for decades.

Of course, he'd never imagined that he'd wake up in a dinky double bed with a kitten perched on his head or when he reached to tickle his fingers across Abby's stomach that he'd get a handful of puppy fur.

At that moment, his cell phone went off, and he grabbed it off the nightstand. Checked the number to make sure it wasn't the Volunteer Fire Department.

Nope.

Mom.

Luckily, it was a text so she wouldn't detect the *"Yes, I stayed up all night making love to my new girlfriend"* gravel to his voice.

The *new girlfriend*—and didn't that just send his heart into a handspring—rolled over and stretched her smooth leg over his. Her warm hand snuck across his chest, and her fingers twirled lazy circles across his skin. He texted his mother back, then tossed the cell on the nightstand. He turned toward Abby, pulling her in so that his erection settled into that soft space between her thighs.

"I like your hat," she said, lifting her hand away from his chest to tease the kitten paw that now dangled over his forehead and batted at her finger.

He slid his hand around her waist, clasped her naked behind in his palm, and gave it a gentle squeeze. The puppy groaned and stretched. "And I like your furry butt."

She laughed. "Guess we need a bigger bed if we're going to have all this company."

"*Or* they could stay downstairs," he said. "I like the close sleeping quarters."

He kissed her slow and sweet, and they didn't come up for air until the puppy began to whine. Abby pulled the little fluff ball into her arms.

"Guess Liberty needs to piddle," she said, nuzzling the pup and cooing as if it were a baby. Which for some reason totally flipped his heart.

"Thwarted by a potty run," he said.

She laughed. "Stay here, and I'll be right back."

"Can't." He kissed her nose. "We've got a date."

"We do?"

"Yeah, I was going to take you to Bud's Diner for some cinnamon-banana flapjacks, but I just got a text and we've been summoned to the ranch."

Her delicate brows pulled together. "We? Or you?"

"*We.*"

"How does your mom know there's even a *we*?"

He lifted his head. "Are you kidding? By now, the entire town knows there's a *we*."

"Oh." She stroked Liberty's head between the ears. "Are you okay with that?"

"Sugar, we've been a *we* for over twenty years. It just took some of us this long to figure it out." He gave her tush a little pat. "On second thought get that pup outside, then come back quick so I can say a proper good morning before we go before the rest of the damn family."

"Okay."

She gave him a quick kiss on the forehead that would barely hold him over until she crawled back between the sheets with him. When she slipped out of bed and sauntered from the room wearing nothing but a smile, he tucked his arms behind his head and called himself a lucky man.

"*Y*ou ready for this?"

In the early-afternoon sunshine, Abby looked up at him, bright-eyed and looking like a Western princess, in her pretty pink sundress and cowboy boots as they stood outside his mother's house.

"Are you?" she asked, wrinkling her nose.

"I asked you first."

"I think I've actually been ready since I was five."

"Then let's get in the house before that damned amorous goat shows up." He took her hand in his and led her toward the veranda.

"I like Miss Giddy," she said.

"Well, it's a good thing, because she sure doesn't take no for an answer."

He opened his mother's front door and kept hold of Abby's hand as they stepped inside. She might have been ready for this since she was five, but it was still new to him, and for some reason, all that bundled up into a wad of nerves in the pit of his stomach. Not that he wasn't sure he wanted to be with her, he did. He'd pretty much always wanted to be with her. But there was still the doubt that—especially after witnessing his breakdown last night after the nightmare—she'd find him lacking.

He'd never *had it all* before, and he was nervous about what all this meant for their friendship. How it would change. If it would change. He was nervous that she'd realized she'd made *him* up in her head. Nervous she'd succumb to the reality that he'd merely been a figment of an imagination he could never live up to.

He snapped his attention back into focus as they moved toward the mounting noise level in the living room his mother had recently given new life with sand and poppy paint and a hodgepodge of antiques from her stash in the barn loft. The moment he and Abby stepped inside the room, conversation stopped. All heads turned their way.

"Hey, everyone," Jackson said. "Look who's here. With me." He looked at Abby, smiled, and held up their joined hands. "Guess what this means."

"You finally got a clue?" Jesse responded.

"Yep."

Next to him, Reno grinned like a proud older brother. "It's about damn time."

Jackson looked at Abby, who was all smiles, and said, "He's got a point."

A volley of laughter, and congratulations, and because it was the Wilder family who, for the most part, were wildly expressive, a round of hugs ensued.

His mother crossed the room and took his face

in her hands. "You're such a smart boy, sugar-plum. I'm so glad you finally figured things out." She gave each of them a hug. "You take good care of each other."

"We will."

After the initial surprise had waned—thank god—Izzy ran across the room and held up her arms. Jackson reached before he realized she wanted Abby to hold her. With Abby chatting and smiling to his baby girl, the two of them took off toward Fiona on the opposite side of the room. And though Fiona gave him a smile, he felt uneasy.

First, he'd put Abby in an awkward position by being there with Fi. Now he'd put Fi in an awkward position by being with Abby.

Geez, he needed a drink.

A strong hand clamped over his shoulder, stopping him from a trip to the liquor cabinet.

"Too late to run now."

Jackson met Reno's smiling eyes. "Wasn't going to run. Just could use a hit from Mom's *secret* cupboard."

"How's this?" Reno handed him a freshly opened bottle of Shiner Bock.

"Perfect." He took a drink, and the cold liquid put out the fire in his chest.

"Congratulations on finally making your move." Reno lifted his bottle in a toast.

"Had to. She was going to kick me to the curb permanently if I didn't."

"Smart girl. Same thing happened with me and Charli."

His big brother glanced across the room to his bride-to-be, and his entire expression changed from happy to out-of-his-mind-ecstatic.

"Which is why I pulled my head out and chased her all the way to Oregon. At least you were smarter than me and saved yourself the gasoline." Reno returned his gaze back to Jackson. "So why the sudden case of the jitters?"

"She's over there talking to my ex-wife."

"Is that *your* problem or Fiona's?"

"I'm not sure. I never wanted to hurt Fi. You know that. She's an amazing woman. She just wasn't the right woman for me any more than I was the right man for her." He took another pull of beer. "Doesn't make it any less awkward, though. For me or her."

"So why don't you stop freaking out and have a talk with her? She's the mother of your little girl. You can't avoid her forever because *you* feel uncomfortable."

"I know that."

"Then talk to her." Reno glanced over to where their mother stood next to her "friend" Martin Lane chatting and doing the high-school-girl hair-flip thing. "Before Mom makes her big announcement."

"What announcement?" He took a closer look at his mother. If he thought he could read her mind from across the room, he'd be wrong.

"Aw, come on," Reno said. "You don't want me to spoil the surprise, do you?"

"Yes. I do."

Reno chuckled. "Go talk to Fiona, Jack. Ease

your mind. Then get back to the task of being happy."

As his brother went to sweep his woman up in an embrace, Jackson looked at the two stunning women and one adorable little girl chatting amiably near the big picture window. While one part of him was happy they all got along, the other part of him knew that his day of reckoning had come. He walked toward their circle, and they opened it up to let him in.

He gave Izzy a kiss on the forehead, squeezed Abby's hand, and turned to his ex-wife just as his mother said, "Can I please have all y'all's attention?"

Chapter 15

"*I* can't believe my Mom's getting married."

Abby sat across the seat in Jackson's truck with both the kitten and puppy in her lap as they headed toward his apartment.

"She's happy."

"She barely knows the guy," he said. "Look at us. We've known each other for a couple of decades, and we're taking it slow."

"*Slow?*" Abby laughed. "Is that what you call it?"

"You know what I mean."

She did know. Jana had only been seeing Martin for a few months. So the announcement today was a bit of a surprise. Well, at least to some of them. Or maybe it had just been that she and Jackson had been too wrapped up in their own business to recognize that something big was going on. She knew none of the Wilder boys were necessarily thinking about their mother's getting married as much as they were thinking that their mother was going to marry a man who wasn't their father.

All the boys had idolized Joe Wilder—with good reason. He'd been a handsome, bigger-than-life solid-gold nugget of a man who was neither too strong to cry or too weak to hold up their end of the world with one hand. He'd had a soft side for his family and a fierce side whenever anyone tried to mess with what belonged to him. He'd had a laugh that came from the heart and a smile that could warm the coldest day. And all his sons had been born from that same amazing mold.

Poor Martin Lane.

He was probably a fine man in his own right. But in Joe Wilder's son's minds, he could never hold a candle to their dad.

"At least they're planning a long engagement. You want your mom to be happy, don't you?"

"Of course I do." He looked at her with that perpetual look of concern pulling at the outer corners of his eyes. "What kind of question is that?"

"I just meant that a guy who's guarded his heart for so long might not be in the best position to judge."

"Ouch."

"Sorry." She reached across the cab of the truck and caressed his arm. "I promise to take the sting out of that owie remark as soon as I get you naked."

A grin shot to his face. "Now you're talkin' my kind of language."

He parked the truck near the barn and helped

her bring the big wire crate up the stairs to his apartment. She set Liberty and Miss Kitty inside, where they both immediately took a little drink of water, then settled in together on the fluffy blanket and instantly fell asleep.

While Jackson cruised through the rooms, flipping on lights, adjusting this and that, Abby stood with her arms folded, watching her furry little friends find comfort in one another and feeling a little out of place in his domain. Finally, he came up behind her and wrapped her in his arms.

"Do you think they'll ever find out they're not supposed to be together?" she asked him as she settled back against his broad chest.

"Who says they're not?" The resonance of his deep voice rumbled across her back.

"Nature."

He kissed her neck and the curve of her shoulder. "When it's meant to be, there's nothing that will stop it. Not even when stubborn heads try to prevail."

"Like us?"

He turned her in his arms, caressed the side of her face with his long fingers, and gently pushed her hair back. And then he smiled. "Exactly like us."

With that smile and in that moment, Abby knew she'd never been happier in her life. She didn't know exactly what the future held, but as long as she was sharing it with the man she loved, all was right with the world.

"You ready for bed?" he asked.

"It's two in the afternoon."

"You promised to kiss my owie."

She grinned up at him.

"On second thought . . ." He pulled her closer. Nuzzled her neck. "I think I might have two owies. Maybe even three."

"Then we'd best get busy."

"My thoughts exactly." He swept her up into his arms, and they did exactly that.

The next morning, while Jackson was in the shower, Abby got up and put on a pot of coffee. She fed her fur babies, then took Liberty outside to go potty. When all was well, she let them out of their crate to play. She made Jackson a breakfast of bacon, eggs, and fried potatoes. And when he walked into the kitchen wearing his blue SAFD pants and shirt and looking mouthwateringly gorgeous, she could picture every day starting just like this.

What she hadn't imagined was staying awake half the night waiting for him to have the nightmare again. Waiting for him to wake up trembling, bathed in sweat, and panic clouding his eyes. She'd waited—ready to give comfort. To console. To protect. But after they'd made love, he'd fallen fast asleep and stayed quietly asleep all night.

Other than the near anniversary of Jared's death, she wondered what set off these nightmares? Obviously, they didn't interfere with his doing his job, so maybe that was the million-dollar question. She wanted to find a way to let him know he could talk about it with her at any time. For now she realized she needed to know a lot more about PTSD than just what she heard on the news.

"Morning." He leaned in and kissed her, bringing with him that fresh, clean, manly, shower scent and a hint of lemony aftershave. "Your cat is biting the ear off your dog. I don't think she realizes that tiny little pup will probably end up being a shepherd or Rottweiler."

She chuckled. "By then, I'm sure they'll both have matured and realize the other one is friend not food."

"You made breakfast." His enthusiastic grin sent her heart spinning.

"I thought it might be a good way for you to start the day in case you have a lot of damsels who need rescuing during your shift."

"The only damsel I'm going to be worrying about is the one who's going to work with my playboy brother all day." He grabbed a folder stuffed with papers off the breakfast bar and tossed it on the table next to his plate.

"No need to worry." She set a steaming cup of coffee next to his plate. "The playboy brother isn't the damsel's type."

"Thank God. Because that boy already sees more action than any sniper rifle I ever used."

Apparently, he didn't know his brother as well as he thought he did. "You were a sniper?" she asked, pulling up a chair next to his.

"Yeah." He looked up, eyes dark. "Not going to start my day talking about it if that's what you're thinking."

Nope. Bad timing.

"Actually. I'm more interested in how your breakfast tastes."

"Perfect." He stuffed a forkful in his mouth, chewed, and smiled. "Aren't you going to eat?"

She lifted her coffee mug. "Got what I need right here."

"I hope you're not going to start that protein-drink stuff again."

"Well, thanks to Bud's Diner and Sweet Pickens BBQ, I have put on a few pounds."

"And they look amazing on you." He cupped the back of her head and drew her in for a kiss.

She sighed. Old habits were hard to break. And going from a man who judged her beyond the norm to a man who loved her the way she was, sometimes gave a jolt to the heart. She didn't want to keep looking back over her shoulder, waiting for the criticism, but sometimes, she just did. So she changed the subject. "What time does your shift end?"

"Day after tomorrow at 0800. Unless we're out on a call. Then it could be anybody's guess."

There was a whole lot about his life she needed to learn. "Does that happen a lot?"

He sipped his coffee and shrugged. "It's unpredictable. Most days we respond to more medical-related calls than actual fires. When it comes to fires—depending on the blaze—we can be on-site for anywhere from two to ten hours or more."

"I had no idea a fire could take that long to extinguish."

He chuckled. "Yeah, Hollywood has definitely

fooled everyone into thinking it's something it's not. Mostly the long hours and weird shifts make it hard for a guy to be a good husband and a good dad. You miss all kinds of important events. It's not like working in an office, where you can just take a long lunch break and run to your kid's soccer game."

"Are you trying to scare me?" She braced her elbow on the table and leaned her chin on her palm. "Because it's not working."

He leaned in and gave her a kiss. "Just trying to be realistic. Divorce rates are about as high for a firefighter as they are for the military. It's not an easy life. And . . ." He lifted the folder and let it drop back down to the table. "For me, it's about to get harder."

"Are those your study materials?"

He nodded, finished off his breakfast, and wiped his mouth. Then he pulled her out of her chair and onto his lap. "And I'd much prefer studying *you*."

"How about we make a deal," she said, pressing a finger to his lips to keep him from kissing her when she *really* wanted him to kiss her. "How about I help you study."

"You'd do that?"

"Of course."

"That'd be great." He wrapped his arms around her. "Like old times. And I'd really appreciate it."

"Then maybe *you* could help *me* figure out how to get the Sweet Reprieve Animal Rescue started."

"Like I said, I don't know much about creating a nonprofit."

"Me either," she said. "But it might be fun sitting down together and studying."

"Yeah."

"*If* you're naked."

He smiled. "Are you really going to throw that at me, then expect me to go to work like this?"

By *this* she knew he meant the erection heating up inside those sexy fireman pants.

She couldn't stop a flirtatious grin from bursting across her face or her hands to start wandering down the front of his shirt. "How long do you have before you have to leave?"

One dark brow lifted. "You ever do it on a kitchen table before?"

"No. But hopefully I'm about to."

"Oh. You are." His big warm hands slid beneath the fabric of the old university sweatshirt she'd borrowed, and he cupped her breast. "And this time *you* can put out the fire."

$\mathcal{S}$everal days later, Abby had fixed Jackson another breakfast—her house this time—and once more sent him off to rescue the good folks of San Antonio. On his days off, while she worked at the pet clinic, he'd completed painting the rooms on the first floor of her parents' house. It looked much better now that she'd gone through everything and moved it out to the storage container. She figured she could have the house completed and the FOR SALE sign up by the following week.

Then what?

She could live there until the house sold, but

after that, she'd need a place to live. At least until they figured out exactly where their relationship was headed. Since they'd started hitting the books and gathering info on nonprofits together, she knew their beyond-the-sheets partnership worked well.

Their between-the-sheets communication was rock solid. And frequent.

Amazingly frequent.

Just a few months ago, she'd never have thought it possible to feel like a horny teenager again. But one look at Jackson naked, half-naked, or even fully clothed, and she was ready to pounce. The night she'd talked him into putting on his extra set of turnouts and red-hot suspenders—sans shirt—had been an exercise in record-breaking, simultaneous, multiple orgasms.

But that wasn't all there was to the man.

His soft side had always been what had captured her heart. Sure, maybe he wasn't the kind of guy to show up at her door with flowers all the time. It didn't matter. She'd had a husband who'd had a florist on speed dial. He used flowers to coerce, to cajole, to control.

They'd never been given from the heart.

Unlike one springtime when she and Jackson had been about fourteen years old and out riding the ranch on their favorite horses. He'd stopped in a field of bluebonnets and picked her a bunch. The gesture had been so sweet coming from a boy at an age where most thought they had to be cool or tough. Those flowers were still pressed between the pages of her memory book.

And then there were the times when Jackson had visitations with Izzy. Abby's own father had always been a good-time Charlie, yet he'd never found it within himself to let loose and play or be silly with his two little girls. Jackson had no problem in that department. Though she hadn't had the privilege of seeing Izzy's amazing drag-queen makeup job again, there were other ways that Jackson shifted his alpha DNA to please his little girl. To see him down on the floor playing dolls with her positively made Abby's heart go wild in her chest with love.

She wanted babies.

Lots of babies.

For her own children, she wanted a man who wouldn't hesitate to go above and beyond to be a good father.

Jackson was an amazing daddy.

While the man himself remained thirty miles away, taking care of business in San Antonio on this gorgeous Saturday afternoon, she threw on a pair of jeans and headed toward his mother's place. The invite from Jana had been to come for lunch with a warning that there would most likely be a nauseating amount of wedding talk.

Abby arrived with a homemade pasta salad. The minute she'd gotten out of her SUV, she'd had to hold the bowl high. It seemed as though aside from being overly affectionate, Miss Giddy—in a spanking-new pink satin bow—liked people food.

"Welcome, sugarplum." Jana met her on the veranda with a hug and a kiss on the cheek. "Just push that old goat aside. You won't hurt her feelings."

Miss Giddy gave a powerful bleat that dismissed the remark.

"Heard you got yourself a kitten and a pup."

"I did. And they are so adorable. Miss Kitty loves to sleep on top of Jackson's head." She stopped in her tracks. "Not that we're sleeping together or anything."

Jana laughed. "If you weren't, I'd figure there was something wrong with you both." She held the door open. "Come on in. The girls are in the kitchen making some roast chicken sandwiches for us and a peanut butter and banana sandwich for Izzy."

When they walked through the entry and hall, Abby again noticed all the fresh personality Jana had recently put into the place. Which raised the question, "After you and Martin are married, where will you live?"

Jana stopped in front of a large family photo taken with the boys in their Marine dress blues and their parents beaming proudly.

"I imagine we'll live at Martin's. He bought the old Pritchard place. It's a bit smaller than this house, so it will fit the two of us better."

"But you've lived here for so long. And you've fixed it up so nice."

"And there are ghosts that live in these walls," Jana said.

"Ghosts?"

"Oh. I don't mean the woo-woo kind. I mean the memories. Everywhere I go, I see Joe or Jared. I thought if I painted the walls. Changed the curtains. Moved things around a bit, it would make it better."

"It didn't?"

Jana shook her head. "I'll be married for the first time in over thirty-five years to someone who isn't my Joe. Martin and I make a great pair, and we'll be good to each other. But not in this house."

"So what will you do?"

"Reno and Jesse have their own homes. I'm guessing that Jackson will build a house sooner rather than later now that he has you. And Jake will be home soon. This house should be his." Jana looked away as though gathering herself. When she looked back she had a smile already in place. "Joe and I made a pledge to each other that our boys would always have the Wilder Ranch to raise their families."

"You're an amazing mother." Abby gave her a hug. "And those boys were so fortunate to have Joe for their father."

"And they know that. Which is why learning to accept Martin and my decision to marry him won't be easy for them. I just hope with time they'll come around."

"I'm sure of it."

"I hope so. Otherwise, I've got some lonely golden years ahead of me. Because as well as Martin and I get along, I won't choose between him and my sons." Jana reached for the bowl in Abby's hands and pasted on a smile that seemed to wobble at the corners. "Now. Let's take this in the kitchen and get snackin'."

The kitchen bustled with the energy of a lively Rascal Flatts song as Charli and Fiona cut up lunch ingredients. Izzy sat up on the counter, clapping her hands to the music. A round of hellos greeted her, and Izzy held out her arms for Abby to pick her up. Abby was happy to comply and gave her a noisy kiss on her little cheek.

"Wheyah daddy?"

"He's working, sweetheart."

"You mawee him?"

"Oh . . ." Abby glanced up to find all the activity in the kitchen had come to a halt, and all females of drinking age stood with arms folded waiting for her response. "Sweetie, I think between your Uncle Reno and Aunt Charli, and your grandma and Martin, there are enough weddings. Don't you?"

Izzy shook her blond curls. "Mo cake!" She lifted her chubby arms up toward the sky and grinned.

Everyone chuckled.

"I agree," Abby said. "There's never enough cake." She hitched Izzy up on her hip and joined the others at the counter.

"Izzy?" Fiona said. "Can you go get your Loopsy doll and bring her in here so we can all have lunch?"

When Izzy nodded, Abby set her down and watched her scamper off.

"Was that just a ploy to allow for some adult talk?" Abby asked.

"Ah, so smart. And such a natural with kids," Fiona said. "You should have a dozen."

"Reno and I are having a dozen kids," Charli said. "Or at least we're going to practice making a dozen kids."

Abby laughed. "Eventually, I'd like at least a couple."

"Which brings me to ask why the quick evasion of the *M* word just now," Fiona said.

"Yeah." Charli pulled some lettuce leaves off a giant head of romaine. "That was some mighty fancy footwork you did there."

"It's only been a couple of days for Jackson and me," she protested politely.

"If you don't count the previous twenty years," Jana pitched in.

"Wow." Abby plopped down into a kitchen chair. "Am I going to get the third degree every time I get around you people?"

Jana laughed. "Not *every* time."

"You know," Abby said, "people don't have to get married to be happy together."

"They don't?" Charli's perfectly arched brows lifted. "Geez. Don't tell Reno that. He's a little freaked out over this whole wedding thing."

"Stage fright," Jana confirmed. "He's always been shy about being the center of attention. Has nothing to do with marrying you."

"Well that's a relief."

Fiona grabbed the loaf of homemade black bread and began to cut neat slices. "We just want to see you and Jackson happy, is all."

The conversation volleyed back to Abby.

"What about you, Fiona?" All the tones were of the teasing sort, but talking about her relationship with Jackson was just too new to feel comfortable to discuss with the three women. Especially when one was his mother and another was his ex-wife. Yeah, she knew there was no lingering crazy-in-love thing between those two, but discussing him

was like bringing everyone else into their bedroom. She just wasn't on board with that yet and
maybe never would be.

"Me?" Fiona pointed at herself.

"Yeah. Why didn't you bid on that hot friend of
Jackson's at the auction?"

"*You* know how much he sold for." Fiona's
brows shot up, and she tossed a look to Jana.

"I'm not going to apologize," Jana said. "It was
for charity."

"Some of us noticed you didn't even bid," Abby
said. "So what's up with that?"

"Yeah, Fi," Charli said. "What's up with that?"

"Yeah," Jana added with a laugh.

"I . . . chickened out." Fiona shook her head.
"I don't think I'm ready to start anything with
anyone yet."

"Who says you have to start something?" Jana
asked.

"Sometimes it's okay to just get laid." Charli's
mouth dropped open on a gasp. "Did I actually
just say that?"

"Loud and clear." Abby was glad the heat had
transferred to someone else even though she was
enjoying the female camaraderie immensely.

"Well, if anyone's interested," Jana said, plop-
ping healthy portions of tomato on thick slices of
black bread, "I've got the 4-1-1 on that handsome
young man. Whose name happens to be Mike
Halsey. Nickname is Hooch."

"Yikes," Charli said. "Must be quite the
drinker."

"Never touches the stuff," Jana said. "If you're

interested, Fiona, I can highly recommend him as a person of quality character."

Fiona shook her head again. "I'm not ready."

"Then you just let me know when you are." Jana gave her a wink. "I've got an *in*."

"So all the guys at the station have nicknames?" Abby asked while she set the napkins and silverware on the table.

"Yeah. It's a fireman thing." Fiona grabbed the plates from the cupboard.

"What's Jackson's nickname?"

"Crash." Every one responded at the same time.

"Well, that's appropriate." Considering how many bones he'd broken in the past.

"Sadly so," his mother said. "That boy just can't help adding to my gray hairs." At the sound of a crash in another room, Jana looked up. "Sounds like Izzy's gotten sidetracked. Fiona, how about y'all go corral her and we sit down to eat before we pull out the *Brides* magazines?"

No sooner had Fiona left the room than Abby's cell phone chirped. She pulled it from her purse and checked the incoming number.

Five minutes later Abby had lost count of the F-bombs her baby sister fired off like bottle rockets. After several minutes of encouragement, Abby had managed to calm her sister down. With a long sigh, she shoved her phone back in her purse.

"Trouble?" Jana's forehead crinkled above her glittery blue eye shadow.

With Annie and her loser boyfriend?

"Always."

Chapter 16

$\mathcal{A}$ long night stretched ahead as Abby put finishing up her parents' house into high gear. Before, time hadn't been of the essence. The phone call from her sister had quickly changed the tempo.

Thanks to Jackson, painting the walls hadn't been an issue. But within the space of a few hours, she'd had to learn to hang curtain rods. And as she gave a final twist of a wrench, she'd learned to install the new kitchen faucet too. In the midst of her home-makeover list, she'd managed to keep Miss Kitty from climbing the new curtains and Liberty from trying to wiggle her now-chubby body up onto the sofa.

All that had come several hours after she'd called her parents and told them the news—that her pregnant sister had been abandoned by her loser-musician boyfriend because he couldn't let her or a baby interfere with his nonexistent career.

It had taken only a heartbeat for Abby to tell her

sister to come home. As soon as Annie packed up her belongings and handed them off to a mover, she would be back within the walls where she'd been raised. Just like Abby.

Seemed you were never too old to come home.

Unfortunately, their party-all-the-time parents didn't feel the same and had chosen to remain in Florida while their youngest child figured out the workings of single motherhood. At least they'd agreed now probably wasn't the right time to sell the house.

In the midst of chaos and bad news, Abby had wished Jackson was by her side. Not that she needed him to resolve her issues—she'd learned to do that by herself over the years. But because she'd just needed his presence. Even if that only meant that he'd be pacing the floor with his usual intensity and wanting to resolve the situation with action.

With every breath she took, Abby found she needed him more.

These long shifts at the fire station were something she'd have to grow used to. Especially if he was to become a captain. His responsibilities would increase and maybe even his time away from home. Maybe he'd have to move to another area of the city or state. She only knew she'd follow him to the ends of the earth as long as he wanted her there.

The late hours of night grew into the early hours of morning before Abby finally laid down her tools and crawled into bed beside her two little fur babies. Luckily, they'd been so busy pouncing and zipping around the house they both zonked right out. As Abby fell asleep with a sense of accomplishment, she allowed herself the reward of fantasizing about Jackson wearing those smokin'-hot fireman pants and suspenders, and nothing else.

At the end of his shift, Jackson stopped by Fiona's apartment to see Izzy before he headed home. He'd caught her and Fiona watching *Tangled*, and since it was—begrudgingly—one of his favorite Disney princess movies, he sat down to watch. When Fiona went in the kitchen to make popcorn, he got down on the floor with his baby girl and drew her into his lap. She stretched her little arms up to his neck and, without taking her eyes away from the movie, gave him a hug.

Fiona came back into the living room with a huge bowl of buttered popcorn in one hand and a smaller bowl of Cheerios for Izzy in the other. She looked at him as if he'd morphed into something other than just a guy in a blue uniform sitting on her floor.

"Troubles?" she asked.

Time to face the music. "I'm sorry."

"For what?" Her head tilted.

"I should have called you before showing up at my mom's with Abby. I apologize. It was . . . insensitive of me."

"Are you serious?" She blinked. "Do you think you need my permission to move on with your life or something?"

"Well . . ."

"Jesus." She leaned down and gave him a quick hug. "Stop beating yourself up. I'm proud that you finally took a step you should have taken years ago. I'm happy for you, Jackson. I want you to be happy. If you're happy, then Izzy will be happy. And that's what matters."

"I want you to be happy too. I know I wasn't the best—"

"Stop." Her hand came down over his shoulder, and she gave it a squeeze. "Everything happens for a reason, Jackson. Your rescuing me and us hooking up was meant to be so we could bring Izzy into the world."

"God." He rolled his eyes. "*Hooking up* sounds so . . ."

"Maybe," Fiona said. "But it's the truth. And if I hadn't gotten pregnant, you and I would have eventually gone our separate ways. We didn't have the normal marriage. We tried. We love each other. We're great friends, and we have our daughter's best interest at heart. We're a great team. We just weren't a great married couple."

He flinched. The truth hurt no matter what kind of spin you put on it.

"Besides, I knew you were in love with Abby the second I heard you mention her name."

"You did?"

"Everybody did. Eventually, you had to catch on too." She glanced toward the TV, then back at him. "Abby's wonderful. And she'll make a great stepmom to our little girl."

"Whoa. Things haven't gone that far."

"They will. And when they do, I'll be there to support you both." She gave him a silly frown. "Unless you'd prefer I behave like a wicked ex-wife instead?"

"No! I'm grateful for who you are. And I hope someday you'll find the perfect guy."

"I'm not in any hurry."

"You were a really good wife, Fi." His chest tightened. "I want you to know that."

"Stop blaming yourself for what happened, Jackson. We just weren't the right fit. And as much as Izzy and I love having you stop by, what are you doing here when you should be home with Abby? She needs you right now."

His head came up. "She *needs* me?"

"Didn't she call you?"

"No." She *needed* him, and yet she didn't call? What was up with that? "What's going on?"

"Not for me to say." Fiona reached down and lifted Izzy off his lap. "I don't think it's an emergency, but it might be a good idea to head home."

Home.

It was funny how that word now meant Abby when for years he didn't even know where she lived. Or what she was doing. Or if she still thought about him.

And here he was now, wondering why—if she needed him—she hadn't called.

He shoved off the floor and stood. Gave Izzy a kiss on the top of her blond curls and tried not to feel slighted when she leaned to look around him, and said, "Daddy. Can't thee."

Fiona walked him to the door. "Just so you

know, I've decided it's best if Izzy and I move to Sweet. She needs to be closer to you and the family. And since my parents live halfway across the country, there's really nothing holding me in San Antonio. I can commute just like you until I find a way to open up my cupcake shop."

"That would be great."

She shrugged. "It will help us both be better parents."

They came together in a friendly embrace that lifted the weight from his chest.

"Now, go home." She laughed as she shoved him out the door.

He got in his truck and checked his cell phone for messages.

Dead battery.

Maybe that's why he hadn't heard from her.

He searched the glove box for his charger cord and couldn't find it. Angry with himself for such a dopey move, he put the truck into gear and headed toward Abby. Whatever the problem—no matter how big or how small—he'd fix it. The last thing he wanted was to give her a reason to leave again. Because for the first time in a long time, he felt like his life finally made sense. Like he could finally breathe without waiting for the other shoe to drop.

When he showed up at Abby's door her smile warmed up all those chilling concerns he'd had during the thirty-mile drive home.

"Is everything okay?" he asked, searching her face for signs of distress. "I stopped by to see Izzy after work, and Fiona told me there might be a reason you needed me. My cell phone was dead, so I didn't know if you'd left a message."

"I didn't call. I didn't want to bother you while you were at work."

"Bother me?" He cupped his hands over her shoulders and drew her into his arms. "Sugar, you could never bother me. I've been worried."

"I'm sorry. I didn't mean for that to happen."

After a brief kiss, he stepped inside, and she shut the door. In the center of the living room, the kitten and puppy were playing a game of tag, and the house looked surprisingly in order. "Looks like you've been busy."

She glanced around and nodded. "Pretty much worked all night and day to get it done. Or at least what I could manage to do by myself."

"What's going on?" Why had she worked so hard to finish the house when she hadn't been in a hurry before? Dread snapped against his spine.

"I got a phone call from Annie."

On the ride home, he'd imagined every scenario from an illness to her going back to her husband— which, even as he'd thought it, he knew was ridiculous. He'd never even given a thought to her sister. "Is she okay?"

"The loser left her. He doesn't want her or the baby to *interfere* with his nonexistent musical career."

He remembered feeling overwhelmed when Fiona had first told him she was going to have his baby. But he'd never once even considered abandoning her or their child. "Selfish bastard."

"Exactly." She glanced away. "I'd like to smash him over the head with his stupid guitar."

And then it hit him. How Mark Rich had treated her when she'd wanted a baby of her own. How he'd abandoned her. Thrown her out with the trash. Jackson took her in his arms, and, as he held her close, he wished he could rewind time to that night before he'd left for Afghanistan. The night they'd made love, and instead of telling her then how he felt, he'd said nothing. And she'd walked. Rightfully so.

When her head came back around, and she looked up at him, he could see all the anguish she'd been trying to hide. His heart broke. In that moment, he wanted to give her the world. To make up for the time they'd lost. To make up for what she'd lost during her marriage to Mark Rich. He loved her so much, it made him ache.

"Want me to go break his kneecaps?" he said with a smile.

"Yes." She laughed. "But you'd look horrible in prison orange."

The break in tension had been apparently what she needed as her smile lingered.

"The reason I didn't call you at work," she said, "was because nothing was on fire and nobody was dying. And in your line of work, that's why the calls come in. I knew Annie's news could wait until you came home."

Home.

There was that word again.

"I appreciate that. But if you need me, call. Please. If I'm fighting a fire or saving a life, you'll get my voice mail, and I'll call you back as soon as possible. And I promise to keep my phone charged from now on." He tucked his fingers beneath her chin and lifted it so her eyes met his. "Got that?"

She nodded.

"I need to hear a " 'Copy that, Crash.' "

She folded her arms. "I am *never* going to use that ridiculously appropriate name of yours."

"Then how about 'Copy that, extremely hot guy whose naked body I can't wait to get my hands on'?"

That got him the smile he'd been looking for.

"Come on." He took her by the hand and led her into the kitchen. "I'm starving. Let's fix some dinner, and you can tell me all about Annie."

Between grilling the chicken and vegetables and making a salad, he realized how well they worked together. All it took was a little communication. *Yes, salt. No, pepper. Yes, you can kiss me while I lean over to grab the zucchini. Speaking of zucchini . . .*

In that enlightening moment—not quite worthy of an Iron Chef episode but extra points for the handling of the tools between dishes—he realized that he was happy. Deliriously, life-is-fucking-awesome, happy. And it felt damn good.

"And so . . ." Abby poured a glass of wine for herself, and for him she grabbed a bottle of Sam Adams from the fridge. "I just told Annie to come home. That's why—minus the new flooring—I finished the house up quicker than planned. I bought her an airline ticket, and she'll be here next week."

"Good." He kissed her forehead. "Don't worry, sugar. We'll get her home, and we'll take care of her and her baby. No worries. Okay? That's what families do. We take care of each other."

"*We.*" She smiled. "I like the sound of that."

"Me too." He drew her into his arms, and his heart gave a great big thump as she wound her arms around his neck. He cupped her face in his hands. Rested his forehead against hers. Held her close. "I love you, Abby. I know I should have told you sooner. It would have spared both of us a lot of heartache."

"Why didn't you?"

"Honestly? I was afraid I'd ruin our friendship. And that meant more to me than anything. Outside of my family, you were the only one I could ever just be myself with. With you, I didn't have to try to compete or impress or find my place in the mix. With you, I had someone to talk to who'd listen. Someone to dream with who wouldn't judge. I honestly didn't know how you felt back then. I didn't tell you I loved you because I was afraid I'd lose you. I lost you anyway."

"Yeah. That really sucked."

"I'm not afraid to say it now." He kissed her. "I love you, Abby."

"I love you too."

He kissed her again. Longer this time. Sweeter. At least it started out that way.

Eventually, she asked, "Are you still hungry?"

"Yeah." But the smile he gave her said he wasn't talking about grilled chicken and vegetables.

Chapter 17

Abby spooned eggs onto Jackson's plate next to the maple sausages and the extra crispy English muffins she'd made. She refilled his coffee mug, then sat down beside him and sprinkled salt on her own eggs.

"I meant to ask last night how the conversation is going with city hall on your rescue center," he asked between bites.

She didn't know why, but sitting down with him like this for breakfast seemed so special. At night, they were eager to relax or study, and touch, and make love. The mornings had become the best time to discuss whatever took place the day before and formulate a new plan.

Like a real couple.

She smiled. "So far so good. Although Mrs. Laupner swears the mayor will shoot it down when it reaches the city council."

"Mrs. Laupner walks around with a half-empty glass. Don't pay any attention to her."

"I won't." As the kitten and pup scampered across the floor in a game of chase, she smiled. "There are too many little guys like them out there that need my help."

Fork halted halfway to his mouth, he curled his long fingers into the front of her fuzzy robe and pulled her in for a kiss. "You're a good woman, Abby Morgan."

She threaded her fingers through his short, soft hair and kissed him back. "As long as you think so."

"I do." He gave her two quick kisses. "I always have."

"Good to know."

"It's my weekend to have Izzy," he said. "I know we talked about taking it slow with her, so she doesn't get confused."

"It's a good idea," she agreed.

"I don't know how I'm going to manage being away from you for three days."

She touched the side of his face with the backs of her fingers. "I know it won't be easy for me, but it's what's best for your little girl."

"Think we can at least have a movie date?" He gave her that smile that melted her from the inside out. "The three of us? I got a new DVD she hasn't seen yet."

"Are you sure?"

"Definitely. You're going to be a part of her life from now on."

From now on sounded permanent. And no words other than "I love you" had ever sounded so good.

"Then count me in and sign me up to bring the popcorn."

"We don't let Izzy eat popcorn yet. Choking hazard," he explained. "But for me you can bring the jalapeño cheese kind."

"Seriously?"

He chuckled as he took his empty plate to the sink, rinsed it off, and put it in the dishwasher.

Who wouldn't love a man who picked up after himself?

"Yeah. I like the hot stuff. And that's exactly where you come in." He came back to the table, wrapped his arms around her, and softly kissed the sensitive skin between her neck and shoulder.

Who wouldn't love a man who showed affection so easily? So effortlessly? And so often?

While she certainly felt like she'd died and gone to heaven, she was very happy to still be alive to enjoy the man she'd waited so long to love.

For Jackson, putting on his uniform and walking out the door to go to work had never been so difficult. On rainy days or Sundays, when others were home with their loved ones, he'd never given it more than a passing thought that he'd like to stay home and sleep in because then his bed had been empty—most of the time. Even when it hadn't been, he hadn't wanted to stay. Spending time with Abby never seemed long enough. He needed more hours in the day just to be with her. To talk with her. To hold her. To make plans for their future.

And there would be a future.

They'd made it through the weekend apart— barely. And though they'd decided to take things slow so as not to confuse Izzy, it seemed she had a less cautious take on the whole relationship.

When Abby had come over for their movie date, Izzy kept finding ways to put them together. When they'd sat on opposite ends of the couch and put Izzy between them, she got up and pushed Abby toward him. Then she sat simultaneously on both their laps—one chubby little butt cheek on each of their legs. When they sat at the table to eat dinner, she pushed Abby's plate closer to his. If he didn't know better, he'd think his little girl had started up Izzy match-making dot com.

The moment he knew his world had really come together had been when he'd tucked Iz into her little princess bed and kissed her good night. She'd looked up at him with a sweet little smile curving her mouth, and said, "Wub you, Daddy. Wub, Mommy. Wub, Abby." After that, she'd listed all the other family members she loved. That she'd put Abby right in there with the rest told him everything would be okay in her book.

Now, as the morning sun streamed in through the window, he walked into the kitchen, wrapped an arm around Abby's waist, and kissed her neck as she removed sizzling bacon from the pan.

"Careful you don't get splattered with hot oil."

"No worries. At least my EMT training will pay off," he said, as she pushed a pile of fried potatoes off onto a plate. "You don't always have to make breakfast for me."

"I know." She gave him a smile. "But I can't bear to send you off to rescue the world with an empty stomach. You need your strength to rescue those damsels."

"The only damsel I want to rescue is you." He pushed the frying pan off the burner, sat down at the table, and dragged her down onto his lap. As he nuzzled her neck, she smelled good enough to eat. "I'll even pay extra if you put on one of those hot little tavern-wench outfits."

She laughed. Kissed him. Then stuck a piece of toast in his mouth. "Eat."

On the counter, her phone chirped, and she got off his lap to answer. She looked down at the number. "Hmmm."

"Who is it?"

"My attorney."

With a hot pink fingernail, she tapped the screen and lifted the phone to her ear. "Hello?"

Jackson picked up his fork and tried to eat his breakfast while she repeated a volley of "uh-huhs," and "yeses," and "nos" into the phone. But the longer she talked and the more the wrinkle between her brows deepened, the worse his stomach knotted up like a pretzel.

By the time she finished the conversation with an, "Okay, I can be there around one," and hung up, he was wound tighter than a new coil of rope.

"What's up?" he asked, trying to sound casual as he pushed away his half-eaten breakfast.

"I have to go to Houston."

"Today?"

"Yes."

Dread curdled in his stomach. "Why?"

Her careless shrug didn't sync with the tension in her shoulders. "Apparently Mark is negotiating some kind of business deal, and there are some papers I need to sign."

"I thought you signed everything with the divorce."

"I did too. It was my understanding he'd done everything he could to wipe me from his life like I never existed."

"Then I don't understand." He wasn't a dumb guy, but none of this made sense.

"I don't either. Which is why I need to go to Houston."

"Will Rich be there?"

"My attorney said both he and his lawyer would be attending the meeting."

Fuck.

She reached past him to pick up his half-empty plate. He laid his hand over hers, halting her progress.

"I don't want you to go." Okay, *that* hardly sounded desperate.

She looked down at him with a hint of disbelief—like she couldn't understand why he'd even say such a thing. Hell, he knew why loud and clear.

"I have to."

"Why can't you just do it over the phone?" he asked. "Why do you have to physically be *at* the meeting?" *Why was she being so stubborn?*

"I told you, there are papers I need to sign."

"They can overnight them to you. What's one extra day? Let the bastard wait." That resolution made perfect sense to him as he folded his arms across his chest.

"I don't think it works that way. The papers will need to be notarized."

"You could take them to the bank and have Mrs. Mayberry notarize them."

She folded her arms across her chest in a mirror image. "I don't exactly want the entire town knowing all my business, Jackson. And no offense to Mrs. Mayberry, but she's one of the bigger gossips."

"The whole town already knows your business, *Abby.*" Irritation sizzled through his veins as he got to his feet. "So what's the real reason you're going?"

With a hard exhale, she grabbed his plate from the table and moved toward the sink with no verbal response.

"Abby? Talk to me. Because I really don't want you to be in the same room as *him.* And at this late notice, there's no way I can get off work to go with you." He wanted to go—to protect her, to be there for her in what would most likely be a difficult moment.

"I'm a big girl. I don't need you to go with me." She dropped the dishes into the sink with a clatter that turned the conversation ugly. "Maybe I just need to go. For myself."

"Why would you choose to put yourself in that predicament?" He felt like he was playing the *Sesame Street* game of one of these things doesn't belong.

"Maybe I *want* to talk to him."

"What?" Jackson whipped his head around. "Why? What could he possibly have to say that you'd want to hear?"

She shrugged, and a long sigh slipped through the lips he'd kissed just mere minutes ago. "Because maybe I just need to. That's all."

"Are you kidding me?" *This wasn't good. This wasn't good. At. All.* "You do remember what this guy did to you. The way he treated you, right?"

"It would be hard to forget."

"Then I'm at a complete loss here, Abby. Unless you still have some feelings for him."

She released a harsh puff of air. "Of course I have feelings."

Not what he wanted to hear. "Don't go." *Please.*

"I have to."

Jackson felt the ground beneath his feet shift, fracture, and, emotionally, he dropped into a giant sinkhole. He didn't understand. Nothing made sense. The anger he'd been trying to keep at bay exploded as he realized this cozy little fantasy world he'd created was about to blow apart.

Crazier things had happened, but if she still had feelings—even volatile—for Mark Rich, there was no guarantee there couldn't be reconciliation. No guarantee that once she went back to Houston, she wouldn't stay. No guarantee she wouldn't leave *him* again, just as he'd feared.

"Fine." Panic reared its irrational head. "Go." He turned on his heel and headed toward the door.

"Jackson," she called out.

He didn't turn.

Didn't dare look in her eyes again.

He didn't trust the emotions bubbling up inside. Didn't want to make a total ass of himself and beg her not to go. If she wanted to go, there wasn't a damn thing he could do to stop her.

Just as he reached the door she caught up to him, wound her arms around his neck, and lifted to her toes. "I love you," she whispered. "Don't worry. I should be back by tomorrow."

He finally looked into her eyes, and he didn't like what he saw. Fear slithered through him.

Should be back.

The only response he could manage before he walked out the door was, "Yeah."

Chapter 18

"Maybe you ought to suck in a little more of that fresh air and blow that bad attitude out of your system."

Jackson glanced up from checking his air pack to find Mike standing there, arms folded, looking formidable as usual.

"Not in the mood, Hooch."

"No shit." Mike propped his boot up on the fender of Engine Eleven. "Trouble in paradise?"

With a twist of the valve, the air flow stopped, and Jackson set the pack in the apparatus bay. "Don't know what you're talking about."

"Yeah." Mike gave him the stink eye. "You do. And since you've already earned the asshole-of-the-day award, what's up? Oh, and before you argue? For the safety of the entire station, I think it's best if you relieve yourself of the agony you are obviously putting yourself through right freaking now and tell me what's going on."

Jackson came up to his full height. "You sayin' I'm a liability?"

"Yeah, buddy. I am." Mike clamped a hand over his shoulder. "So how about we get a cup of coffee and have a little one-on-one?"

With every intention of refusing, Jackson looked up and noticed the captain standing across the garage with his arms folded and a stern look on his face. Maybe Mike was about to save his sorry ass.

Wouldn't be the first time.

Inside the kitchen, they both grabbed a mug and filled it with the muddy brew.

"Looks like Hot Rod made the Joe again." Mike took a big gulp anyway, then grimaced when the liquid washed down his throat. "Damn, that's horrible shit."

Any other day, Jackson would have smiled.

They leaned against the counter even though there were empty chairs everywhere.

"I don't know what's going on, my man," Mike said, "but for your sake and everybody else's in this crew, you need to get it under control."

Jackson emptied his lungs of air, then sucked in a fresh batch. "I know."

"Abby?"

He nodded. "She got a call this morning. Something to do with her ex. She had to go to Houston."

"So? She's done with the bastard, right?"

"She *wanted* to go. To talk to him."

"About what?"

Before Jackson could get the words out of his mouth, the loudspeaker activated the station for a multiple-alarm fully involved structure fire. A familiar energy surged through the station as the crew jumped into action. For the moment, Jackson was regretfully thankful for the distraction.

They'd all dressed in their fireproof gear on the way to a blaze so many times they had it down to an art. By the time they arrived at the two-story roofing manufacturer, along with four other engines, two trucks, and a paramedic squad they were ready for the smoke that had risen into the sky in a huge black plume and the flames that shot out the windows of the bottom floor.

"This is going to be an ugly mother," Tim "Meat" Volkoff, the engine driver, said as they rolled up into the parking lot.

Nothing but routine, Jackson thought as he climbed out of the engine, down to the pavement, and got to work.

Keep your head clear.

Stay focused.

Each firefighter went about their duties as the captains and the battalion chief assessed the situation and informed them of the plan of attack. From somewhere inside the building, a loud explosion reverberated, and the concrete beneath soles of their insulated boots shuddered. The acrid smell of smoke tickled the back of Jackson's throat as he looked up to see the aerial ladder move into position.

"Hot Rod. Meat. Ground-level check," the captain instructed. "Crash. Hooch. Hit the roof. We've got missing victims and a lot of hazardous material in there. While we do a search, let's see if you can get us some ventilation before it gets any hotter."

Within seconds, Jackson put on his helmet and air pack and led the way up the aerial with Mike close behind. Like most factories or warehouses, the roof was flat, which often made hacking through the thick composition difficult.

Joined by a team from another station they began a roof check. Searching for the safest route and the best place to plant the axes. Though they were equals, Jackson took charge. He'd been a firefighter for a long time. Had been studying every chance he got to move forward in his career. What better time than now to prove himself?

While the additional team took the south side of the roof, he judged the position of the fire below and motioned Mike to the north.

"You sure about this spot?" Mike asked. "Looks like we're right above it."

"I'm sure." Jackson raised his arms and took a whack. Took two more.

The roofing composition split. The lumber cracked. Smoke billowed through the fractured structure. Moments later, another explosion rocked the building, and the crew on the roof staggered from the impact.

Mike gave him a *holy-fuck* look.

They needed to get ventilation ASAFP. From the walkie, Jackson heard the captain's signal to retreat. Jackson hesitated. There were victims inside. If they opened up a big enough hole, it would help with the rescue.

"Let's hit it again," he yelled to Mike.

Mike shook his head. "Cap said to retreat."

Blatantly ignoring the order, Jackson lifted his arms. Brought the ax down just as an explosion shot a fireball out the factory windows.

The building shuddered.

The roof beneath their feet buckled.

Broke.

Collapsed.

And they plummeted.

Chapter 19

Amid heavy traffic, Abby pulled off I-10 to grab a bottle of water and a pack of gum for the remaining drive to Houston. In the convenience-store parking lot she tapped Jackson's name in her contacts list and received his voice mail. She'd texted him earlier too and gotten no response.

Hadn't he been the one to tell her to call if it was important?

On the list of *big things*, an apology might barely register, but to her it was important. Of course, she realized his lack of response could be due to the fact that he was busy and not because he'd left her house pissed off to the point where he'd left a long black tire burn on her street.

The phone call from her attorney that morning had been a surprise. Still, she viewed it as an opportunity she'd long been denied.

An opportunity to vent.

To tell the man who'd treated her as though she

was no more significant than the manure that fed the vegetables he ate—to go to hell.

For months after the humiliation of the divorce, she'd replayed the fantasy of telling off Mark Rich over and over in her head. Yet now, as she headed toward Houston, she wondered at the lack of enthusiasm she'd once felt. What had changed?

Easy answer.

He didn't matter anymore.

After all these years, she finally found herself right where she dreamed she'd be—in Jackson's life. In his arms. In his future.

Sure, he'd gone into total alpha mode after her attorney's call had come, and she could understand his concern. He didn't want her to go alone—the drive was long, and at the end of it, she'd come face-to-face with Mark.

He didn't want her to have to deal with that at all, let alone by herself. She knew he wanted to protect her and lend his support. But even though the face-to-face was something she wasn't overly passionate about doing anymore, she still felt the need to lay it all out there. To cleanse her soul and polish her pride, which had once been so devastated.

Where Jackson was concerned, she didn't deny there would be some ruffled-feather smoothing to do when she saw him again. But that could be an exercise in sensual fun. With his quick temper, she didn't expect it would be their last disagreement. Which would lead to more kissing and making up. Not such an awful burden in her mind.

No sooner had she pulled back onto I-10 than

her phone chirped. Her heart did an eager little dance to hear his voice.

"Abby?"

Jana. Not Jackson.

"Hey," Abby said. "I was about to call you."

"Are you watching TV?"

Jana's voice sounded odd. Clogged. Weak.

"No. I'm actually on my way to Houston. Why?"

"There's a factory fire in San Antonio. Jackson's station is on scene." The long pause sent a river of chills down Abby's back. If it was on TV, it had to be bad.

"Tell me," she said, even though she wasn't sure she wanted the news.

"The roof collapsed. Two firefighters are missing."

Abby sucked in a huge gasp. Her heart seized. "Oh, God."

"He's always the first damn one to rush in," Jana said in a broken whisper. "I know it's him."

Judging from the cold sweat breaking out on the back of her neck, Abby knew it too. She looked up at the next exit sign.

"I'm on my way."

The walls of University Hospital ER were the same as every other hospital in America. But no one noticed. Nor did they notice the standard paintings on the walls. Or the color of the floors.

For hours, the Wilders, associated friends, and emergency-service family members had clogged the trauma waiting room—impatient for news about the firefighters being treated beyond the swinging steel doors. Several more besides Jackson and Mike had received burns and smoke inhalation. But there'd been no specific news or details on Jackson's or Mike's condition.

The initial report Abby caught as Captain John Steele had spoken to Jana was "It's bad."

After that, she'd shut down.

Hours later, nervous energy and worry buzzed through her system, and she'd done whatever she could to keep from going insane. She picked off all the nail polish she'd painted on just yesterday. Paced the long hallway. Stepped briefly outside for a breath of air that didn't smell like some kind of disinfectant, medicine, or illness. Her heart ached like a giant fist had been rammed through its core and left a gaping hole in its wake.

The tick-tick-tick of the clock grew longer and louder until, finally, the double doors swung open, and a nurse in blue scrubs stepped through and called for Jana.

Abby's first instinct was to jump up. To beg to speak to the doctor first. To find out about the man she loved. She wanted to burst through the doors and demand to see him. To touch him and make sure he would be okay. But when the nurse insisted "family members only" she realized she didn't have that right.

When Jana turned to give her an apologetic look, Abby gave her an "It's okay, I understand" nod even though it truly wasn't. Impatiently, she waited while Jana, Reno, and Jesse followed the nurse through those doors and disappeared.

Martin got up from his seat and came over to

sit beside her on the row of padded chairs her butt had stuck to long ago. He patted her hands and gave her a fatherly smile. "Stop chewing on your lip, my dear. Or you won't have anything left to kiss the boy with when you see him."

Abby fought the tears that clouded her eyes and lost. "I'm so worried."

He wrapped an arm around her shoulders. "You just need to hold on a little bit longer. We don't know the extent of his injuries, but whatever they may be, you're going to need to be strong for him. I have a feeling a young man as tough and virile as Jackson isn't going to do well with any kind of weakness."

He was right.

She had to stop freaking out. She had to be strong. For Jackson. He needed her. And until he walked out of that hospital, she wasn't going anywhere without him.

Jackson woke to an infuriating beep beside his ear and a pounding in his head. As his eyes fluttered open, his stomach teetered on the edge of nausea. He blinked several times to clear the fog from his brain. But even that could not help him focus. He closed his eyes.

What the hell had happened?

Where was he?

He opened his eyes again. Blinked. Lifted his head and found Abby sitting beside him. Blue eyes wide. Brows furrowed. Bottom lip snagged between her teeth.

"Hi." Her voice was soft. Sweet. Relieved.

He looked around at what was obviously a hospital room. "Where am I?"

"University Hospital."

He lowered his head back down to the pillow and flinched at the pain that burst between his eyes. "What happened?"

"There was an explosion at the roofing-factory fire your station responded to. You and Mike were on the roof opening up ventilation, and a portion collapsed. You both fell through."

"Where's Mike?" Panic stabbed his heart. "Is he okay?"

"They released him to go home yesterday."

"Yesterday?" He swung his gaze toward the window, but the blinds were closed, and he couldn't tell the time of day. "How long was I out?"

"You've been drifting in and out for about . . ." She glanced down at the pink watch on her wrist. "Forty-six hours."

"Holy shit." He lowered his pounding head back to the pillow. "You said Mike's okay?"

"Like you, he has a concussion. His was milder. He suffered smoke inhalation and also a dislocated shoulder. But he'll be okay."

"A concussion?"

She nodded.

"Guess that explains the pounding in my head." Eyes closed to ward off the dizziness; he lay there quiet for a moment. When he looked up, she was still there.

Watching him.

Waiting.

He didn't like the concerned way she looked at him—as if he was weak. Pathetic.

He wasn't weak.

Only hours ago, he'd been on a rooftop battling a bitch of a fire.

He wasn't weak.

Except when it came to her.

Bitter realization hit him below the belt. He remembered standing on that roof blatantly ignoring orders to retreat and telling Mike to take another strike at the roof. He'd been angry. Trying to prove himself.

Mike could have been killed.

Guilt sent another wave of nausea through his stomach.

He tried to sit up. An excruciating pain streaked down his side and shot through his leg. He dropped right back down to the mattress.

Abby settled her hand on top of his. Her warmth seeped through his skin, and he fought the urge to turn his palm over and hold her.

"Don't try to get up," she said. "You broke several ribs and your leg."

Shit. "Femur, fibula, or tibia?"

"Not the femur."

"The other two?"

"Yes."

"Great." Hell. Not only was he weak, he was broken.

"You had surgery yesterday. The doctor inserted some pins and screws to hold you together until your leg heals."

"Does Izzy know?"

"She sensed something was wrong. Fiona told her that you slipped on Curious George's banana peel and that you had to rest for a couple of days."

"Creative." He inhaled and found the action excruciatingly painful. "I don't want to scare her."

"Once she sees you and knows you'll be fine, she'll be okay."

Nothing was fine.

Like a bad dream, the memory of their argument roared back. It flashed through his drugged system and caught fire in the pit of his stomach.

He'd asked her not to go.

She'd chosen to go to Rich, ignoring *his* pleas and concerns.

Like it or not, Abby had a habit of walking away. Even if he thought he could bear the anxiety of worrying about when she'd leave again, he couldn't be that selfish. He had Izzy to think about. He didn't want her to get too attached to Abby and get her little heart broken. Not if he could help it.

Disconnect, he thought. Now. It was easier. Less painful.

"What are you doing here?" he asked. "I thought you went to Houston."

"I love you." She curled her fingers over his hand. "Where else would I be?"

In a thoughtless reflex he pulled away.

"Jackson, I'm so sorry. I—"

He didn't want to hear what she had to say.

He was tired.

Exhausted to the depths of his soul.

He'd made many mistakes.

He couldn't bear to make another.

"Go home, Abby." His next words drilled a stake into the heart of whatever had been between them. "I think . . . we're done here."

"Done?"

He nodded.

For several minutes, she sat there, begging him with her tear-filled eyes to take back his harsh words.

He did not.

$\mathcal{T}$he following day, the doctors agreed to release him as long as he stayed at his mother's house, where she could look after him. He couldn't go back to his apartment because he'd been put on stair restriction.

On a positive note, they'd kept him so pumped full of medication he barely registered the misery sucking the life out of him. A misery caused not only by his physical injuries but because of the deep ache in his soul.

No medication on earth could take away that pain.

The weakness he hated so much became even more apparent as he had to allow them to push him out of the hospital in a wheelchair. Hospital rules, they said. Even so, like it or not, it looked like he was about to become compadres with a pair of crutches and some serious couch time.

As the nurse pushed him down the hall, and his family followed close behind, he realized he had a lot of soul-searching to do.

Mike's injuries were his fault. Hell, he could have gotten the entire team on that roof killed. He knew in his state of mind he shouldn't have been in such a hurry to prove himself or to rush in and try to save the day. Mike had been right. He'd been a risk. He shouldn't have been on duty at all. He was a father, and he needed to be around to protect his little girl. He couldn't do that if he was falling through roofs and getting himself killed.

Though Mike had called, and they'd talked things out, and Cap had come in to see him too, their forgiveness didn't lessen his guilt. Somehow, he'd find a way around it. For now . . .

In front of them, the elevator doors whooshed open. The nurse pushed him out into the hall and rolled him past the gift shop.

"Want me to get you some flowers?" Jesse teased.

"Or chocolates for those long hours you're about to bank as a couch potato?" Reno added.

"Or maybe Mom will just fill you full of cobbler, and you'll get a big fat belly."

Looked like his sympathy reprieve had been short-term.

"You boys stop that." Their mom swatted at the two instigators. "A few days ago, you were worried sick about him."

"Yeah," Jesse said, "but now that we know he's alive, we have to make up for lost time."

"Jackasses." Their comments brought a sense of normalcy and made Jackson smile. It took his mind off everything else that had his gut tied up in a knot.

As they passed through the lobby, Jackson caught a flash of curly blond hair.

All alone and perched at the edge of one of the brown chairs sat Abby. Without moving, she watched him as they slowly rolled across the carpet.

"What's she doing here?" he asked.

"Abby?" his mother responded. "Oh nothing. Just waiting for you to pull that gigantic stick out of your ass."

"What?" Jackson's head jerked up so fast, it made his broken ribs scream in protest.

"She's been sitting there in that chair since you threw her out of your room," his mother said. Obviously, the fact that he had several broken ribs and a busted leg weren't going to stop her from speaking her mind.

He dropped his hands down to the wheels of the chair to stop the forward motion. "What do you mean she's been sitting there?"

Reno let the nurse know that he'd take over, and with a nod, she silently eased away.

His mother folded her arms and shifted her weight to one hip in her signature "Don't mess with mama" way. "Did y'all break your ears in that fall too?"

"No."

"Then open them and get a clue, son. You might have kicked her out, but she wasn't about to leave your side. Since they brought you into this hospital, she's either slept in that chair or in the chair by your bed. She loves you. What's she supposed to do? It's not her fault your head is as hard as a brick."

"Jesus. Can't an injured guy get a little mercy here?"

"No." Both his brothers chimed in on that response.

He glanced across the lobby again and met Abby's hopeful gaze. He got a little dizzy just looking at her, but he'd conveniently blame that reaction on the concussion. "Then push me over there and give me a couple of minutes, will you?"

Reno took the handles of the wheelchair and pushed him forward with the warning, "Don't fuck this up, little brother."

Jackson knew better than to respond. He had too many emotions racing around inside him to say the right thing. Which did not bode well for coming face-to-face with Abby.

When Reno parked the wheelchair directly in front of her, she smiled, and his brother made himself scarce.

"What are you doing here?" Jackson asked.

"Funny. You already asked me that." She got that stubborn look in her eye. "Not so surprising? My answer is still the same. Because I love you."

Instead of reaching for him or touching him with those soft hands as she usually did, she sat completely still, with her hands folded in her lap. The light streaming through the window behind her highlighted the dark circles beneath her eyes. Her clothes were rumpled. She looked like she'd been down a hundred miles of bad road.

Her words banged his heart against his busted ribs.

"Abby, I—"

She lifted her hand. "Earlier you didn't give me a chance to explain. I'm taking it now." Her slim shoulders lifted on a sigh of either utter exhaustion or frustration. "I understand you didn't want me to go to Houston and why. I appreciate your wanting to protect or defend me. But I wish you'd been confident that my actions had nothing to do with wanting to see Mark again out of any kind of affection. I admit they were purely selfish. But unless you've walked in a person's shoes, you can never fully understand how something makes them feel."

She glanced away, then brought that sharp gaze right back. "I chose to go to Houston because I thought it would give me the opportunity I'd long been denied. I wanted to unleash on Mark. Cuss him out. I never got that chance when he left me standing on that front step, locked out, clutching a letter that dismissed me as if I meant nothing more than a bug that crawled beneath his shoe. I never got the chance during the divorce because his attorney handled everything, and he was never present in the courtroom. From the moment I was told I wasn't wanted anymore, I never had any retribution."

She let go another sigh that tore through his soul.

"I wanted to get all that anger off my chest, Jackson. I needed to do it for me." Those eyes narrowed. "Surely, someone as fiery-tempered as you can understand that."

Her clasped hands trembled. "I was halfway to Houston when your mother called to tell me about the fire. And you know what? Not for one minute did I hesitate to turn my car around. Because *you* were more important."

Jackson swallowed the lump in his throat.

"You've been my best friend for most of my life," she continued. "I thought if anyone might understand how I felt, it would be *you*."

"Abby, I . . . I don't know what to say."

"Well, *I* do," she said, her jaw tight. "I love you, Jackson. With all my heart. I've always loved you. I'm *in* love with you. And I've waited my whole life for you to love me back. But you can't keep pushing me away when things don't go just right. I know you've had some devastating moments in your life. And I know it's easier to pull back and feel safe than if you put yourself out there to possibly feel that pain of loss or failure again. But in my opinion, it's always worth a try."

"I thought . . ."

"That I was leaving you like before?"

He could only nod.

"Never even entered my mind."

The sincerity in her eyes brought everything home in the center of his chest. He thought of the kisses they'd shared, and he wasn't at all surprised to realize he wanted to take her in his arms and kiss her now.

"When I thought you needed me, I came back as fast as I could," she said. "To be here for you. To try and make you understand how much you mean to me. But if you're not willing to fight for what we have . . ."

She rose to her feet. He found himself looking up at her and knew he'd never forget the pain in her eyes. She stood there as if waiting for him to jump in and say something. To rescue the moment. Their relationship. Live up to that act-first, think-later behavior he'd honed over the years.

But the power and passion of her words rendered him speechless.

She let go a disenchanted sigh. "Then I guess you're right. We're done."

A helpless weight crushed down on him as he watched the woman he loved so much it was like a tangled ache in his chest walk through the hospital doors and out of his life.

$\mathcal{T}$he battles of his soul seemed nothing compared to battling a pair of crutches while trying to open the heavy doors to the old shed. Days after he'd left the hospital, Jackson stood in the bright sunlight looking into the darkness as his gaze ping-ponged back and forth from his father's white Ford truck to his brother's green Chevy.

After their deaths, his mother hadn't been able to get rid of the vehicles, and she'd put them in storage. Over time, Jackson had been glad. While Reno and Jesse often visited the two graves up on the hill, he'd always felt closer to the two men who'd meant so much to him by driving their trucks. And while they might no longer be around to hand out advice, he hoped they could still listen.

He tossed the crutches into the bed of Jared's truck, hobbled up into the cab, and stuck the keys in the ignition.

Beside him on the seat lay his brother's thread-bare USMC T-shirt. Hanging from the rearview mirror—his dog tags. And crumpled on the dashboard, the pack of Marlboros that signified his brother's one and only fault.

Jackson threw the truck in reverse and backed out of the garage. When he put the four-wheel drive into gear and pulled out onto the road, he pushed in the CD left by his brother and grinned at Waylon Jennings's outlaw way of turning a song. Jared had always been an old-time Waylon, Willie, Merle, and Hank fan. He'd laughed, as the rest of them moved toward country pop and called him a redneck.

Cranking the volume up to ear-shattering, Jackson sped out onto the gravel. For miles and miles, he burned up the backroads, kicking up dust, and letting his troubles fade into the sunset. He could almost feel his brother right there beside him, grinning, and yahooing it up as Waylon launched into "I've Always Been Crazy."

When the gas gauge ran low, Jackson headed to the creek and parked in the shade of the tree house. He turned off the engine, and the music died. For several minutes, he looked out over the water, where the sunlight danced on the ripples and whitewashed rocks. Then he laid his head back and closed his eyes.

I fucked up, Jared, and I wish you were here to tell me what to do.

In his mind, he imagined his brother's deep laughter.

You've always known what to do.

Jackson slowly shook his head.

Yeah. You do. You let go. You live. You love. You be happy. And someday, when you're a bald old fuck with more wrinkles than hard-ons, we'll meet again. And I'll still beat you at poker.

Jackson laughed.

Something brushed his fingers, and he opened his eyes. There, lying on top of his hand, was the old snapshot that had been tucked into the sun visor.

The photo was of all five of them before they'd gone off to boot camp. They'd stuck Abby in the middle. "Beauty and the beasts," Jared had joked. They all stood side by side, arm in arm. Jackson to Abby's left. Jared to her right. While he and all his brothers looked into the camera and grinned like fools, Abby looked up at *him.*

He could deny it all he wanted, but it was there. He could see it now. The love of a woman he should be fighting *for* instead of fighting off.

You live. You love. You be happy.

Jackson smiled. "I hear you, brother," he said. "Loud and clear."

Chapter 20

For two weeks, Abby got up each day for work. She put in eight hours behind the desk at the clinic, then managed to put in another two hours of research for her rescue center.

Annie had made it home and, after several tearful days and nights, she seemed to settle down and accept that she and her baby were probably going to be much better off without the *loser* in their lives. Abby had done her best to keep her mouth shut about the little worm. Because really, who was she to hand out advice? She'd made plenty of her own mistakes. She'd trusted all the wrong people, then tried to blame them for her own inadequacies.

Things were different now.

She knew where she'd been. And now she knew where she needed to go.

Understanding hadn't come easily, but it was hard to think when your heart was clogged up with love for a man who needed to come to his own conclusions.

You didn't stop loving a man because he wouldn't admit he loved you back. A man brave enough to rush into a burning building yet fearful to live in the moment and allow himself to be loved. To fail. To realize, above anything else, that he was human. With faults a mile long.

She didn't know what he planned to do after his bones healed. She hoped he'd find a soft part of that thick skull to let in the important things in life.

He was an amazing father.

A wonderful soul.

But he needed to learn to let go.

To trust himself and the love she had to offer.

In his mind, he'd failed the day he hadn't been able to save Jared from the bullet that had taken his life. He hadn't been able to stop his father from giving up. And he hadn't been able to rescue a marriage that seemed doomed from the start. She couldn't change the events in his life. But at some point, he had to recognize the need to move past them.

All she could do was hold on to hope and keep moving forward—one shaky footstep at a time.

When her phone had chimed that morning, and she heard his voice on the opposite end of the line, she'd been surprised.

When he'd asked her to meet him out at the tree house, she'd been suspicious.

But that hadn't stopped her.

With the sun on her face, Abby got out of the SUV, shaded her eyes with one hand, and glanced across the meadow to where yellow caution tape had been strung to form a great big rectangle. She couldn't imagine what it was for and wouldn't even attempt to guess.

Instead, she strolled over to the creek and looked up at the tree house, where so many memorable moments in her life had taken place. Alone, she looked around and took in the beauty of the oaks and elms, the tall grass, the occasional clusters of prickly pear, and the gentle, rolling hills.

The Wilder Ranch had always given her a sense of happiness, belonging, and peace. Even when there had been five ornery little boys playing Army, with their plastic guns and helmets.

Moments later, Jackson's big silver truck pulled up and parked beside her SUV.

Though she'd kept tabs on him via his mother and the rest of his family, she hadn't seen him since the day she'd walked out of the hospital. In a loose pair of jeans—one pant leg cut up the side to make room for his cast—and a blue T-shirt that matched his eyes, he looked good. Tanned. Healthy. That last day at the hospital, he'd looked pale and in pain.

Her heart took a little trip as he came toward her, his crutches making circular dents in the sandy soil.

"Progress," she said, as he carefully made his way over to her.

"I've got a long way to go," he said with a tenuous smile, and she wondered if that comment might have deeper meaning.

He stopped in front of her, and his gaze dropped to her mouth. Every hormonal cell in her body reacted, and she had to cross her arms to keep from flinging them around his big, muscular body.

"Thanks for meeting me here," he said in a businesslike manner.

"Sure." She ignored the swarm of nerves in her stomach and shrugged. "It will be impossible not to see each other around town, so I figured . . . why not."

"I hope that's true."

"Why did you ask me out here? I don't imagine you can climb the ladder to the tree house."

"Yeah." He glanced over his shoulder to the wooden structure and sighed. "Not for a while."

His gaze came back to hers, with the outer corners dipped down, displaying the distress that matched the deep furrows in his forehead. "I wanted to apologize to you," he said.

"You could have done that over the phone."

"I could have. But . . . if you'll just let me have my say, I'd really appreciate it."

"Go ahead." She tried to sound indifferent but probably failed.

"I'm sorry I didn't call you sooner. I just needed some time to get past what happened. I realize now that I've blamed myself for failing at a lot of things I really had no control over. The rest, I just continued to beat myself up. And then I was just plain frozen in fear to move forward. I think I finally understand that I've just been getting in the way of myself."

He reached down and took her hand. Placed her palm against his heart.

Her own heart reacted with a wild thump.

"Everything you said was true. I have been pushing you away," he said. "And I haven't been honest. I didn't realize *I* was the one with the problem. I've always trusted *you*, Abby. I just didn't trust myself."

His big shoulders lifted on another sigh, and it took everything she had to just stand there and let him talk.

"I'm stubborn," he said. "And I'm rash. And I'm a million other things that should make you run as far away from me as possible. But I hope you won't. You make me want to be a better man, Abby. With you, I *am* a better man."

"Jackson, I—"

He pressed a finger to her lips. "Let me finish. Please. Then if you want to get in your car and drive away, I'll try to understand. Okay?"

Emotion clogged her throat, and she could only nod.

"You see that yellow tape over there in the middle of those live oaks?" he asked.

"Yes."

"That's where I plan to build a house. And I wanted to know what you thought about that."

Confused at the shift in conversation, she looked across the tall grass. "I think it's a perfect spot."

"I'm glad." He smiled. "Because that's where

I want to build *our* house. I'm thinking a two-story." His smile widened, vividly reminding her how useful stairs could be for something other than getting from one floor to another.

"*Our* house?"

He nodded. Cupped her face in his big hands. "I love you, Abby. I always have. I always will. I don't want to dwell on the past anymore. I want to live, love, and be happy. With you. I want you with me always. If you still love me, I hope you can find it in your heart to forgive me."

If?

There was no *if.*

"I just . . . want to make *you* happy," he added.

"Maybe we could find a way to make each other happy."

His smile lit her up on the inside.

"Maybe we can start with this." He reached into his pocket and withdrew a beautiful diamond ring that sparkled in the sunlight. "I'd get down on one knee, but I'd probably do more damage. And I want to be healthy enough to carry you across the threshold very soon. If you'll say yes."

Behind her tears, his handsome face blurred.

"Marry me, Abby. Be my wife. My happiness. The mother of my children. My best friend forever." He took a breath. "Let's make a promise to love, honor, and cherish each other for as long as we both shall live."

Without waiting for her response, he slipped the ring on her finger and looked up, with hope brightening those amazing blue eyes. "Say yes, Abby. Say yes, and I promise to spend every day of the rest of my life proving how much I love you."

"You make it very difficult for a girl to say no."

"Then please don't."

"I wouldn't dream of it." Heart bursting, she wove her arms around his neck. "I love you. I've always loved you. And nothing will ever stop me. Not even that hard, stubborn head of yours."

Then she rose to her toes and took the kiss she'd wanted from the moment he'd gotten out of his truck and hobbled his way over to stand before her and bare his soul.

"Yes, Jackson, I'll marry you. I'll be your wife. Your happiness. The mother of your children. And your best friend forever."

When he bent his head and kissed her, a ray of sunlight shot rainbow sparks off the ring on her finger.

Jackson Wilder was all she'd ever wanted.

And now he was hers.

It didn't take a genius to figure out that the day she'd walked out of his life had been her biggest mistake.

Finding her way back?

Definitely the sweetest.

Something Sweeter

A dream come true . . .

To the single women of Sweet, Texas, former Marine, Jesse Wilder is hot, hunky perfection, with six-pack abs and a heart of gold. He's a veterinarian who loves animals and kids, is devoted to his family, and financially stable.

The best part? No woman has yet snagged him or put a ring on his finger.

The problem? Jesse's been down a long, bumpy road and isn't the least bit interested in setting his boots on the path to matrimony.

*Comes heart-to-heart with a wedding
planner and her big secret . . .*

Sure, Allison Lane makes a living helping others plan their big day, but that doesn't mean she has to actually believe in matrimonial bliss. Her family's broken track record proves she just doesn't have the settle-down gene swimming in her DNA. And though she finds Jesse fantasy material, why should she take the word of this confirmed playboy that all roads lead to "I do"?

In their battle for a happily-ever-after

Coming Summer 2014